Highland Wolf

E-Rights/E-Reads, Ltd. Publishers
171 East 74th Street, New York, NY 10021

www.ereads.com

Highland Wolf

by Hannah Howell

E-Reads®

Prologue

Scotland—spring, 1477

Sir James Drummond, once laird of Dunncraig, once a husband and a loving father, crawled out of his hiding place deep in the Highlands' most remote mountains and slowly stood up. He felt the hint of spring in the air, the promise of warmth in the moist dawn breeze, and took a deep, slow breath. He felt like some beast waking from a long winter's sleep, only his had lasted for three long, hard years. He was ragged, filthy, and hungry, but he was determined not to spend another season slipping from hollow to hollow, afraid to venture near friends or kinsmen because he had death at his heels and afraid to exchange even the most fleeting of greetings with anyone else—because they might be the one who would recognize and kill him. It was time to stop running.

He clenched his hands into tight fists as he thought on his enemy, Sir Donnell MacKay. Even though he had never liked or fully trusted the man, he had allowed Donnell to come and go from Dunncraig as he pleased, for he was Mary's kinsman. That simple act of courtesy and his wife Mary's own sweet innocence, the sort that never saw evil in anyone, had cost her her life. James had barely finished burying his wife and was thinking how he could prove that Donnell had killed her when the man had made his next move. James had found himself declared guilty of murdering his wife; soon after that he was declared an outlaw, and then Donnell had claimed both Dunncraig and little Margaret, James' only child. The few people who had tried to help him had been killed and that was when James had begun to run, to hide, and to keep himself as far away from those he cared about as possible.

Today the running stopped. James collected up the sack holding his few meager belongings and started down the rocky slope. As he had struggled to survive the winter, living no better than the beasts he had hunted for food, James had come up with a plan. He needed to get back to Dunncraig and find the proof he required to hang Donnell MacKay and free himself. There was still one man at Dunncraig that James felt he could trust with his life, and he would need that man's aid in beginning his search for the truth and the justice he craved. He would either succeed and then reclaim his good name, his lands, and his child, or he would lose it all, including his life. Either way, at least he would not be running anymore.

At the base of the hill, he paused and stared off in the direction of Dunncraig. It was a long, arduous journey away, one that would take him weeks because he had no horse, but he could see it clearly in his mind's eye. He could also see his little Meggie with her fat blond curls and big brown eyes, eyes so like her mother's. Meggie would be five now, he realized, and felt his anger swell as he thought of all he had missed of his child's growing because of Donnell's greed. He also felt the stab of guilt born from how he had thought mostly of saving his own life and not what his daughter might be suffering under Donnell's rule.

"Dinnae fret, my Meggie, I will come home soon and free us both," he whispered into the breeze and then James straightened his shoulders and began the long walk home.

Chapter One

Dunncraig—summer, 1477

"Pat the dirt o'er the seed verra gently, Meggie."

Annora smiled as the little girl patted the dirt as slowly and carefully as she patted her cat Sunny. Margaret, who stoutly preferred to be called Meggie, was all that kept Annora at Dunncraig. Her Cousin Donnell had wanted someone to care for the child, and her family had sent her. That was no surprise, for she was poor and illegitimate, a burden every kinsman and kinswoman she had was quick to shake off whenever they could. At first she had been resigned, but then she had met little Meggie, a child of only two with huge brown eyes and thick golden curls. Despite the fact that Annora thought Donnell was a brutish man, even feared him a little, and had some doubts about his rights to claim Dunncraig, three years later she was still at Dunncraig and not simply because she had no better place to go. She stayed for little Meggie, a child who had stolen her heart almost from the very first day.

"Seeds are precious," said Meggie.

"Aye, verra precious," Annora agreed. "Some plants just grow again every spring all by themselves," she began.

"Cursed stinking weeds."

Bending her head to hide a grin, Annora quietly said, "Young ladies shouldnae say cursed." Neither should ladies of four and twenty, she mused, fully aware of where Meggie had heard those words. "But, aye, weeds grow all by themselves in places where ye dinnae want them. Some plants, however, cannae survive the winter and we must collect the seeds or roots, storing them away so that we can plant them when it is warm again."

"'Tisnae warm yet."

Annora looked up to find Meggie scowling at the sky. "Warm enough to plant seeds, love."

"Are ye certain we shouldnae wrap them in a wee plaid first?"

"The earth is their plaid."

"Annora! The laird wants ye to go to the village and see how good that new mon makes a goblet!"

Even as Annora turned to respond to young Ian's bellow, the youth was already heading back into the keep. She sighed and carefully collected up all the little bags of seeds she had intended to plant this afternoon. Ian was probably already telling Donnell that Annora was going to the village and, of course, she would. One did not say nay to Donnell. Taking Meggie by the hand, Annora hurried them both into the keep so that they could wash up before leaving for the village.

It was as they were about to leave that Donnell strode out of the great hall to intercept them. Annora tensed and she felt Meggie press hard against her skirts. She fought the urge to apologize for not having raced to the village without hesitation and met his dark scowl with a faint, questioning smile.

Her cousin should be a very handsome man, Annora thought. He had thick dark hair and fine dark eyes. His features were manly but not harsh. He even had good skin and no visible scars. Yet Donnell constantly wore such a sour or angry expression that his handsomeness was obscured. It was as if all that was bad inside the man left some irrevocable mark upon his looks. The way Donnell looked now, Annora could not see how any woman could find him attractive.

"Why arenae ye going to the village?" he snapped.

"We are going right now, Cousin," she said, doing her best to sound sweet and obedient. "We but needed to wash the dirt of the garden off our hands."

"Ye shouldnae be working in the gardens like some common slut. Ye may be a bastard, but ye come from good blood. And ye shouldnae be teaching Margaret such things, either."

"Someday she will be the mistress of some demesne or keep with a household to rule. She will rule it much better if she kens just how much work is needed when she orders something to be done."

The way Donnell's eyes narrowed told Annora that he was trying to decide if she had just criticized him in some way. She had, all too aware of how little Donnell knew or cared about the work he ordered people to do. He never gave a thought as to how all his needs and comforts were met, except to savagely punish the ones he deemed responsible if they failed in some way. Annora kept her gaze as innocent as possible as she met his look of suspicion, breathing a silent sigh of relief when he obviously decided she was not clever enough to be so subtle.

"Get ye gone, then," he said. "I have been hearing a great deal about what fine work this new mon does and I seek a goblet or the like so that I may see his skill with my own eyes."

Annora nodded and hurried past him, little Meggie keeping step close by her side. If the fool was so interested in this man's skill, she wondered why he did not go and have a look for himself. It was the fear of saying that thought aloud that made her hurry away. Donnell's response to such words would be a hard fist, and she preferred to avoid those whenever possible.

"Why does the laird need a goblet?" asked Meggie the moment Annora slowed their fast pace to an almost lazy stroll.

"He wants to see if the man who carves them is as good at what he does as everyone says he is," replied Annora.

"He doesnae believe everyone?"

"Weel, nay, I suspicion he doesnae."

"Then why will he believe us?"

"A verra good question, love. I dinnae ken why he should if he doesnae heed anyone else's word, but 'tis best if we just do as he asks."

Meggie nodded, her expression surprisingly solemn for one so young. "Aye, or he will hit ye again and I dinnae want him to do that."

Neither did Annora. Her Cousin had come close to breaking her jaw and a few other bones the last time he had beaten her. She knew she ought to be grateful that Donnell's second-in-command, Egan, had stopped him from continuing to punch her, but she was not. Egan did not usually care who Donnell beat or how badly he did so, was in truth just as brutish as Donnell was. The fact that the man did not want her beaten, at least not too severely, made her very nervous. So did the way he always watched her. Annora did not want to owe that man anything.

"Neither do I, love," she finally murmured and quickly distracted Meggie from such dark thoughts by pointing out the cattle grazing on the hillside.

All the way to the village Annora kept Meggie entertained by drawing her attention to every animal, person, or plant they passed by. She exchanged greetings with a few people, yet again regretting how closely watched and confined Donnell kept her and Meggie. Although she would have preferred choosing the times and reasons she traveled to the village, Annora enjoyed the pretense of freedom, able to ignore the guards she knew were right behind her. She only wished she would be given enough time and freedom to come to the village more often and get to know the people of Dunncraig better.

Annora sighed and inwardly shook her head. She had not been given any chance to become a true part of Dunncraig, but that was only part of her regret about not getting to know the people as well as she would like. Something was not right about Donnell's place as laird, about his claim to these lands and to Meggie. Annora had sensed that wrongness from the start, but after three years, she had not uncovered any truth to give some weight to her suspicions. She knew someone at Dunncraig knew the answers to all the questions she had, but she had not yet found a way around Donnell's guard long enough to ask any of them.

Approaching the cooper's home and shop, Annora felt her spirits lighten just a little. Edmund the cooper's wife, Ida, might be at home and Annora knew the woman would readily sate her need to talk to another woman. Her pace grew a little faster in anticipation. She dearly loved Meggie, but the child simply could not satisfy the need for a good, long woman-to-woman talk.

"Rolf, she is coming."

This time James did not hesitate to look up from his work when Edmund called him by his assumed name. It had taken James longer than he had liked to become accustomed to being called Rolf. He hated to admit it but Edmund had been right when he had counseled patience, had warned him that he would need time to fully assume the guise of Rolf Larousse Lavengeance.

Then what Edmund had just said fully settled into James' mind. "Meggie?"

"Aye, but to ye she must be Lady Margaret," Edmund reminded him.

"Ah, of course. I shallnae forget. Who comes with her?"

"Mistress Annora and, a few yards behind, two of Donnell's men."

James cursed. "Does the mon think there is some danger to the woman or Meggie here?"

"Only to him, I am thinking. MacKay doesnae allow the woman to talk much with anyone. Nor the bairn. Some folk think the lass thinks herself too good for us and is teaching the bairn to be the same, but I think Mistress Annora is forced to keep to herself. E'en when she has a chance to talk to someone, there are always some of MacKay's men close at hand to try to hear all that is said."

"'Tis his own guilt making him think everyone is eager to decry him."

"I think that may be it. My Ida says the lass is clever and quick. MacKay may fear she has the wit to put a few things together and see the truth. 'Tis a big lie he is living and it has to weigh on the mon."

"I hope it breaks his cursed back," James muttered as he tried to clean himself up just a little. "Better still, I want it to hang him."

"So does most everyone at Dunncraig," said Edmund.

James nodded. He had quickly seen how cowed his people were. Donnell was a harsh, cruel laird. He was also unskilled in the knowledge needed to keep the lands and the stock thriving. There were all too many signs that the man glutted himself on the riches of Dunncraig with little thought to how his people might survive or the fact that care must be taken to ensure that there would be food in the future. The people might be afraid of the man seated in the laird's chair, but they did not hold silent when they were amongst themselves, and James had heard a lot. Donnell was bleeding the lands dry to fill his belly and his purse.

Ida stuck her head into the room. The lass says the laird sent her. He is wanting a goblet made by Rolf."

Before he could say anything, Ida was gone. For a moment James simply sat at his worktable and breathed slowly and evenly to calm his excitement and anticipation. This was the first step. He had to be careful not to stumble on it. He knew Donnell spent a lot to make Dunncraig Keep as fine as some French king's palace. That required a skilled woodworker, and he wanted to be the one who was hired.

"That one," said Edmund, pointing toward a tall, richly carved goblet.

"Aye, I think ye have chosen the perfect one, old friend," James said and smiled.

"I havenae seen that expression for a while."

"'Tis anticipation."

"Aye. I can fair feel it in the air. The mon is a vain swine who spends far too much of your coin on things he doesnae need, things he thinks make him look important. Ye guessed his weakness right. Do ye really think the mon would leave some proof of his guilt around, though?"

It was a question Edmund had asked before, and James still was not confident of his feeling that the truth was inside the keep. "I cannae be sure but I think there has to be something. He cannae be rid of all proof. Mayhap I will but hear something that will aid me." He shrugged. "I cannae say. All I do ken is that I must be inside Dunncraig if I am to have any chance of getting the truth."

"Weel, then, let us get ye in there."

Annora looked up as Edmund and another man stepped out of the workrooms in the back of the little shop. She stared at the man with Edmund wondering why he so captivated her attention. He was tall and lean, even looked as if he could use a few good meals.

His hair was a light brown and hung past his broad shoulders. There was a scar on his right cheek and he wore a patch over his left eye. The right eye was such a beautiful green she felt a pang of sorrow for the loss of its mate. His features were handsome, cleanly carved yet sharpened a little by the signs of hunger and trouble. This man had known hardship and she felt a surprising tug of deep sympathy for him. Since she had no idea what sort of trouble may have put that harshness on his handsome face, she did not understand why she wanted to smooth those lines away. The way his slightly full lips made her feel a little warm alarmed her somewhat. The man was having a very strange effect upon her and she did not think she liked it.

Then she saw his gaze rest on Meggie and put her arm around the child's shoulders. There was such an intensity in his look she wondered why it did not make her afraid. A moment later, Annora realized that the intensity held no hint of a threat or dislike. There was a hunger there, a need and a grieving, and she wondered if he had lost a child. Again she felt a need to soothe him, and that need began to make her very nervous.

She looked at the goblet he held in his elegant long-fingered hands and gasped softly. "Is that the one ye wish to sell to the laird?" she asked.

"Aye," the man replied. "I am Rolf, Rolf Larousse Lavengeance."

Annora blinked and had to bite her lip not to say anything. It was a very strange name. It roughly translated to wolf, redhead, and vengeance. It was also strange for a poor workingman to have such an elaborate name. There had to be a story behind it and her curiosity stirred, but she beat it down. It was not her place to question the man about his name. As a bastard, she was also all too aware of the hurt and shame that could come from such questioning, and she would never inflict that upon anyone else.

"It is verra beautiful, Master Lavengeance," she said and held her hand out. "Might I have a look?"

"Aye."

As she took the goblet into her hands, she decided the man had been in Scotland long enough to lose much of his French accent and pick up a word or two of their language. If Donnell hired the man to do some work at the keep, that would make life a great deal easier. Donnell had absolutely no knowledge of French and could easily become enraged by a worker who had difficulty understanding what he said. And, looking at the beautiful carvings of a hunt on the goblet, she suspected Donnell would be very eager to have the man come and work at Dunncraig Keep. The thought that she might have to see a lot of the man in order to translate orders for him made her feel a little too eager, and Annora felt a sudden need to get away from this man.

"I believe this will please my cousin weel," she said. "Your work is beautiful, Master Lavengeance. The stag on this goblet looks so real one almost expects to see him toss his proud head."

James just nodded and named his price. The woman named Annora did not even blink, but paid it and hurried Meggie out of the shop. Moving quickly to look out the door, James watched her lead his child back to the keep, two of Donnell's men in step a few yards behind them. He felt a hand rub his arm and looked to find Ida standing at his side, her blue eyes full of sympathy.

"Annora loves the wee lass," Ida said.

"Does she? Or is she but a good nursemaid?" James asked.

"Oh, aye, she loves the lass. 'Tis Lady Margaret who holds Mistress Annora at Dunncraig and naught else. The child has been loved and weel cared for whilst ye have been gone, Laird."

James nodded but he was not sure he fully believed that. Meggie had looked healthy and happy but she had said nothing. There was also a solemnity to the child that had not been there before. Meggie had been as sweet and innocent as her mother but had had a liveliness that Mary had never possessed. There had been no sign of that liveliness and he wondered what had smothered it. He would not lay the blame for that change at the feet of Mistress Annora yet, but he would watch the woman closely.

He inwardly grimaced, knowing he would find it no hardship to watch the woman. Mistress Annora was beautiful. Slender yet full-curved, her body caught and held a man's gaze. Her thick raven hair made her fair skin looked an even purer shade of cream, and her wide midnight-blue eyes drew a man in like a moth to a flame. After three years alone he knew he had to be careful not to let his starved senses lead him astray, but he was definitely eager to further his acquaintance with Mistress Annora.

Suddenly he wondered if Mistress Annora was Donnell's lover and wondered why that thought enraged him. James told himself it was because he did not want such a woman caring for his child. It might be unfair to think her anything more than she seemed, but her beauty made it all too easy to think that Donnell would not be able to leave her alone. Mistress Annora's true place in Dunncraig Keep was just another question he needed to answer.

Stepping more fully into the open doorway of Edmund's shop, he stared up at the keep that had once been his home. He would be back there soon. He would enter the keep as a worker, but he meant to stay as the laird. For all her beauty, if Mistress Annora had any part in Donnell's schemes she would find that her beauty did not buy her any mercy from him.

Chapter Two

Rage swept over Annora so quickly she had no chance to shield herself from it. It clouded her mind and churned her stomach. She placed one shaking hand on her stomach and the other hand flat upon the cold stonewall of the upper hall to steady herself. It took several minutes of concentration and slow, deep breathing to push the feeling away until she simply recognized it and was no longer consumed by it. It was proving to be very slow work to rid herself of it all, however. It was times like these that she truly hated the strange ability she had to sense the feelings of others, for it did seem as though the most distasteful ones were the strongest and hit her the hardest.

Frowning, she looked around and realized she was only a few steps away from Donnell's bedchamber. Her first thought was that someone had sparked Donnell's considerable temper again, but then she inwardly shook her head. She had been slapped by the harsh, bitter taste of her cousin's rage before, more times than she cared to count. This did not have the same feel to it or the same taste. Yet, aside from Donnell and Egan, Annora did not know anyone else at Dunncraig who had ever revealed such a fierce anger.

Finally feeling steady again, Annora crept toward Donnell's bedchamber. The door was open yet she heard no raised voices, no sounds of fists hitting flesh, not even the softest of pained whimpers. That made no sense. Where was the consequence of such rage? If it came from Donnell or Egan, there should not be such calm, such quiet, inside the room. In truth she should be hearing, and probably feeling, some poor man's or woman's pain as a harsh punishment was meted out.

Suddenly she was afraid that Donnell had seriously injured someone, perhaps even killed the object of his anger. She silently hurried closer and cautiously peered into the room. Even as she did so a small voice in her head scolded her for doing something so foolish, for she knew that she could do little to help anyone who had stirred up the rage of either her cousin or his fist, but she did not heed that warning voice and looked anyway. Annora barely stopped herself from gasping aloud in surprise and giving herself away.

There was no broken, bleeding body on the floor. There was no sign of any confrontation at all. Not even a tipped-over stool. Donnell and the handsome wood-carver from the village stood before the massive fireplace studying the mantel and talking quietly. Annora warily allowed herself to reach out to find the source of the rage that had so affected her and abruptly stood up straight in the doorway. It was coming from the wood-carver.

"What are ye doing here?" demanded Donnell.

Annora blinked, feeling as if she had just been rudely awakened from a deep sleep. In a way she supposed she had been. Shock over the fact that the soft-spoken man standing so diffidently in front of Donnell was actually seething with fury had thoroughly stunned her. Her abrupt movement must have given away her presence in the doorway. Unfortunately she was now the object of Donnell's attention and irritation, something she usually did her utmost to avoid. Rousing irritation in Donnell tended to leave one with a lot of bruises.

"I beg your pardon, Cousin," she said, taking a step back in the start of what she hoped would not appear to be an ignominious retreat. "I heard voices and saw that your door was open. Since it isnae your habit to be in your bedchamber at this time of the day, I felt compelled to see what was going on in here."

"The only thing ye should feel compelled to do is what ye were brought here to do—watch o'er Margaret. Naught else at Dunncraig is of concern to ye save for doing what ye are told."

"Of course, Cousin."

The humiliation Annora felt over being spoken to so dismissively in front of Rolf Lavengeance bit far deeper than she thought it should. After all, Donnell always spoke to her in such a manner. She had thought she had become accustomed to it. This time, however, it took every scrap of willpower she had to subdue the urge to blush in shame. If nothing else, she refused to give Donnell the satisfaction of seeing just how he had hurt her. Her pride might be badly battered after three years at Dunncraig, but it was not dead yet.

"Margaret isnae with ye, either, is she? Just why is that?"

"She went down to the great hall to wait for me. I but needed a moment to fetch her cloak from Mary, who had taken it away last eve to clean it."

"A lot of time is wasted in cleaning that child and her clothing. If ye find it too difficult to care for her properly, mayhap 'tis time I found her a better, more capable nurse, aye?"

Donnell's voice was dangerously soft and he watched her closely as he spoke. A chill snaked down Annora's spine. He had never struck at this particular weakness before. She had thought she had kept her love for Meggie well hidden, but she suspected he had finally sniffed it out There was even a chance he had known about it all along, had just been waiting for the perfect moment to strike and use her feelings for Meggie just as he used his fists—as a way to keep her cowed. It was working. Meggie was her only joy, and even the thought of being separated from her terrified her.

"I shall strive to do better," she said, praying that she sounded appropriately submissive yet revealed none of the fear gripping her heart.

"See that ye do."

Annora curtsied and walked away. What she really wanted to do was race to the great hall, grab Meggie, and flee Dunncraig. So strong was that urge she trembled as she forced herself to walk away with a steady, even pace. All she could do was try even harder to stay out of sight, to be meek and quiet when in Donnell's presence, and to hide how desperately she needed to stay with Meggie.

"I thought ye got lost."

That sweet, high voice pulled Annora from her thoughts and she looked down at Meggie as the little girl tugged gently on the cloak Annora held. Crouching down she helped Meggie into her cloak and studied every soft curve of the child's sweet face. It always astonished her that Donnell could have helped to make such a pretty, sweet child, which was one reason she questioned his claims.

Meggie had become her life, her joy. Somehow she had let her cousin see that. Considering how strong her feelings were for the child, Annora supposed she ought not be so surprised. One could never completely hide such deep feelings. Donnell could simply have realized how often she shielded Meggie from his anger and brutality and wanted it known that he had noticed it. She knew she could never stop doing that, but there might be some way to do it in a less obvious manner. If she had to become some spineless ghostie slipping in and out of the shadows of Dunncraig to stay with Meggie, she would.

"Where are we going to today, Annora?" Meggie asked.

Standing up, Annora bit back the urge to say they were going to run away to France. Dunncraig under Donnell's rule was not a good place for such a sweet child as Meggie, but it was more than Annora could ever offer the child. It was a roof over Meggie's head, a bed to sleep in, and food to eat. On her own and fleeing from Donnell, Annora doubted she would be able to meet even one of those meager needs. It galled Annora to admit it but they were trapped, forced to stay beneath Donnell's brutal rule just to stay alive. She just had to try harder never to draw Donnell's attention or stir his anger. Before this day, she had done so to avoid a beating, but this new threat terrified her even more than Donnell's brutal rages. Donnell's fists simply hurt her body. If he sent her away from Meggie, it would tear the heart right out of her.

"We are going to just walk about outside the walls and look round at the beauty spring always brings to the land," Annora told Meggie as she took the child's small hand into hers and started out of the great hall. She silently wished that, one day, she would find the means to just keep on walking with Meggie at her side, right past the walls of Dunncraig, past its boundaries, and far, far away from the fear that had become her constant companion.

James did his best to hide all expression as he listened to Donnell speak so coldly to Annora. Even though she revealed nothing in her expression when MacKay threatened to replace her as Meggie's nurse, she was not completely successful at hiding her distress. James had seen it flash briefly in her eyes and watched some of the healthy glow abruptly fade from her beautiful skin. Although he did not dare guess at the reasons, it was obvious to him that Annora MacKay did not want to be separated from Meggie. The smug look on Donnell's face as Annora walked away told James that the man knew that and was pleased with the success of his threat.

"I fear my cousin of times thinks she is more than she is," said Donnell.

"More than she is?" murmured James, hoping that speaking only a little would keep everyone from noticing what an appalling French accent he had.

"Aye, more than some bastard get of one of my kinsmen. I have kindly opened my home to the wench and given her a coveted position as my child's nursemaid, but Annora still tries to act as if she is my equal, a true lady born and bred."

James clasped his hands tightly behind his back to quell the strong urge to strike out at Donnell MacKay. The way the man spoke so condemningly concerning Annora's illegitimacy was enough to earn him a thrashing. From what little James had heard and seen thus far, Annora MacKay was all a lady should be. He was not sure he should trust her yet, but hearing someone fault anyone for the sins of their parents was something that had always angered him.

It was Donnell claiming Meggie as his child that truly enraged James, however. The urge to kill the man, here and now, alarmed James a little. He had never considered himself a bloodthirsty man and he had also thought he had learned to control his temper.

It was not that control that stopped him from lunging at MacKay and wrapping his hands around the man's thick neck, however. James had to prove his innocence before he sought any retribution from this vain, officious man. He sternly reminded himself of that until his rage subsided to a more manageable level. Once he was no longer condemned as an outlaw, James would seek the justice he craved. Snapping MacKay's neck right now might make James feel good for a little while, but he knew that pleasure and satisfaction would be very fleeting indeed. It could well cost him all chance of removing the taint of outlaw from his name. Regaining Dunncraig, reclaiming his daughter, and living as a free man again were far more important things to reach for than MacKay's throat.

"The child appears to like her," was all James dared to say on the matter.

"Weel, aye, but what does a lass of five ken, eh? She is nay more than a wee bairn."

James simply nodded, not trusting himself to say another word. He had been feeling very pleased over how quickly MacKay had demanded his presence at Dunncraig. It had taken only a week and James suspected most of that time MacKay had spent his time thinking of all the things he would have James do. It had taken James only minutes to know that dealing with MacKay was going to require every ounce of willpower he had.

Even if Donnell MacKay had not been the one to destroy his life, James knew he would never have liked the man anyway. The visits MacKay had made to Dunncraig while Mary had been alive had not revealed the true nature of the man until too late, only hinted at it. Donnell MacKay was brutal, vain, and venal. James was surprised that the man had lived so long, that no one had murdered him yet, and he suspected only a sharp, animal cunning had protected him.

"Come, I will show ye where ye are to sleep and work," said MacKay as he started out of the room. "I have gathered some fine wood for ye to work with."

As James followed MacKay, he kept a sharp eye out for the men who served as MacKay's guards. Very few of the men James had used had remained at Dunncraig. That could make things very difficult, but James had anticipated it. A man like MacKay would naturally be very careful in choosing the ones who would guard him.

After seeing the workshop he had been allotted, as well as some of the wood chosen by MacKay, James settled into the small room he had been given in one of the towers. He had been hard-pressed to hide his surprise and delight when he had been given a room within the keep itself. It was a room that had been used for storage while he had been the laird, and James wondered where everything that had been stored there had been taken. A moment later, he cursed. The way MacKay used up supplies with no thought to the future, James suspected the bolts of cloth, threads, and other household supplies that had filled the room had already been used up and never restocked. It was going to take a lot of time and coin to replenish all that had been lost to MacKay's gluttony.

There was only a tiny, narrow arrow-slot for a window in the room, a simple cot for a bed, and a small brazier to supply heat if it was needed. On a rough table set in a far corner of the room was a jug of water and a bowl for washing up. MacKay obviously considered Rolf Lavengeance to be somewhat better than a common man. If bitterness did not have such a tight grip on him, James suspected he would laugh.

Shaking free of his dark thoughts, James carefully put his meager possessions into the small battered chest beside the bed. Since it was still early in the day, he went to the workshop MacKay had prepared for him. It had once been the room where the women did the laundry and hot baths were prepared. Not only had it allowed the women easy access to heated water, they could stay out of the wind or the hot sun while they were scrubbing the clothes. It had also saved them having to run up and down the stairs time and again with buckets of water when someone wished a bath. James hoped the loss of this room did not stir too much resentment. To prove his innocence he could not afford to make any of the servants his enemy, and it would help him immensely if they felt they could talk freely to him.

One good thing about the arrangement was that he would not be expected to bathe in this room now. Since he knew he would be bathing or washing up far more than any other common man would, James tried to think of some explanation for that oddity. There was a chance that many would just assume it was because he was French. Having to bathe in his room also meant he could maintain his privacy, something that might also seem very odd to people. Seeming odd was just something he would have to risk, however. The very last thing he needed was for anyone to see him naked.

Opening the wide heavy door that led to the outside, James welcomed the flood of light caused by an unusually sunny day. The gardens behind the kitchen had already been planted and he inhaled deeply of the smell of the still damp laundry waving gently on the lines it had been hung from. He had never really taken much notice of such things before, but now they filled him with a sense of homecoming and made him even more determined to wrest hold of Dunncraig from Donnell MacKay's greedy hands. This was his home and he should never have allowed himself to be driven away.

"Weel, it appears ye are enjoying the comfort of your room. Fine working quarters ye have gotten yourself, aye?"

James turned slowly to face the owner of that querulous voice and felt himself tense with the fear of discovery. Big Marta stood scowling at him, her thin but muscular arms crossed over her thin chest. It should have occurred to him that, while the men-at-arms he had known might all be gone, at least some of the servants would still be around. Big Marta being an excellent cook, it was no surprise MacKay had held fast to her. Unfortunately, she was one who had known him the longest and the best. He hoped the way she was narrowing her dark eyes was due to a rising temper and not that she was beginning to recognize something in him.

"It was not my choice, eh?" he mumbled and shrugged his shoulders.

Big Marta rolled her eyes. "Now, isnae that a fine thing? Ye cannae e'en speak our language weel, can ye? And here I was just thinking that there was something familiar about ye. 'Tisnae likely as I have ne'er kenned a Frenchmon. Ne'er wanted to. I suspicion I cannae really blame ye for this," she said and sighed. "'Tis just another thing that fool has done to make our lives a misery." She frowned at him. "Can ye understand better than ye can speak?"

"*Oui.*"

"Since ye are nodding your head, I will assume that means
aye."

"Aye."

"Weel, ye are a handsome laddie so I will tell ye what I have
told the others, stay away from the lasses who work for me. 'Tis
hard enough to get all our work done without ye and those fools
MacKay has gathered round him sniffing at the skirts of every
maid in Dunncraig. I can reach ye a lot quicker than I can them
and best ye remember that."

James nodded again. It was an easy promise to make. After
more than three years of celibacy he was certainly hungry for a
woman, but the risk of his disguise being revealed was too great.
Before that, the risk of being betrayed or caught unawares had
kept him from taking any lovers, even some tavern maid who
took a man's coin, gave him ease, and then was forgotten. Even if
he were free to indulge himself, he would not do so with a maid
who worked within the walls of Dunncraig anyway; never had.
It was a rule his foster parents had made very sure he and his
foster brothers had learned well.

"Humph. Nay sure I believe ye any more than I do MacKay's
dogs, but we will see." Big Marta looked around the room. "Just
what has the fool got ye doing for him?"

"Carving." James pointed to the wood and then the tools. "He
liked my goblet."

"Ah, I see. That was a verra fine goblet. Good work, verra
good. Havenae seen any better. More fine things for our great
laird. The bairns can cry themselves hoarse from the hunger in
their wee bellies, but MacKay will have a finely carved chair to
sit his arse on and a fancy goblet to swill his wine from." She
shook her head, her graying brown hair bouncing with the
movement. "Just dinnae bother my lassies and keep your messes
to this room. Dinnae let all those wood chips and all get into my
kitchen."

Before James could nod again, Big Marta left. He breathed a
slow, hearty sigh of relief. If she had noticed anything familiar
about him she was keeping it to herself.

He moved to run his hands over a large piece of oak. It would
serve to make one of the elaborately carved mantels MacKay

was so eager for. James did not really mind doing the work as he had often bemoaned the lack of time to indulge his skill. Perhaps while he sought the proof he needed to rid Dunncraig of MacKay, James could finally get a few of the things done that he had often dreamed of. MacKay might think it was all for his aggrandizement, but James would know that when he was once again free and laird of Dunncraig, he, too, would be well satisfied with whatever work he had accomplished.

"I just need time and a wee bit of luck," he whispered to himself as he studied the piece of wood, trying to decide exactly what sort of design he would carve into it.

Just as he picked up one of the tools neatly laid out for his use, Big Marta stomped back into the room. She slapped down a tray of bread and cheese on the table and then looked at him. James felt a trickle of sweat go down his back as the woman stared right into his face, a gleam of amusement and satisfaction to see in her clear, intelligent eyes.

"I am thinking ye will need your strength for what lies ahead, laddie," she said and then marched out of the room again.

James stared down at the tray of food and the tankard of ale. She knew; he had no doubt of that now. The question was, how did she know? He was sure his disguise was a good one. Big Marta had known him for a long time, but so had Edmund and Ida and they had thought his disguise a good one, too.

"Best ye keep your gaze cast down a wee bit more, laddie. Them green eyes of yours be the sort a woman remembers."

He turned to look at Big Marta but only caught sight of a piece of her skirts as she disappeared back into her kitchens. James cursed softly. Obviously covering one eye with a patch was not enough. Now he was going to have to act shyly around any lass who tried to talk to him, at least the ones who had been at Dunncraig when he had been laird. When this was all over, his family would find that very amusing.

He was going to have to pretend to be humble, even shy around women, unable to speak the language clearly, and reveal none of his love for his own child. He was also going to have to play the servant and one with an inclination to remain celibate. Add all of that to the fact that he could not simply kill MacKay as he ached to do but had to search out some proof of the man's crimes, and James began to feel as if he had taken on a burden he could never carry far. He hoped he could prove his innocence quickly or he might be too maddened by all the games he had to play to care.

Chapter Three

"What are ye doing?"

James was glad he was not doing any carving at that precise moment. The sweet, high child's voice was so familiar, and the sound of it so longed for, that he could easily have badly marred the huge piece of the mantel he was working on. Slowly, he turned to look at little Meggie and clenched his fists in an attempt to quell the fierce urge to brush the child's thick, tousled curls off her face. He had been at Dunncraig for a full week and this was the first time Meggie had come near enough for him to talk to her.

"I make the mantel for the fireplace, eh?" he replied.

Meggie cautiously stepped into the room. The way she kept a wary eye on him made James' heart ache. Meggie had always been a happy, trusting child. Life at the Dunncraig that Donnell MacKay had created had obviously taught his child fear and caution. The latter was something all children could afford to learn and learn well, but fear, especially while within the walls of her own home, was not. MacKay's temper, the one the man revealed several times a day, had bred that fear in Meggie as it had in so many others at Dunncraig. James had no doubt about that and he added that to the long list of crimes Donnell MacKay had to pay for.

"I am carving the mantel to put in the lord's bedchamber, *oui*?" he repeated when she just stood there and frowned at him.

"Oh, I understood ye, sir, e'en though ye do talk a wee bit odd, aye? Nay, I was just wondering why Sir MacKay wants ye to do that. He has one now, doesnae he? He doesnae need another one."

Meggie inched closer to the wood James had been working on. "'Tis verra pretty."

"You are much kind." He smiled when she giggled and then he clasped his hands behind his back to resist the urge to hug her. "Why do you say Sir MacKay? Is he not your papa?"

"He tells everyone he is, but he isnae." Meggie suddenly looked nervous. "But ye must ne'er say that I said that, please."

"I will never do so. It is to be our secret, *oui?*"

"Aye, our secret. I ken he kissed my mother, but that doesnae make him my father. He has kissed a lot of women. My da was handsome and kind and laughed and smiled. Sir MacKay just yells and hits people. He isnae a nice mon at all."

Stunned by the words *I ken he kissed my mother*, James had to take a moment to clear his mind enough to respond coherently to Meggie's confidences. "*Non*, kissing does not make a man a papa. Where is your nursemaid?"

"Annora? She is working in the gardens. See?" Meggie held up her very dirty hands. "I was helping her but I needed something to drink. Big Marta gave me something. Why do ye think they call her Big Marta? She is a wee woman, nay a big one."

"I am thinking the name is a jest, *oui?* Something to make people smile."

"Oh. They tease her? Do ye think it hurts her feelings?"

"*Non*. I think she carries the name well, eh? She is big in spirit, *oui?*"

Meggie smiled and nodded, causing her thick curls to do a wild dance around her head. "She *is* verra strong and everyone does what she tells them to." She looked back at the wood James was working on. "'Tis verra, verra pretty. When I have clean hands can I touch it?"

"*Oui*. I am in here most days, working. You may come whenever you want."

"Meggie!"

"That is Annora. I better go back to her. She worries 'bout me, ye ken."

Before James could say anything, Meggie was gone. James stared at the doorway she had just fled through, but saw nothing. His own thoughts consumed him until he was blind and deaf to all else. The innocently said words of his child pounded in his brain.

I ken he kissed my mother.

He tried to tell himself that Meggie was imagining things, that she had only been two years old when Mary had died. It had to be impossible for a child that age to know what she saw and recall it for three years. Yet, he could not shake the words from his head.

Mary unfaithful? It was impossible to believe. Mary had been painfully shy. She had blushed and tensed even during the most restrained form of lovemaking. He had not wanted to believe that she had found his touch distasteful, had even hoped that after a few years of marriage she would begin to enjoy the more intimate side of their union. Now he had to wonder if what he had seen as an intense shyness had indeed been distaste, a distaste born of the fact that Mary had been in love with another man.

James tightened his grip on the awl he held until his hand threatened to cramp. He had never understood Mary's acceptance of Donnell MacKay, but perhaps he should have looked more closely. It was hard to think he had been made a fool of, but it was time to look back over his brief marriage with a more critical eye. Although it was difficult to believe the Mary he had known had had any part in his destruction, James knew he could not ignore the possibility.

Once he accepted that Mary might not have been the sweet, shy wife he had thought her to be, James then wondered if she was really even dead. The body he had buried had been the right size, but the fire had burned that body beyond true recognition. He had accepted that it was Mary, for witnesses had placed her in the tiny cottage at the time of the fire and one small, charred hand had still been adorned with the wedding ring he had slipped on Mary's finger. There had even been a few charred remains of the gown she had worn that day. That still left a lot of room for doubt, however. The biggest doubt was stirred by the fact that he did not think Mary had the clever deviousness needed for such a plot and he could not believe she had the patience to remain hidden from sight for so very long.

Shaking away the questions clogging his mind, James turned his attention back to his carving. The slow, meticulous work would calm him as it always did and allow him to think more clearly. There were obviously a lot more secrets to uncover at Dunncraig than he had thought. He would need to remain calm and avoid drawing any suspicions his way as he hunted for the truth. James just hoped the truth would not reveal that he had been a blind fool who had fallen victim to a sweet smile and pretty blushes, thus bringing his enemies into the heart of his home.

"Where have ye been, Meggie?" asked Annora as the little girl skipped up to her side. "Did ye need to drink a bucketful of water?"

Meggie giggled and shook her head. "Nay, I was talking to that mon who carves wood into pretty pictures."

Annora glanced back toward the keep and then frowned at Meggie. "Ye shouldnae pester the mon whilst he is working."

"He didnae mind."

"He may have been too polite to tell ye to leave him be."

"Nay, he talked to me."

"Weel, that was verra good of him, but ye should still leave him to do his work."

"He said I could come back and touch the wood once my hands were clean."

Annora's first impulse was to say a resounding nay, but she bit back the word. The man did do some exquisite work. She could easily understand Meggie's interest. It would also be wrong to deny the child the chance to make a friend just because she held so many fears for Meggie's safety. Such fears could smother the child's spirit, and simply living at Dunncraig under Donnell's rule did enough of that.

"Weel, then, ye may go and look at his work when ye are clean again," Annora finally said. "E'en more than once if he says it is all right. But ye are nay to pester him too often, and no talking to the mon until his ears burn."

"I like to talk."

"Everyone likes to talk, but he is a mon who has work to do.

Your father has hired him to make things, things that will make Dunncraig beautiful."

"Dunncraig is already beautiful."

"Aye, I think it is, but——"

"And that monisnae my father."

Annora had a few doubts about Donnell's claim of paternity as well, but she would never admit that to Meggie. "Donnell says he is," she murmured.

"He lies."

He did, Annora thought, and suspected it was more often than even she could guess, but she could not say such things to Meggie. "Meggie, ye were but a wee bairn when your mother died," Annora began even though she was not sure about what she should or could say to the little girl.

"The monisnae my da! I ken that he kissed my mother, but that doesnae make him my da!"

Quickly pulling Meggie into her arms, Annora held the tense child close and stroked her hair. "Then he isnae your da. Now, ye must calm yourself ere ye make yourself ill. I wasnae crying ye a liar. 'Tis just that I was puzzled o'er how such a young bairn, as ye were then, could ken, with such utter confidence, just who her father was."

"Because *my* da wouldnae hit me. Or ye. My da was handsome, and he smiled and laughed and gave me kisses."

That certainly did not describe Donnell, Annora mused. "'Tis also that ye have ne'er denied it before."

"Because he would hit me. Or ye. I didnae want that." Meggie stared down at her hand as she threaded her fingers through the laces of Annora's plain, aging gown. "And I thought he might be like my da someday, after he learned to love me. But I dinnae think he e'er will. I dinnae think Donnell loves anyone."

Annora's heart felt as if someone had stuck his fist into her chest and was squeezing it. There was such painful longing in Meggie's voice, a longing Annora understood all too well. Even though no one was certain if Sir James Drummond was dead yet, Meggie was an orphan. Her mother was dead and her father had to remain hidden or he soon would be. Poor Meggie wanted and needed a family and all she had gotten was Donnell MacKay.

Annora also knew that no matter how much love she gave the child it simply could not compensate for the loss of her parents.

"Meggie, sweet lass, ye must continue to play the game. Ye can understand that, cannae ye?"

"Aye, I can. I ken that Sir MacKay would be verra angry if he heard, and I dinnae want him to be angry."

"Nay, we ken weel that that would be a verra bad thing. So we must keep this just between the two of us." Annora wondered about the fleeting look of guilt on the child's face but decided enough had been said on the subject for now. "Now, shall we finish our work?"

Meggie nodded and returned to the small section of the garden she was planting. Annora watched her for a moment and then turned her attention to her own work. Her mind would not rest, however. Meggie was so adamant that Donnell was not her father. Annora knew that a child might turn a wish into her own fact when she was unhappy, but Meggie was not a child who carried pretending to such lengths. She was unhappy at times, but mostly she just avoided or ignored Donnell and all of his unkindness.

The problem was that Meggie's belief that Donnell was not her father fed Annora's own doubts about her cousin's claims. And the thought of Mary being Donnell's lover made her shiver with such distaste she preferred not to think about it at all. Unfortunately, she had not known Mary very well and knew she could have been easily fooled. Yet, could the woman have fooled her own husband for very long? Inwardly shaking her head, Annora decided it was just another puzzle she had to unravel. Considering how long it was taking her to even begin to unravel the others, Meggie could be married and have several children before the full truth was known.

Perhaps it was time to cease being so timid in her search for the truth, she decided, disgusted with her own cowardice. Annora had thought that she could uncover the truth about Donnell's sudden rise in wealth and stature by getting to know the people of Dunncraig and speaking to them. However, Donnell was doing an excellent job of ensuring that never happened. She doubted she could elude his guards very often and it would probably raise some suspicions if she did. So, instead of looking to others to answer all the questions she had, she would look inside Dunncraig itself.

Once the idea settled in her mind, Annora decided it might not be too difficult. Most of the men who were loyal to Donnell stayed close by his side, so once she knew where Donnell was, she ought to be able to poke about undeterred. The question was where to look. Donnell had a very rigid schedule and so she knew exactly when he would be in his ledger room and when he would not. It would probably be the best place to start. All she had to do was make sure she had a route of escape or a very good excuse for being there if she was caught.

"Why do ye do this sort of work?"

At the sound of that deep voice, Annora was so startled and afraid that somehow the man guessed her plans that she nearly screeched. It took all of her control to hide how much Egan's sudden appearance had frightened her. She kept her gaze upon the ground as she sat up straight and, once sure that she was composed, she looked up at him. Kneeling at his feet and looking up at him tasted far too much of subjugation, but Annora quelled the urge to get up and look him straight in the eye. Even though she would still have to look up, that could prove far too confrontational, so she resisted the urge. Egan always reacted to any sort of confrontation in the same way—with his fists.

"I like working in the garden," she said. "It is soothing and it produces something worthwhile."

"'Tis work for one of the other lasses, one of the ones what doesnae come from such good blood as ye," Egan said.

"And they would ne'er hesitate to do it if I asked it of them, but I truly enjoy doing it myself. And 'tis good to get out in the sun now and then."

She kept her voice soft and calm and her gaze fixed upon his pockmarked face. Annora had quickly learned that it was as unwise to annoy Egan as it was to annoy Donnell. He had yet to do more than slap her once or twice, but he had nearly beaten to death several other women at Dunncraig for what were very small mistakes.

Annora wondered why the man was such a brute. Despite the

pockmarks on his face he was not unhandsome. His eyes should have been lovely, for they were a soft hazel color, but they were the coldest eyes she had ever seen. Egan's features were a bit rough, but even and well placed. Yet, when he was angry, he looked cruel enough to scare anyone who saw him. She did her best never to make him angry.

She just wished he had not taken such an interest in her. Thus far she had been fortunate, for he had not tried too hard to force his attentions on her. Sadly, she knew of a few women who had found out the hard way that Egan did not like to be refused and was not above simply throwing the woman down and taking what he wanted. Annora feared that one day he would do the same to her. She sincerely doubted that Donnell would do anything to stop the man or even punish him if he was successful in raping her. If not for Meggie, she would have fled Dunncraig within weeks of arriving and minutes after receiving that first lust-filled look from Egan.

"So they should do because, until the laird finds himself a wife, ye are the highest born lady here."

"Many women of high birth work in the garden. Tisnae as if I am out plowing a field."

The way his eyes narrowed told Annora that her words had come out a little sharper than she had intended them to. When Egan crossed his thick arms over his chest, she inwardly breathed a sigh of relief. Such a position showed arrogance, which annoyed her, but held no real threat of violence.

"Best ye dinnae stay out in the sun too long or ye will be as brown and wrinkled as one of those women. Now, Donnell has been looking for ye."

"Oh, I see." She stood up and brushed off her skirts. "He needs me to go to the village again?"

"Nay. Seems someone is coming to visit and he needs ye to be sure everything is done as it should be for guests."

"Do I ken who is coming? Such knowledge could aid me in deciding what should be served at the meal."

"Laird Chisholm and his sons."

Annora barely repressed a shiver of distaste. Ian Chisholm, laird of Dubhuisge, was big, hairy, and smelly. His two hulking sons were no better. He was eager to join with Donnell in trying to expand their holdings. It made Annora afraid for those clans nearby who were not as strong or as brutal. They had already suffered from raids made by Donnell and the Chisholms; they did not need the deprivations brought by these men to get even worse. All three Chisholms also thought she should be part of the courtesies offered them as Donnell's guests. It had not happened yet and she had the feeling it was because of Egan. She just wished she could feel grateful for that.

"Weel then, I had best go and speak to Big Marta."

"Aye, and tell that old woman that we want plenty of meat on the table and it had better be cooked right."

It was hard, but Annora resisted the urge to stick her tongue out at the man as he walked away. Big Marta was a very good cook. Such criticism of her work was unwarranted and she had no intention of repeating it. She had the feeling that Egan, and Donnell, used such criticisms and insults to keep people subdued and eager to please. The man had not seemed to notice that such tactics did not work with Big Marta.

Collecting Meggie, Annora took the child up to the nursery and cleaned her up. She left her in the care of Annie, a young girl of thirteen who liked to help in the nursery, for it kept her out of sight of Donnell's men. After cleaning up herself, Annora then hurried down to the kitchens.

"Big Marta," she began as she walked up to the woman who was stirring a thick stew that smelled delicious, "there are to be guests for dinner."

"I ken it," Big Marta snapped, her expression suggesting that she would like to spit. "That old lecher Chisholm and his drooling laddies."

"Ah, so there is no need for me here."

"Aye, I ken who be coming and what the fools need to eat, but that doesnae mean ye cannae be useful. I could use someone to chop up those apples I brought out of storage."

"I should be glad to help," Annora said even as she sat at the huge worktable, picked an apple out of the basket set there, and set to work. "Is Helga ill?" she asked after looking around and realizing that Big Marta was missing one of her helpers.

"Humph. Ye might say that. The laird was feeling lecherous last night. Unfortunately, he was also feeling drunk and mean. T'will be a few days before Helga recovers."

Annora sighed and shook her head. "It wasnae like this before, was it?"

"Nay. Dunncraig was a fine place and the laird cared for all his people. He didnae expect the lasses working in the keep to warm his bed, either, though many a one would have jumped between the sheets with him had he but smiled at her."

It appeared that Big Marta was in a mood to talk and Annora meant to take full advantage of that "Yet, they say he killed his wife."

"Nay, that bonnie lad would ne'er have done that. I have ne'er kenned how anyone could e'er think he would. I am nay sure anyone e'en kens exactly what happened to Mary Drummond."

"I have ne'er heard anyone question how she died."

"Weel, ye wouldnae, would ye? That cousin of yours doesnae let ye talk to anyone. If ye were allowed to speak to some of the people who work these lands, ye would hear the truth about Sir James Drummond. He was good to us, and good for Dunncraig."

Glancing around, Annora realized that one reason Big Marta was speaking so freely was that none of Donnell's men were at hand. Somehow, Annora had managed to get to the kitchens without her usual guard. She had no doubt that soon someone would notice that she had gone somewhere without her usual escort, somewhere where she might hear things Donnell did not want her to, so she proceeded to take full advantage of her sudden freedom.

Annora nodded and kept on working as she asked Big Marta question after question. Sometimes she just let the woman talk on uninterrupted. It shamed her that she had not shared more than a few words with the woman in the three years she had been at Dunncraig, even though she knew it was not her fault. This was what she had wanted to do from the start, however, and as more and more information flowed out of Big Marta, Annora saw just why she had been kept secluded from the other women of Dunncraig. She almost cursed when her guards finally stumbled into the kitchen, but, since she had finished chopping the apples, she really had no obvious need to linger anyway.

By the time she returned to her bedchamber, Annora felt full to bursting with the knowledge Big Marta had imparted. None of it matched what Donnell had told her about the previous laird. If everything Big Marta had said was true, then Donnell was even worse than Annora had suspected. If one believed all that Big Marta had said, Sir James Drummond had been cruelly wronged and the people of Dunncraig were suffering for that injustice.

It all strengthened her own doubts and Annora knew she had to be careful. She wanted it to be the truth and she knew that could make her blind to anything that might contradict her own opinion. One thing she was sure of was that she was going to do more to dig up the whole truth about the previous laird and Donnell's possession of Dunncraig. Her curiosity demanded it and the people of Dunncraig deserved to be freed of the tyranny of Donnell MacKay.

Chapter Four

He was sweating and James found that annoying. That hint that fear had taken hold of him made him want to curse and then boldly stride into the ledger room he was creeping toward. To be afraid or even uneasy about entering any room in his own keep pricked at the rage he tried so hard to control. The fact that it had been a fortnight since he had arrived at Dunncraig and this was his first chance to get into the ledger room only added to his anger.

Glancing around when he finally reached the door, he saw no one and quickly slipped into the room. Except for new tapestries and a thick rug, the room had changed very little from when he had used it, but there was no ignoring the luxury of those tapestries. The rug had also had to cost MacKay dearly, of that James had no doubt. He shook his head at those signs that MacKay was spending far too much money on his own comforts.

Everything pointed to the fact that MacKay was bleeding Dunncraig dry. James had seen clear signs of it while he had stayed with Edmund and Ida. Big Marta had also complained about it. It made him almost reluctant to look at the ledgers, for he feared he would discover that MacKay had not only squeezed every coin he could out of the land and the people, but sunk Dunncraig deep into debt.

Shaking off that sudden reluctance to know the whole ugly truth, James sat down at the worktable and began the tedious work of reading through the ledgers. As he read, he listened closely for any sound that would indicate someone approaching the room. It soon became clear that MacKay was doing exactly as James had feared he was. Worse, it appeared that MacKay was regularly raiding his neighbors, stealing what Dunncraig could easily have provided if the man had simply cared for the land, as a laird should. There would be a lot of work needed to soothe those neighboring clans when he regained Dunncraig.

James found a small ledger tucked in amongst the larger ones that detailed the accounts. What he read in that small book chilled him to the bone. Edmund had had little news to offer on the fate of the men who had been loyal to James, but he had feared that only a few had survived the change in lairds. Edmund had been right to fear that. In MacKay's crabbed handwriting James read the fates of his men. A few had managed to flee Dunncraig. The rest had been killed. Too many of those had been brutally tortured by MacKay, who sought information on where James may have fled. Along with that gruesome tally was a careful record of each and every person who lived at Dunncraig, on its lands, or in the village. The notations by each name told James that MacKay kept a close eye on every man, woman, and child he sought to rule.

Anger and grief over the loss of so many good men blinded James to all else for a little while. It was the sound of someone slowly moving the door latch that pulled him free of that dark mire, awakening him to the danger he was in. He quickly closed the ledgers and moved away from the worktable as the door eased open. James readied himself to give a plausible reason for why he was in MacKay's ledger room only to gape when Annora slipped into the room, backward. While she took one last careful look up and down the hallway before closing the door, he crept up behind her.

Her heart pounding so hard she could hear it in her ears, Annora carefully closed the door. She breathed a big sigh of relief. The first step to uncovering the truth had been taken. She had gotten into Donnell's ledger room unseen. Now all she had to do was search it thoroughly and not get caught. Annora grimaced and wondered if her curiosity had finally led her into a trouble she would not be able to get out of.

Stiffening her backbone, determined to find some answers to all the questions she had, she turned to go to Donnell's worktable and found herself staring at a broad chest. In fact, her nose was lightly touching the coarse linen shirt covering that broad chest. The only clear thought she had was that it was not Donnell or Egan. It was certainly not one of the Chisholms. She would never be able to have her nose so close to one of them without her eyes watering from the smell. Slowly she lifted her head and found herself staring into a beautiful green eye. It dismayed her a little to find that she was not really surprised. She had recognized both his scent and the sense of a barely leashed rage tinged with sadness and frustration.

"What are ye doing in here, Master Lavengeance?" she demanded, feeling that, this time, going on the offense was better than babbling excuses or running away.

Since he now knew that Annora spoke perfect French, James did not see the need to try and sound like a Frenchman speaking English, something he did badly. "I think I should ask what *you* are doing here," he replied in French.

"I asked ye first."

"Ah, but I believe your answer will be far more interesting than mine."

It felt a little odd to speak in English while he spoke in French, but Annora had guessed almost from the start that Master Lavengeance understood most of what was said in English. She knew several Gaelic speakers who did the same, understanding but not speaking English. Or, she thought, simply refusing to speak a language used by their oldest enemies. Shaking aside that idle thought, she frowned at the wood-carver.

"I need to write a few letters," she said.

"You can write?" James asked, knowing he was doing a bad job of hiding his surprise. The Murray women were all well educated, but it was very unusual for women to be taught much more than how to care for their home, their husband, and their children.

"Of course I can write. And read."

"Do not get so offended. Many women cannot do either and many men prefer it that way, making certain that the women in their households can do no more than scratch out their names, if that."

Annora finally took a step back, wondering why she had been so slow to move away from the man. "Weel, I stayed in the homes of several women who believed a woman should learn all she can. They finished the work my mother had begun. Not that ye have any need to ken that. Now, I believe I will leave ye to whate'er ye are doing creeping about in here."

She did not even complete her turn toward the door. He grabbed her by her upper arms, his strong, long-fingered hands nearly encircling them. After three years of learning how to avoid the worst of Donnell's anger, Annora did not struggle. Yet, as Master Lavengeance pushed her up against the door, acting quickly but in a way that held her captive without hurting her, she wondered if she should have fought him.

"Do you mean to run to your lord and tell him I was in here?" he demanded.

James moved closer, pinning her against the door with his body and loosening his grip upon her arms. He quickly decided that was a mistake. The moment his body touched hers, need flared inside him, rushing through his body with every beat of his heart, and reminding him of just how long it had been since he had fed those needs.

He nearly grimaced and barely stopped himself from hurriedly backing away when his mind refused to allow him to ignore the truth. It was more than a blind need for a woman that caused him to feel nearly dazed with desire. It was she. It was her scent, her midnight-blue eyes, and even the sound of her voice. It was also the way she could make his too solemn and wary Meggie smile and giggle.

Pushing aside the passion clawing at his insides, he studied Annora's face and almost grinned. When he had first grabbed her she had gone as still as a terrified bird. He knew she had been anticipating some sort of violence, maybe even bracing herself to endure the pain. It pleased him that she had obviously realized that he would not treat her so unkindly. The fact that she would expect such a thing angered and saddened him, however. He decided it was best to concentrate on the look of annoyance and outrage on her lovely face. Having been well trained by the women in his foster family, the Murrays, he knew it could be fatal to tell her that she looked adorable when she was angry.

"So, do you intend to set your lord after me?" he asked again.

"Why? Have ye been doing something that would harm Dunncraig?"

He noticed that she did not say anything about harming MacKay. "No. I but wondered why the man pays me so well to make carved mantels and fine furniture yet the people in the village are but one bite away from starving."

"That is a puzzle easily answered. The fool thinks he should live like a king, that all that is grown, made, or earned in Dunncraig is meant solely for his comfort. Ye have been inside this keep for a fortnight and at the village before that. Ye shouldnae have to come peeking in here to ken that hard truth."

Annora felt her breathing quicken as Rolf pressed just a little closer. She could sense that he spoke the truth, just not the whole truth. She could also sense that he was no threat to Dunncraig and its people. If he was a threat to Donnell and his minions, she did not really care. None of that alarmed her. What did was that she could sense his desire and, as he pressed even closer, she could feel the proof of it. The fact that she liked how it made her feel astonished and frightened her.

"I willnae say anything to Donnell, so ye may release me now," she said, feeling quite pleased with how calm her voice sounded when she was trembling inside.

"Are you sure you wish me to let you go?" James brushed a kiss over her forehead and felt her tremble faintly. "I do not think I want to. I think I am going to kiss you, Annora."

"I dinnae think that would be wise."

"You may be right, but at this moment I do not care. I just want—"

Before she could say a word his mouth was on hers. It was soft and warm. She not only tasted his desire but felt it flow into her, heightening her own. It was as if, for just a moment, his heart and soul were bared to her, his feelings mingling with and strengthening her own. The emotions in the man were strong, and not all good ones, but his desire for her was real. Despite knowing that a man's desire could be a shallow, fleeting thing, she did not hesitate to open her mouth when he nipped gently at her bottom lip. The stroke of his tongue inside her mouth was enough to make her toss aside all caution and she wrapped her arms around his neck. Whether his desire was shallow, deep, or even devious, she did not care. She just wanted him to keep on kissing her.

He pulled her hard against his tall, lean body, his hand moving down to her backside to push her close to his groin. The feel of his long, hard manhood pressing against her in a pantomime of the act he so clearly craved should have had her running for her life, or at least for the sake of her virtue. Instead, Annora pushed back and heard herself moan softly.

When he ended the kiss, Annora briefly followed the retreat of his mouth, trying to bring it back to hers. A tiny flicker of common sense halted her and she slumped back against the door. She could feel how hard he struggled to rein in the desire that had flared between them and knew she ought to be pleased about that. Unfortunately, common sense did nothing to douse the fire his kiss had started. She also wondered why he had stopped when she had been so willing.

"Do you hear that?" he suddenly asked, his whole body tensing as if prepared to fight.

"Hear what?" she asked, still trying to shake the haze of desire from her head.

"Someone is coming this way."

Annora was just beginning to panic when he grabbed her by the hand and started dragging her toward the wall near the small fireplace. "We must get out of here," she said.

"That is exactly what we are going to do."

She watched in amazement when he stopped, pressed a few bricks surrounding the fireplace, and the wall moved inward. The only thing she could think of as he dragged her into a very small room was that it was a good thing that Donnell obviously did not know everything about Dunncraig. She was sure the man would have made some very nefarious use of such things as hidden rooms and passages. She then tensed as Rolf pushed on something to the side of the door and it closed, leaving them standing very close together in total darkness. She did not mind standing so close to him, but she had an old and deep fear of the dark.

"Is this it?" she asked in a wavering voice, that sign of her growing fear embarrassing her. "Is there no passageway we now creep away in?"

"Well, there is a passage," he whispered against her ear, "but it would not be safe to use it without any light."

"Can he hear us?" she whispered back, hoping that conversation would keep her fear from growing too large to control.

"Not if we whisper very, very softly. We will be able to hear anything said in the ledger room, however."

"That could be useful."

James wrapped his arms around her and pulled her back, hard up against him. It was a sweet torture, but he was able to control his desire because he could sense her growing fear. He also suspected she was a virgin and a hasty rutting in a tiny dark room with people only feet away was not the way to introduce her to passion, even if it was a way that would allow him to hold fast to his disguise.

"Are you afraid of the dark, Annora?"

"Aye, the dark and small places with no clearly visible route of escape." She shivered as dark memories of her Cousin Sorcha arose from where she had buried them. "One of the women who took me in after my mother died felt time spent in a small dark space was the best way to discipline an unruly child." She immediately wondered why she had told him that as it was not something she spoke about to anyone.

James held her a little closer, feeling a strong urge to hunt down that woman and slap some kindness into her. It astonished him that he should feel such outrage on Annora's behalf. He barely knew this woman and was not yet sure he could trust her. Just because her kiss had curled his toes did not mean she was someone he could trust with all his secrets. And if they made love as he ached to do, that was exactly what he would have to do. He was going to have to forget how sweet she tasted.

The sound of MacKay's voice pulled him from thoughts of how right she felt in his arms. James tensed and strained to listen closely, not wishing to miss a word. He was a little surprised to feel Annora do the same. Annora did not like or trust her cousin and he wondered why, but knew questions about that would have to wait until later.

"When are those cursed Chisholms going to leave?" demanded Egan.

"When our business is done," replied Donnell.

"They are causing too many people to look our way, Donnell. They dinnae try to hide what they are doing. I wouldnae be surprised if they boast about all we have done in every alehouse they step into."

"That doesnae matter. I dinnae think anyone will heed them if they speak out against us. They are kenned weel for being lying thieves. It willnae be hard for us to convince people that they are just trying to take someone down with them."

"That may be, but are ye willing to take that risk? If ye are wrong we hang right beside them."

Donnell snorted in derision so loudly it was clear to hear in the tiny dark room where Annora hid wrapped tightly in a pair of strong arms she found far too enticing. She was trying very hard to ignore the man holding her and only listen closely to Donnell and Egan, but ignoring so much man pressed up against her back was impossible. The best she could do was listen and hope she would recall enough of what was said to think about it later.

Rolf Lavengeance was a dangerous man, she decided as Donnell and Egan argued over the perils of continuing their alliance with the Chisholms. She had known she was attracted to him from the start but had seen so little of him it had not troubled her much. It was a safe attraction, one enjoyed from afar, and adding a nice romantic glow to a few dreams. It was no longer safe. Now she knew he desired her. Worse, now she knew how he tasted and how he could make her feel. She was going to have to keep as much distance between them as possible now.

Annora closed her eyes as a sudden sense of loss swept over her. She told herself that was foolish as she did not really know this man who held her safe against the darkness and she was not free to explore such things as desire. There was Meggie to consider, for Annora knew that any hint of impropriety on her part and Donnell would use that as an excuse to separate her and Meggie. There was also the danger she could put both Rolf and herself in if she allowed this attraction any freedom, for she doubted Egan would like it. And finally there was the fact that she did not want to find herself in the same situation that had destroyed her mother, left unwed and carrying a child who would suffer her whole life for the sins of her parents. No, it was necessary to step away from Rolf Lavengeance and stay away. Far, far away.

When a little voice in her head said she could wait to do that until they were out of the little dark space they were hiding in, she grimaced and then inwardly shrugged. There was no place to retreat to at the moment anyway. And the way he was nuzzling the place where her shoulder curved into her neck and stealing slow caresses of her body wherever his hands rested made it a little difficult to ignore him.

"This last time a laird's eldest son was killed, Donnell," said Egan.

Those words yanked Annora free of her thoughts about Rolf and she tensed. She had known that Donnell was involved in raids on other clans although she had not known how deeply or how often, but it appeared that he had recently been involved in one and it had caused some blood to be shed. Going on a raid or two was obviously why the Chisholms were lingering at Dunncraig. Since such crimes were usually committed during the night she had never paid all that much attention, but it was evident that they were putting Dunncraig and its people in danger. They were putting Meggie in danger.

The way the man holding her tensed told her that he was probably thinking the same things. She was not sure why he would be concerned, but perhaps he had decided to make Dunncraig his new home and simply feared that Donnell and his men were threatening the peace of his chosen home. Peace was an elusive thing in Scotland under any circumstances, but it was madness to do things that invited retaliation and stirred up bloody feuds.

"Ease your mind, Egan," said Donnell, his footsteps passing by the hiding place she shared with Rolf. "I will soon have that old bastard tied to me in a way that will make him shut his mouth, e'en if he is caught."

"I hope ye are right about that," Egan said, his footsteps following Donnell's.

"E'en if I am wrong about Old Ian, I am nay wrong about his sons. They would turn on their own father to protect their own arses or gain the power he denies them. Once I have one of those fools tied to me, he will do his best to ensure that I am nay taken down, not e'en by his own kinsmen."

The sound of the men leaving the ledger room, the door closing behind them, almost disappointed Annora. She was glad they were gone as she needed to get out of her place of captivity and out of Rolfs embrace. However, she would have liked to have the men talk long enough to let her know just what weapon Donnell thought he would soon have to hold over the heads of the Chisholms, one or all, to force them to protect him.

Several tense, silent moments passed and Annora was about to ask if they were getting out of there, when Rolf opened the door and nudged her back out into the ledger room. As she blinked against the sudden light, it was a minute or two before she could see Rolfs face clearly, and what she saw surprised her. The man was furious. Since she always sensed some rage inside him, she had not paid much attention to that underlying feeling of anger. It was clear that this anger was fresh and had been stirred to life by hearing of the crimes Donnell and Egan were involved in. She was just thinking that it was nice to meet a man who could be upset by crimes and injustices when she realized he was cursing, low and long and viciously. In the Scots tongue,

"So ye do speak our language," she murmured and faintly smiled. "And verra colorfully."

"My apologies," he murmured in French, his attempt to sound calm and polite marred slightly by the underlying throb of fury in his deep voice. "I can curse fluently in your tongue, but speaking as a gentleman should to a lady is more difficult."

She nodded but knew she was as detached from the conversation as he was. Now that she was no longer in his arms, the conversation she had overheard was filling her mind and demanding that she think about it. It would also be a good idea to put some distance between him and herself as quickly as possible. Annora started inching toward the door.

"I think it would be a verra good idea if we got out of here as soon as possible," she said.

"Yes, it would be."

James strode past her and eased open the door. He looked out into the hallway, saw no one, and signaled her to follow him as he slipped out of the room. Once outside, he grabbed her by the hand as she started to move away from her and kissed her hard before letting her go again.

He almost smiled at the way she blushed and nearly ran from him. It was undoubtedly a mistake to remind her of what they had shared before Donnell and Egan had interrupted them, but he found he did not want her to go away and force it from her thoughts. That brief kiss had been a little reminder and a warning that this was not the end of it, simply the beginning. He needed to be cautious but he decided he could not completely ignore what had flared between them.

He could not ignore what he had just heard MacKay and Egan talk about, either. Hurrying back to his workshop, he fought against the urge to go straight to MacKay and demand to know whom he was raiding and who had died. The man was threatening to draw Dunncraig and its people into a long, bloody feud. It could be something it would be impossible to fix once James proved his innocence and regained control of Dunncraig. Unless he could serve MacKay's head on a platter to the aggrieved party, he thought with a hint of anticipation.

Reaching his workshop, James looked at his tools and the mantel he was working on and knew it was going to be hard to find the calm he needed no matter how hard he worked. Dunncraig was in danger. The death of a laird's heir was no small thing that could be talked or bought away. He would have to get rid of MacKay and regain his good name as fast as possible. It was time to stop moving quite so slowly and cautiously. If he did not put a halt to the man's crimes soon, all he would have when he did regain his good name, his child, and his lands, was a smoking ruin.

Chapter Five

A soft curse escaped Annora as she entered the great hall to break her fast. The Chisholms were still at Dunncraig. She had hoped that they had left with the dawn. From what she and Rolf had overheard yesterday, their bloody work had been accomplished, so there was no need for the men to linger. Yet, here they were, ruining her morning.

Sitting down in her usual seat at the head table, she found herself seated across from the Chisholms. That was not far enough away for her comfort, but she could not simply move, for it would be an obvious insult to Donnell's guests and cause her a trouble she would rather avoid. Worse, she now had Egan seated to her right. Since it was a very small bench she sat on, it meant that Egan was constantly rubbing against her, touching her, and she knew he did most of the touching and rubbing on purpose. Her appetite was suddenly gone, but she knew she had to stay, had to pretend that sharing a table with five brutal men did not disturb her.

The moment her bowl was filled with oatmeal, Annora did her best to ignore the men. It was not as easy as it should have been. Egan kept rubbing up against her and pressing his thigh against hers. The Chisholms loudly revealed their utter lack of table manners and Donnell seemed oblivious of everything except the vast quantity of food he was shoving into his mouth. For a man who was expending so much coin and effort to make the keep equal to any royal palace, Annora wondered why he did nothing to improve himself. She had the sinking feeling that her cousin was so vain he thought he was already quite perfect.

Annora was just helping herself to some fruit when Meggie

was brought into the great hall by Hazel, one of the many maids Donnell had working inside the keep. Most of the women were hardworking, but others, ones who willingly leapt into Donnell's bed, did whatever they wished to. They obviously thought that sharing the laird's bed gave them some special place in the keep and some privileges. The one leading Meggie over to Donnell's seat was one who still held some kindness and conscience, and Annora was glad of that. Meggie always felt afraid when she was brought before Donnell, and one of the more cocky and callous maids would have made it even worse.

Poor little Meggie looked as confused as Annora felt when Donnell introduced her to the Chisholms. His voice was so gentle when he spoke to Meggie that it made Annora nervous. Whenever he deigned to speak to the child he claimed as his, kindness never softened his tone. The way Meggie's eyes began to widen told Annora that the child also found such a change in Donnell's manner toward her more alarming than welcoming. Meggie was right to be worried. Such a change in Donnell's manner was a sure sign of trouble.

Abruptly a chill went through Annora's body. There was only one reason a man dragged his mere child of a daughter to a meal with guests, or at least only one reason a man like Donnell would have. He knew nothing about Meggie's accomplishments, likes, or dislikes, and so he could not be attempting to boast about any of those. Donnell was displaying a possible bride before his friends. The mere thought of one of the Chisholms getting his hands on sweet little Meggie made Annora feel ill.

As she carefully peeled and cored an apple, Annora surreptitiously watched the Chisholms. It had to be them that Donnell was trying to impress, perhaps even bribe, for Egan had known Meggie nearly all her life and had shown no more interest in her than Donnell did. The way the younger Chisholms studied Meggie, as if trying to decide how she would look when she was fully grown, made Annora want to grab Meggie and run for the hills.

When Meggie was finally sent away, Annora calmly finished her apple and then politely excused herself. She did not go far, only far enough so that the men in the great hall would think she had retired to her bedchamber or joined Meggie in the nursery. Then, as silently as she could, she crept back to the great hall, pressing herself hard up against the wall just by the doorway. If Donnell did have a plan to marry Meggie to one of the Chisholms, there would be some talk of it now that the prize had been shown around.

"A bonnie wee lass," said Ian Chisholm, his deep, scratchy voice easy to recognize. "What do ye think, Wee Ian?"

"Aye, she could weel grow up to be a bonnie lass," replied Ian's firstborn son.

Annora almost cursed aloud and clapped her hand over her mouth to prevent her anger from taking voice. Donnell was indeed attempting to arrange a betrothal between Meggie and one of Ian Chisholm's ugly sons. There had to be something Donnell would gain from such an arrangement. Even though Ian and Donnell had become close allies in stealing from the neighboring clans, Annora felt they were on even footing as far as the crimes they had committed were concerned. Therefore she doubted it was because of blackmail that Donnell would offer the Chisholms what Donnell always claimed was his first and only child.

"Why does Wee Ian get to choose?" growled Halbert, the younger son. "He has already had two wives."

"Because he is my heir, ye half-wit," snapped Ian. "Those weak lassies he married didnae give him the son we need ere they died. Young as she is, wee Meggie looks a sturdy, healthy female."

"Fiona is a cursed sturdy and healthy female, too. Why doesnae Wee Ian marry her?"

"What does Fiona have to do with this?"

"Wee Ian has been sharing her bed and showing her that he isnae so verra wee after all, aye? Word is that she is carrying his bairn."

There was the sound of a fist hitting flesh and then someone crashing to the floor. Annora fought the urge to run from those sounds of violence, a caution she had learned early on in her life at Dunncraig. Thinking of the fate that might await Meggie, Annora found the strength to stay where she was and silently began praying that the Chisholms would keep their attention centered upon the fruitful Fiona. If that woman was carrying Wee Ian's child, the whole matter of Meggie wedding one of Ian Chisholm's unwholesome spawn might be forgotten for now.

"Why did ye knock me down?"

Annora thought that, for a full-grown man, Wee Ian could whine just like a small child.

"Why didnae ye tell me that ye got a bairn on Fiona?" demanded Ian.

"Because she is a whore, ye ken. I cannae e'en be sure tis my bairn she is carrying."

"'Tis your bairn and ye ken it weel," said Halbert, sneering triumph filling his voice. "The minute ye got your arse in her bed she ne'er e'en spoke to another mon. Everyone kens it."

"Then ye will be wedding Fiona, Wee Ian," said Ian.

"But she could bear a lass!" protested Wee Ian.

"So ye get her with bairn again and again until she gets it right. She looks a good breeder. Halbert will be the one betrothed to Margaret. If, by the time the lass grows, ye have no son and Fiona has joined your other wives, then we will talk on this matter again."

"Then let us discuss the possibility of a betrothal, a joining of our houses," said Donnell.

Annora had to force herself not to run into the great hall and scream nay. Another part of her still wanted to just grab Meggie and run away. She had to fight both urges so hard she was trembling. Realizing how long she had stood there, she finally found the strength to move and fled to her bedchamber. She knew Meggie would be waiting for her, wondering where she was, but Annora needed time to calm down, time to push away all thought of that sweet, innocent, and bright child being given to one of those hard, cruel men.

Once in her room, she threw herself down on the bed and took slow, deep breaths until her heartbeat slowed and she could finally think more clearly. Her first thought was that the threat to Meggie was not imminent. She was only a child of five years. At the very least, she would not be of an age to marry for another eight years and a lot could happen between now and then. She repeated that fact to herself over and over and felt her fears slowly fade away.

Sitting up, Annora stared at the door to her room and decided that she needed to make plans. Since she could not be certain she would be allowed to stay with Meggie for all of those years, several plans needed to be made to cover every possibility. The knowledge of what Donnell planned for Meggie gave Annora even more incentive to find out the truth about Donnell, his possession of Dunncraig, and his claim to Meggie. If Donnell was no longer a laird, might even be proven to be a thief and a liar, or worse, then Meggie would be freed of all promises Donnell had made.

Destroying Donnell would rob Meggie of her life at Dunncraig, but that realization caused Annora to hesitate for only a moment. Even the sort of life Annora had led, or one where food and shelter were of a poor quality, had to be far better than life as the wife of Halbert Chisholm or one of his brothers. Determined that no matter what she had to do, she would keep Meggie safe from the Chisholms, Annora finally went in search of her charge. When it came to the safety and happiness of Meggie, Donnell might soon discover that his cousin, the unwanted bastard child, was not the meek, obedient soul he thought she was.

The sound of a little girl's laughter drew James to the door of his workroom. He had to step all the way outside to get a clear view of his child. As always, Meggie was with Annora. It seemed to him that there was something a little different in the way Annora treated Meggie today, but it was several moments before he realized what the difference was. Annora was acting far more watchful, more protective, of her little charge. James suddenly wanted to know why, what had changed, and he actually took a step toward them, only to feel someone grab the back of his shirt and stop him. He glanced behind him to find Big Marta slowly shaking her head.

"Nay, laddie, ye best nay be doing that," she said.

"Oh? I cannae just wander o'er there to greet them, mayhap remark upon the fine weather we are having?" James had given up trying to hold fast to his disguise in front of the sharp-eyed

Big Marta, but he spoke softly so that no one else heard the clear proof that he was no Frenchman.

"Dinnae ye see those two hulking fools watching o'er the lassies?"

"MacKay has Annora and Meggie watched closely e'en inside the walls of Dunncraig?"

"When those bastards the Chisholms are here, aye. And it isnae just MacKay who wants the lassies watched. Egan doesnae want them to catch Annora alone. In the keep itself she isnae followed about much, for a good scream could save her if anyone was fool enough to try to grab her and nay many of us talk much to her for fear MacKay will find out. One doesnae want that mon thinking ye ken something ye shouldnae. Aye, and every mon, woman, and child here kens that neither of the lassies is to be touched."

"It surprises me that MacKay would be so protective of a child he kens weel isnae his."

Big Marta crossed her arms over her chest. "Och, aye? Who better to watch than the daughter of the mon ye ken weel must want ye dead?"

James grimaced, realizing that his resentment over MacKay's false claim of being Meggie's father could obviously make him blind to a few simple facts. "And Annora? He couldnae think that I kenned her at all. She ne'er came here when I was wed to Mary."

"As I just said—Egan doesnae want Annora touched."

"He wants her."

She nodded. "That he does and he has wanted her from the first day she walked through the gates of Dunncraig. It took a while for the lass to see that."

"As MacKay's first and a mon who doesnae seem to hesitate to take what he wants, why has Egan left Annora alone all this time?"

"She may be a bastard but she is higher born than he is and he wants her to accept him without being forced. 'Tis his vanity, I suspicion. He wants all to ken that she chose him, that she willingly went into his bed because he is such a big, important mon."

At first James was furious, and the derision clear to hear in Big Marta's voice as she spoke of Egan did nothing to diminish that anger. It took him a minute to realize that a lot of it was born of what tasted so much like jealousy he could not deny it. It was a bad time to be feeling possessive about a woman. It was particularly bad to feel so about Annora MacKay, a woman who was cousin to the man who had destroyed him and was dependent upon that same man for her livelihood.

"Do ye think that will happen?" The noise Big Marta made, one rife with scornful amusement, eased something inside him this time.

"Nay. I think she wouldst rather be in a gutter and begging ere she took him as her mon. The lass isnae allowed to have much to do with the rest of us, ye ken, but after three years one can still ken what sort of lass she is despite that. Aye, and wee Meggie loves her. The wee maid Annie who helps her with the child says Annora is a fine lady, sweet and kind and patient with Meggie. To me, weel, the first time she made Meggie giggle, I kenned she was a good sort." Big Marta sighed. "Your bairn was a sad wee lass ere Annora came. And Annora does her best to be sure Meggie isnae under Donnell's eye much, ye ken, turning his anger to her own self if needed."

"He beats them," James said quietly, a renewed anger tightening his voice.

He avoided people and tried to speak as little as possible, afraid to risk his disguise. Even so he had learned a lot. People seemed to like to talk to a man they did not think understood all they said or, at least, could never repeat it correctly. One man had quietly told James, after a long rant on all that had gone wrong since MacKay had taken Dunncraig, that there was something about him that made a person feel he could be trusted. James was not sure he fully believed that, but was glad that it was so, for it was proving very helpful.

One thing he had learned was that Donnell MacKay and his first were brutal men. They used their fists and worse to enforce their rules and strengthen their hold over the people of Dunncraig. James expected that the torture and death of so many of his guard had been enough to make people understand the danger of complaint or resistance. Hearing strong, brave men scream was something that made many pause for fear of sharing that fate. It was hearing that MacKay took his fists to Annora and Meggie that had enraged him and nearly made him do something foolish. It had taken hours to calm himself after that. The fact that he could not immediately do something about it, might even have to stand back as it was done again, caused a hard knot of bitter anger to lodge in his belly.

"Aye, he beats them but nay so badly that there is much damage," Big Marta said quietly.

"And that is supposed to make me feel better?"

"Just said it to make ye nay try to do anything that might help them yet lose ye all else. Only once did MacKay become so enraged with Annora that he wasnae careful, but Egan pulled him away ere he could do too much damage. I took care of the lass then and it was bad, but naught was broken. Nay, not e'en her spirit. I realized then that she had some, quiet and weel hidden that it is. 'Tis what keeps her here. That and her love for wee Meggie."

"I am nay finding out what I need to ken fast enough," he muttered, dragging a hand through his hair.

"Ye didnae think the mon would leave a written confession lying out for all to see, did ye?"

"Impertinent wench."

"Aye, and proud of it. The proof is there, I am sure of it. There is something or someone who can expose all that bastard's lies and trickery."

"Ye sound so sure of that."

"I am. He is too careful. A mon that careful kens that there might be something out there that can hurt him. He is a mon who has secrets he needs to keep anyone from guessing."

James just nodded as he watched Annora and Meggie play some skipping game around the back garden. "If I could prove my innocence, MacKay could then be hanged many times o'er for the killing of so many good men."

Big Marta sighed heavily. "Aye, that was a verra dark time. I think I may ken where some of the few who escaped are hiding."

A flicker of hope danced in James" heart, but he had had too many disappointments lately to allow it free rein. "Where?"

"I will ken the whole of it soon. Need to be careful about such things as I wouldnae want to be the one who caused the death of any of those few lucky ones who survived MacKay's arrival."

"Nay, of course not."

James sighed and started to turn back toward his workroom only to have Meggie suddenly look straight at him. She smiled at him and waved. James returned the gestures and then caught Annora staring at him. He could still taste her on his mouth, feel her soft curves in his arms, and hear her soft sighs in his ears. His dreams had been filled with the sort of images that left him hard with need when he woke. When Meggie looked at her, Annora gave him a hasty smile and a little wave before hurrying his child away.

For a moment James actually considered accepting the smiling offers that had been made by several of the maids. His body was starving for a woman, but he realized it wanted only one woman. In one way, that was a good thing, for dallying with a maid could all too easily prove a serious mistake, exposing him for the fraud he was. On the other hand, he was not sure he liked the fact that Annora MacKay held his body in thrall.

"She would be a good choice when ye are laird again," Big Marta said quietly.

Refusing to blush over being caught staring longingly after Annora MacKay, James snorted and walked back into his workroom. "She is a MacKay."

The noise Big Marta made clearly revealed the scorn with which she viewed that answer. "Only because her mother was. The lass hasnae been treated weel by her kin. She certainly hasnae been treated weel by this part of the family. She doesnae trust MacKay and hasnae from the start. And ye didnae think ye were the only one asking questions about the mon, did ye?"

Thinking of how he had caught Annora sneaking into MacKay's ledger room, so obviously intent upon spying on the man's writings, James just frowned. "Who else is? Aside from me and mayhap Annora MacKay?"

"Weel, your kinsmen tried but they couldnae get close enough."

"Aye, and I made it clear that this was my trouble and they shouldnae risk their lives, at least until I had some way to prove that MacKay had committed the crime I was accused of."

"Didnae stop them. But they couldnae get close. I dinnae ken how but MacKay could almost sniff them out. After a few times when your kinsmen barely escaped with their lives, I think they finally decided to sit back as ye had asked them to. I doubt they have done naught, though."

"I doubt that, too. Unfortunately, the truth is hidden here. I am certain of it"

Big Marta nodded. "That it is, laddie. That it is. But, mayhap, it isnae hidden as weel as that bastard thinks it is. 'Tis muckle hard to keep something secret for long in a keep, isnae it? There is always someone who saw or heard something and one day they admit it."

"Have ye heard something?"

"Whispers, laddie. Just whispers for now. I am keeping this old ear to the ground and will let ye ken when I hear more than a wee rumor or an I *think*."

James sighed and nodded. He watched the woman disappear back into the kitchen and resisted the urge to drag her back and demand to hear what rumors she had heard, even every little suspicion. That was foolish and he knew it. He would not win his freedom with rumors and suspicions. Moving too quickly could also silence those who were doing the whispering and they might well lead to something he could use.

As he returned to his work he thought about Egan's pursuit of Annora. It roused something very primitive inside him, some chest-thumping thing that kept grunting *mine*. He would have to be careful there for several reasons. Egan could cause him to be thrown out of Dunncraig if he thought Annora had an interest in him, or worse. And Annora was such an innocent, he could hurt her feelings if he went from hot to cold and back again once too often.

He cursed and shook his head. No matter how much he told himself that it was bad to feel so attracted to Annora, the attraction did not fade. He had the sinking feeling that he had met his mate. There was a strong belief amongst his foster family the Murrays that everyone had a mate, and thus far, in the matches he had seen, there seemed to be some truth to that feeling. He had not had it with Mary, something that still stirred a deep feeling of guilt, but that strong sense of *mine* that came over him whenever he saw Annora MacKay made him think he may have found it with her.

Not only stupid but a very poor sense of timing on fate's behalf, he mused. As a declared outlaw, he was a walking dead man. Accepting a mate now meant that he placed the woman under that same death sentence. He was going to have to try harder to control that part of him that wanted to grab Annora and claim her in every way a man could claim a woman.

Forcing all thought of her from his mind, he concentrated on his carving. The work did bring him some peace and he welcomed the lessening of the tension that had gripped his body. It was not until he paused to study what he had done that his tension returned full force. In the far corner of the piece of the mantel he had been working on was a woman's face. It was Annora's, every soft curve of the face already as familiar to him as his own.

"'Tis some fine work ye have done there, laddie," said Big Marta from behind him, and James inwardly cursed. The woman had a real skill at arriving at his side at just the wrong moment.

"Aye, it will do," he murmured, hoping the woman would leave it at that.

"That face looks verra familiar."

"Does it, now?"

"Aye, it looks just like our wee Annora."

"Weel, she has a fine face."

Big Marta laughed, slapped him on the back, and walked away. "Och, laddie, dinnae fight it too hard."

James groaned and rested his head against the carving that was now permanently etched into the wood of the mantel that would adorn the fireplace in the laird's chamber. He would probably still fight what was becoming very clear. It was a man's natural inclination to fight a thing as binding as what was growing inside him. Unfortunately, he was sure it was a battle already lost.

Chapter Six

Annora woke to her cat sitting on her chest and staring into her face. She gave the big, gray torn a sleepy smile and scratched behind its ragged ears. It had been on a bit of a wander for a few days and she feared there would be some kittens born in a few months. She would have to try to find them and see if she could save them from a drowning.

Mungo, named after a boy who had been her friend when she was a child, was a well-kept secret. Annora had absolutely no doubt that Donnell would use her love for her cat against her if he found out about Mungo. He had already shown that he could use her feelings for Meggie to keep her obedient.

Sitting up, she uncovered the small plate of venison bits mixed with a cooked egg that she had scavenged for her pet and set it down on the bed beside her. Purring deeply and loudly, Mungo moved off her to eat and she idly stroked its back as she shook free of the last tenuous grip of a long, deep sleep.

Oddly enough, despite the depth of her sleep, she could recall a very vivid dream, one she had had many times before. This time, however, the ruddy, green-eyed wolf was watching her as she kissed a tall, dark-haired man. A man with the same color eyes as the wolf, she thought and frowned. That kiss she had shared with Rolf had certainly added new warmth to her dreams, but it was only now that she realized he had those same eyes as the wolf that had haunted her dreams for a little over three years.

"How verra strange, Mungo," she murmured as the cat curled up by her side, resting its head on her chest. "Do ye think my dreams are some kind of, weel, a vision? Nay, that cannae be. Wheesht, I have enough trouble trying nay to feel what everyone round me is feeling. I dinnae need to become afflicted with the sight as weel."

Mungo yawned widely and began to lazily wash a paw.

"He kissed me, Mungo. Oh, I ken that I have been kissed before and one or two times I actually wanted to be kissed, but, wheesht, none kissed me like he kissed me. I have certainly ne'er dreamed of any mon who kissed me. Most of them I wouldnae want to dream of, true enough, but, aye, one or two didnae repulse me. But e'en they didnae make me dream of them. Rolf kisses me but once and I cannae shake the memory of it; it e'en invades my dreams of my wolf." She grimaced. "I fear my heart may be readying itself to do something verra, verra foolish."

Seeing that Mungo was asleep, Annora carefully slipped out of her bed. Despite losing its comfortable pillow on her chest as well as her warmth, the cat barely blinked. It was a sad state of affairs when one was reduced to discussing one's troubles with a cat, Annora mused as she hurried to get washed up and dressed. Talks about kisses and men were best had with other women, but Donnell had made certain that she had no close confidante amongst the women of Dunncraig.

Refusing to become maudlin over all she lacked, Annora went to say a good morning to Meggie. The little girl was all smiles and chatter when Annora reached the nursery. Meggie's plans for the day ran one into the other as she babbled. The small grain of sadness and self-pity that had taken root in Annora's heart was soon banished. The maid Annie quietly let Annora know that their *guests* had left at dawn and Annora smiled with relief at the thought of breaking her fast without having to face the Chisholms again.

After telling Meggie to heed the young Annie who had prepared her such a fine meal to break her fast with, Annora headed down to the great hall to break her own. She wondered if one reason she was so cheerful was simply that the Chisholms were gone and, as was their usual habit, would not be back for a few months. From what little she had been able to discern, and the lack of any hastily performed ceremony, no final agreement had been made with Donnell concerning the betrothal of Halbert

Chisholm to Meggie. Donnell obviously wanted to dangle the bait before the Chisholms for a while longer.

The evening meal the night before had been a torment for Annora, one that she doubted she would soon forget. She had spent every minute of it expecting Donnell to announce that Meggie was now betrothed to Halbert Chisholm. The conversation she had overheard between the Chisholms and Donnell had certainly made it sound as if it was all settled between them, but now she had to wonder. Since she did not know what each man wanted or held over the head of the other, she suspected the why of it all would be very hard to discern. It was tempting to simply confront Donnell and demand some answers, but she knew that was just her frustration talking. She knew it was absolute foolishness to think a confrontation with Donnell about anything was a good idea, and it was certainly unwise to think he would calmly accept her opinion on anything.

Stepping into the great hall, Annora breathed a silent sigh of relief. The Chisholms were really gone. There was no sign of them in the great hall and they never missed a meal. Donnell was there talking to Rolf, but even Egan was absent. It was a little unsettling to face a man she had so recently kissed and clung to with such abandon, but it was better than facing Egan and the others again. The little bench where she always sat to eat was beautifully empty. She approached cautiously, however, for she did not know if Donnell would want her to be there while he discussed work with Master Lavengeance. When Donnell only briefly glanced her way and then continued to talk to Rolf, she was relieved. She sat down quickly, and helped herself to some food as surreptitiously as possible.

Pretending not to listen to the conversation between the men going on so close to her was difficult. Donnell was discussing the making of chairs. He talked of how he had seen some at some rich man's keep and wanted a full set of something similar for his head table. Annora badly wanted to gape at the man, revealing her astonishment, but she quickly filled her mouth with oatmeal to smother the urge.

A quick glance at Master Lavengeance tempted Annora to reach out with her gift to see if she could sense what he was feeling. There was certainly no hint of how he felt about Donnell's elaborate plans upon his handsome face, and Annora felt strangely compelled to know what was going on behind that smooth, calm mask of a face. The moment she let herself reach out to him, she began to think it had been a mistake to do so. The rage she had felt before was now sharp and boiling up inside him. Annora was astonished that no sign of that revealed itself upon his face. There was also a wealth of scorn inside him, directed at Donnell, but Master Lavengeance's fine voice was soft and polite.

Suddenly Master Lavengeance rubbed his hand over his mouth as if he was thinking and then he spoke quickly in French. Annora nearly choked on the oatmeal she had just put into her mouth. She glanced at Donnell, and the faint frown of confusion on his face told her that Donnell had no idea of how vilely he had just been insulted. It took every scrap of willpower she possessed not to blush over the coarse words Master Lavengeance had spoken in his deep, calm, and courteous voice. The man detested Donnell so deeply and completely that she had to wonder why this wood-carver was even at Dunncraig. How could he work for a man he loathed so thoroughly?

"Curse it all," muttered Donnell and then he scowled at Annora. "What did he say? Are the things I am asking beyond his capabilities? Come now, ye understand him, dinnae ye?"

Annora took a deep drink of her goat's milk to drown the urge to repeat Master Lavengeance's insults word for word. She was sure a beating would be the very least Donnell would give the man for those words. Donnell may not have loved his mother, but Annora was sure he would not want to hear anyone say that the woman had been the lover of goats. So she decided the best thing to do was to tell Donnell some of what she had been thinking as she had listened to his grand plans.

"Master Lavengeance but wonders if the design ye spoke of putting onto the back of the chairs would make them uncomfortable to sit in." Out of the corner of her eye she saw the faintest glint of amusement in Master Lavengeance's eye. "T'would be a wee bit, weel, bumpy, aye?"

Donnell frowned, obviously struggling to picture what he

wanted in his mind and failing. "Humph. That wouldnae be a good thing. Weel, I will leave the design up to ye, then," he said to Master Lavengeance. "I expect ye to show me what ye plan first, however. What else?" he then demanded of Annora. "I ken that wasnae all he said, for there were a lot of words there."

Weel, he also said that he thought your father was the king's whore, she mused, but simply said, "He says ye need to decide if ye want to use a heavy wood or a lighter one."

"Heavy. I want good sturdy chairs." As if realizing that he was having to ask for Annora's help simply to make his wishes understood to a mere wood-carver, Donnell scowled at Annora. "Why do ye ken this language anyway? What does a wee lass need to ken such things for?"

"I suspect I dinnae really need to ken it," she said in an attempt to keep his annoyance from growing, "but when I was but a child and still living with my grandsire, I had a friend named Mungo. His mother was French." The memory of Lady Aimee made Annora feel both sad and comforted, for the woman had been very kind to her, and kindness was something she had received little of as a child. "She taught me."

"Ah, I suspicion she wanted someone to talk to, eh? Easier to gossip in her own tongue."

"Aye, I suspicion that was it."

Pleased that Donnell's annoyance had lessened and he turned his full attention back to Master Lavengeance, Annora finished her meal. She also pulled back from the wood-carver, understanding the harsh feelings he had toward Donnell, but finding them very uncomfortable to share. She had enough of her own to deal with. The moment she was done eating she excused herself, but as she stood up to leave the table, Donnell grabbed her by the arm. Annora tensed, afraid that she was about to pay dearly for knowing something that her Cousin did not She saw Master Lavengeance's whole body tense and forced herself to squarely meet his gaze, trying to convey to him that it would be useless, even dangerous, to interfere in whatever Donnell planned to do now.

"Best ye dinnae go too far, Cousin," Donnell said to her. "I may have need of ye to help me understand the mon again."

Even though she could hear the resentment in Donnell's voice, Annora felt weak-kneed with relief. "As ye wish, Cousin. May I go to Meggie now?"

"Aye, get away with ye."

Bobbing in a swift, shallow curtsey to both men, Annora fled the room as fast as she could without actually running. It bothered her that Donnell wanted her help, for the resentment he felt for even having to ask for it would only grow each time she had to come to his aid. She decided it might be wise to try to find a moment to speak privately with the wood-carver. It was a little amusing to hear Donnell vilified, but she knew she could easily pay dearly for that brief amusement If Donnell ever discovered exactly what Master Lavengeance was saying, the wood-carver would pay even more dearly. The last man who insulted Donnell had died slowly and painfully while hanging in a cage from the battlements of Dunncraig Keep. Since the mere thought of the handsome wood-carver meeting the same gruesome fate made her feel horrified and deeply afraid for him, Annora knew she would be cornering the man at the earliest opportunity.

James watched Annora leave the great hall, enjoying the gentle sway of her hips. He felt a little guilty about what he had said to Donnell even though it had eased the strength of the anger churning inside him. For a moment he had forgotten that Annora understood French. He never should have spoken so crudely in front of her. Worse, he had the feeling that he had just caused her some trouble with her cousin. He would have to be more careful, he thought, as he turned his gaze back to Donnell only to find the man staring at him. MacKay did not really look angry, but there was a narrow-eyed warning easy to read in the man's expression.

"That one isnae for ye, laddie," Donnell said as he poured himself and then James a tankard of ale. "Best ye dinnae let your gaze rest on her too much."

"She sits too high?" James murmured and then took a drink of ale.

"Aye, I suspicion she does although ye have a verra fancy name for a common mon. But she is meant for Egan. He wouldnae like to see that look ye had in your eye as ye watched her fine arse swish out of the room."

It was hard not to strike the man down for speaking so crudely about Annora. "They are betrothed, eh?"

"Weel, they will be soon if Egan has his way. Now, let us try and make each other understood as we talk some more on these chairs I am wanting."

James nearly rolled his eyes. If he did not hold fast to the hope that he would soon be sitting back in the laird's chair, he would probably be even more upset over MacKay's scramble for elegance at the expense of all the people of Dunncraig. There was nothing he could do about the neglect of his lands and his people until he had proven his innocence and regained the right to rule his lands. If he increased the beauty of the keep as he worked to destroy MacKay, he could perhaps find some comfort in that. He also knew that the moment he regained his good name and his lands, his family would help him begin to restore Dunncraig lands to the efficiency they had once enjoyed. It was the only thing that held him back from acting too quickly.

Rubbing at the ache in the small of her back, Annora looked over the finished garden. If there was enough rain and sun over the next few months, Dunncraig would have all the herbs it needed for cooking and healing. There would also be some flowers to enjoy. Satisfied with her work, she praised Meggie for all her help and sent the little girl off to the nursery to get cleaned up. Annora began to collect up the little bags the seeds had been stored in and the tools she and Meggie had used to plant them. As she straightened up, someone grabbed her from behind, causing her to drop everything, and then she was dragged over to the wall of the keep. It was all done so quickly she had not had time to gather her wits enough to say anything before she found herself already near the wall.

For just a moment, Annora thought it was Rolf despite the roughness of the treatment, but she quickly realized her mistake. The feel was wrong, as was the smell. By the time she felt herself thrust up against the wall, she knew that Egan had her. The brief look she got of his face before he forced a kiss on her mouth told her that he was tired of playing the gentle wooer.

This time, she thought, he would not stop. She could almost smell the lust in him. Unlike the desire she had felt in Master Lavengeance, Egan's did not stir a similar wanting in her. The feel of his hard mouth bruising hers, the taste of him as he shoved his tongue into her mouth, and the way he rubbed his groin against her had her feeling nauseated and terrified. Worse, because it was late in the day and she was in the far rear bailey of the keep, she did not think anyone would be coming along to disturb them, something that had worked to make Egan back away in the past. For some reason he did not want people to think he had to force himself on her despite his reputation as a brutal rapist, someone who had left far too many women at Dunncraig and elsewhere bruised, bleeding, and afraid of men from then on.

Annora tried to push him away but he was too big and too strong. Trapped against the hard wall as she was, she could barely move. Kicking her feet proved useless and he had her hands pinned tightly against the stones, so tightly that she felt a slow trickle of blood run down her wrists. There was a sense of harsh, brutal hunger in the man, something almost feral and very frightening.

Then, suddenly, he was gone and she was free. While she stood there gasping, she watched Master Lavengeance knock Egan unconscious with one powerful punch to the jaw. For a moment she was stunned both by the fortunate appearance of Master Lavengeance, but also by the powerful rage filling the air around him. Then she saw him grab the unconscious Egan by the front of his shirt and yank him up out of the dirt, pulling his fist back in preparation for another blow.

"Nay," she gasped and stumbled forward to grab at Master Lavengeance's arm.

"Do not tell me that you were enjoying that," James growled, even as he fought to conquer the blind rage that had engulfed him at the sight of Egan pinning Annora against the wall and grinding his body against hers. He was surprised that he had retained enough of his wits to speak in French.

"Men can be such idiots," she muttered. "Nay, fool. One punch can be explained away as a mon who thought he saw a woman being raped and paid little heed to who the couple was. More than that and it looks to be a verra personal beating, aye?"

James knew immediately that she was right and he threw Egan back down. He put his hands on his hips, kept his gaze fixed on the unconscious Egan, and took several deep breaths to further push aside his fury. When he looked at Annora again, however, it almost all returned. Her lips were bruised and swollen and there was a fear in her eyes that was new. He had heard of Egan's reputation for brutalizing women and suspected she had thought she was about to be another of his victims.

"Are you hurt?" he asked in French.

"There will be a few bruises but nay more than that. Thank ye," she added in a soft, tremulous voice.

Annora felt a strong urge to cry and did not understand that. She had been saved. She should be feeling relieved and happy. There was some of that, but mostly she was still afraid and she wanted to hurl herself to the ground and weep like a heartbroken child. It took her a moment to realize what ailed her. Egan had finally crossed that fine line that had always kept her safe from his brutality. She could no longer think that he would not treat her as he did too many others. There was little doubt in her mind that she would be flinching at every movement she caught out of the corner of her eye and searching every shadow for some sign of him.

"Are you able to lock your bedchamber door?" James asked her.

"Aye. I usually do."

"Good. Make that always instead of usually."

Despite the fact that French was a soft language, Master Lavengeance's command sounded very hard and cold. There was still a lot of anger in him and not one that was part of that rage that she could always sense inside him. This was new and it was aimed directly at Egan. Egan deserved it, but Annora became afraid for Master Lavengeance. Egan was Donnell's first, and perhaps his most loyal, friend and minion. It was not wise to make an enemy of either man.

"Ye had best be verra careful, Master Lavengeance," she said as she stepped forward to take him by the arm and tug him away from where Egan lay sprawled facedown on the ground.

"And you must call me Rolf." James wished he could hear her say his real name, say it in a soft voice made thick and husky with passion.

Annora blushed, but nodded. "And ye must call me Annora." She glanced back at Egan as she continued to tug Rolf to the door leading back inside the keep. "But nay in front of him or Donnell, aye?"

James hesitated in their retreat long enough to tug free of her grasp, take her by the arm, and become the one leading them away from the place where Egan had tried to rape her. "He has already told me that you sit too high for me and that Egan is wanting you."

Stumbling a little because the shock of his words were so great, she stared at him as he now led them through the door and into the keep. "Donnell said that? Wheesht, I dinnae sit too high. I am a bastard and my mother didnae sit that high e'en before her fall from grace. As for Egan wanting me, weel, that is just too bad."

Although he wanted to tell her she was being naive, James decided now was not the time to have that discussion. She was still trembling even though her voice had now lost that wobble that indicated tears were close at hand. He had the feeling that Annora either did not know Egan's plans for her aside from getting her into his bed or she was trying to ignore the truth because it was too ugly for her.

Once outside the great hall, James gently pushed her toward the stairs. "Go. I am going to tell MacKay what happened."

"Do ye think that is wise?" she asked, pausing on the first step to look at him.

"It is wise to be the first to tell him what happened. Then he has that tale in his mind when Egan comes to him demanding justice or revenge. Go, it will be fine. You were right to stop me from beating him more even though it was what he needed. I but stopped him and even your lord cannot argue with the right of that. You are Margaret's nurse, not some whore of a maid like Mab."

Even as she went up the stairs, Annora kept her gaze fixed upon him until he disappeared into the great hall. She wanted to go after him, to stand beside him, and try to keep Donnell from getting angry, but knew that was useless. She had never been very good at stopping Donnell from getting angry. And Rolf was right. Being the first to tell the tale was best. It would put Egan on the defensive.

As she entered her room to clean up and change for the evening meal, Annora thought of what Rolf had claimed Donnell had said about her. For Donnell to imply that she was too high a reach for a man like Rolf was ridiculous. Donnell did not see her as a wellborn maid. It was the fact that Donnell had implied that she was meant for Egan that really troubled her. It might have been just some ruse to keep Rolf from wooing her. After all, Donnell found her useful as Meggie's nurse.

But if Egan claimed her she would still remain at Dunncraig, she thought, and felt a chill go through her so quickly and fiercely she shivered as if caught outside in a snowfall. The more she thought about it, the more she feared Donnell and Egan had plans for her that they had not yet informed her of.

Suddenly anger pushed aside the lingering fear stirred by Egan's attack. They had no right to plan who she would marry or who would have her in any manner. Donnell was her kinsman but far from close kin, and at four and twenty she was far past the age where a man needed to arrange her future.

A new determination took hold of her. She was going to find out what these plans were. It would mean more sneaking around and listening to things not intended for her ears, but, she thought as she changed her gown, she was getting rather good at that. The sooner she knew what Donnell and Egan planned, the sooner she could act to protect herself. She would not have years to come up with a way to thwart them, so she would have to act fast. If Donnell intended to give her to Egan, she was going to have to answer just one question. Was becoming Egan's chattel too high a price to stay with Meggie?

Chapter Seven

Leaving Meggie with Annie to have her bath, Annora hurried to her bedchamber to prepare for the evening meal in the great hall. For reasons of his own that Annora had never really understood, Donnell had refused to allow her to stay in the nursery with Meggie, or to sleep anywhere near it. The only reason she could think of was that Donnell did not want her and Meggie to grow too close to each other. If that was his intention he had utterly failed, for spending every day together had made her and Meggie as close as mother and daughter. Annora could only hope that Donnell never noticed that.

Shaking aside that puzzle, she began to hurry. She did not want to be late for the evening meal. Her intention of finding out what Donnell had planned for her had met with utter failure last evening, but she was not one to give up too easily. Seeing Egan with a badly bruised face had offered her some compensation for that failure, but not enough. The way the man had glared at her all evening would have suited her just fine, as it was far better than having him try to woo or seduce her, but there had been such menace in his eyes it had spoiled her appetite. Tonight she would not allow him to intimidate her.

Just as she started down the long, poorly lit hall that led to her bedchamber, Annora met up with a buxom maid named Mab. She smiled politely at the woman who frequently shared both Donnell's and Egan's beds. If the whispered rumors she had heard had any truth in them, she had sometimes entertained both men at the same time. Annora decided that was not something she really wanted to think about.

Noting the direction the woman was coming from, Annora

knew it was neither one of those men Mab had been visiting. Annora suddenly realized one could reach the wood-carver's small room if one continued down the hall to the very end and turned left. The mere thought that Mab had been romping with Master Lavengeance made Annora feel both hurt and angry. It should not matter to her who the man bedded, but it did; it mattered a lot.

"Ah, the wee nursemaid," sneered Mab.

A little taken aback by the animosity that filled the woman and stripped her voice of all softness, Annora asked, "Is there something I might help ye with?" Annora was pleased at how calm and polite she sounded, for she refused to add to the woman's inexplicable dislike.

"Wheesht, there be naught ye can help me with unless ye want to tell me how good that fine Frenchmon is atween the sheets."

"Dinnae ye ken that?" Annora decided that courtesy was completely wasted on this woman.

"I ne'er said I didnae. I was just wondering if ye wanted to have a wee woman-to-woman talk o'er how verra fine that mon is. I hear ye can understand what he says e'en when he gets too, ah, impassioned to speak our language."

Annora wondered where a woman like Mab had learned a word like *impassioned* and then felt guilty for being so unkind, even if it was only in her thoughts. "I am afraid I cannae answer that question."

"Nay? Ye would have me believe that ye havenae been sniffing round that fine mon? That ye arenae trying to see if he is better in the bed than Egan?"

"I cannae tell ye how weel or how badly Egan performs, either." And Annora prayed to God that she would never find out.

"Bah, arenae ye the sweet innocent? Weel, I ken what ye are thinking. Ye are thinking that I am naught but a whore and ye are looking down your fine nose at me, aye? Ye are naught but a bastard who goes from home to home doing work nay better than what I do. Just what makes ye think ye are so much better than I am?"

I occasionally bathe, Annora thought and immediately

wondered why she was consistently thinking such unkind things about this woman. It was so unlike her. At best she would think little or nothing at all about someone goading her as Mab was now. If she did think of anything, it was only about how quickly she could extract herself from the conversation and get far, far away.

It all tasted far too much like jealousy to her. Reluctantly, Annora had to admit to herself that she loathed the very thought of Master Lavengeance and Mab doing anything more than shaking hands. She was not even sure she would like that, for it would mean he was touching the woman. Such feelings had to be some form of madness. True, she did find the man very attractive and she still felt warm all over when she recalled how he had kissed her, which was far too often for her peace of mind. That did not excuse this growing urge to do violence to Mab, or to feel as possessive of Master Lavengeance as she did. If nothing else, anything that grew between herself and the wood-carver could have no future and could even cause them a great deal of trouble with Donnell and Egan, dangerous trouble.

"This is a foolish conversation," Annora suddenly said and pushed Mab aside so that she could continue on to her room. "I do nay more at Dunncraig than care for Meggie. 'Tis all I do and weel ye ken it."

Mab's derisive snort echoed down the hall, following Annora and making her leave-taking taste a little too much like a retreat. Annora muttered a curse to herself and refused to rise to that bait. A heavy, but soft sigh of relief escaped her when she heard Mab hurry away and she refused to look to see which direction the woman took. Mab was one of those women who had to have every man in reach, and Annora suspected that, even if the woman had never touched Master Lavengeance, she would dislike her. No one liked a greedy person, Annora thought, not caring if she sounded a little childish even to herself.

Just as she walked by a small alcove near some steps that led to one of the tower rooms, Annora was grabbed by the arm and pulled deep into the shadows. A warm, soft mouth quickly smothered her instinctive scream. For a brief moment she was terrified that Egan had found her again. But then Annora recognized the taste of the man kissing her. She knew she ought to fight Rolf, knew she ought to be alarmed at how readily she recognized the man holding her so close, but she simply wrapped her arms around his neck and gave herself over to the kiss.

The moment the kiss ended, she struggled to regain her good sense, only to lose what little she had grabbed hold of a heartbeat later. He began to kiss her throat, pulling her hard up against his strong body even as he pushed her against the wall. She had the wild, fleeting thought that perhaps people did not need to be prone to make love.

When Rolf nibbled on her ear, teasing it with his tongue, Annora shivered. She felt as if pure fire was rushing through her body. A touch of fear mixed with the passion that had taken complete control of her. Something so strong, so overwhelming, was something that she should not and did not trust.

James felt a hint of tension enter the soft body he craved and quickly kissed Annora again, eager to banish whatever resistance she was mustering. It was madness to grab her like this, but his need for her felt like madness. He had escaped any punishment for hitting Egan, but James had a feeling it was because MacKay wished to strike out at Egan in some small way. Whether it was a need to assert his power over his first or something else, James did not know and was not sure he cared. One thing he was sure of was that both MacKay and Egan were now watching him closely. Especially Egan, who undoubtedly sought a chance to make him pay dearly for putting such an abrupt ending to the man's attempt to rape Annora and for beating him in front of her.

It did not please James to admit it, but some of his great need to hold Annora and kiss her was to mark her as his own. He wanted to banish the taste and feel of Egan from her lips. He also wanted to make sure that Annora was not left with a fear of such intimacies because of what Egan had tried to do to her.

He kept kissing her as he slowly slid his hand up her rib cage and stroked her breast. She tensed for just a moment and uttered a protest against his mouth, but to his delight it was a very short-lived resistance. The feel of her breast in his hand, the weighty fullness of it, left him hungry for so much more. He wanted to feel her skin, to taste her, and he wanted to do so right now, but he fought to restrain himself.

When Rolf ended the kiss and began to spread hot kisses along the neckline of her gown, Annora fought to regain some control of herself. What he was doing felt so good it was a little difficult to recall that it was all wrong. A maid should not allow a man to corner her in a dark hallway and touch her so intimately. In this case, it could also be dangerous. She had not yet discovered what Donnell's plans were for her future. If Rolf did anything to ruin those plans, he would pay for it with his life and she could not allow that. To cool her passion as quickly as possible, she began to think of Mab and recall the chance that the woman had been returning from sharing Rolf's bed. It acted almost as good as a bucket of cold water.

"Nay," she said as she pushed at his chest, idly wondering why she felt such a strong urge to rip his shirt from his body and touch the skin beneath it. "I willnae be another Mab for ye."

James leaned back a little and stared at her. "Mab?"

Finally able to think clearly, although his body ached all over to make love to her, James cursed softly. He then muttered an apology when Annora blushed. Mab had obviously been trying to get into his bed again and Annora had met up with her. Mab was becoming a nuisance. James also wondered if Mab's persistence was because one, or even both, of her lovers was trying to use her to keep him occupied. MacKay and Egan were not the sort of men who could understand how any man could want only one woman.

"I have not bedded Mab. I do not care what the woman says. Yes, she seems eager to crawl into my bed"—he gave Annora a quick, hard kiss—"but I want something better, something sweeter. I think your lord or that fool Egan keep sending her to me in the hope that it will keep me well occupied."

Annora knew he spoke the truth. Her ability to sense the truth or a lie was one of the few things she actually appreciated about her gift. "Why would they do that?"

"To keep me away from you."

Since he had stepped back a little, Annora busied herself with the needless chore of brushing down her skirt with her hands. It gave her a moment to calm herself as his talk of wanting her both flattered her and made her uneasy. Although she did not sense any taint in his desire for her, she knew a lot of men felt a woman who was bastard born did not deserve the respect and courtesies offered a wellborn lady. There was no use in mentioning to such men that her mother had been a true lady born and bred. The fact that her mother had born a bastard diminished her in a lot of eyes. They also seemed to think that her mother's apparent immorality was passed on to her daughter. None of that attitude shaded Rolfs desire, but she had to turn him away and that made her very sad.

"It would probably be best if ye did stay away from me," she said, hoping the regret she felt over the need to push him away did not show in her voice or in her eyes as she looked at him.

James gently stroked her cheek, pleased when she did not flinch away from his touch. He knew that many people thought French was the perfect language for lovers, but he was rapidly growing weary of it. He wanted to talk to Annora in his own tongue. Soon, he hoped, he would be able to.

"You do not wish me to be near you?" he asked.

Annora sighed. "What I want isnae important, is it?"

"It is to me."

She smiled faintly. "Ah, weel, that is verra fine, but we arenae free to do as we please."

"I am not a MacKay."

"Nay, but I am and ye are a mon who was hired by MacKay."

"So you do think you sit too high to kiss a wood-carver."

"Dinnae be a fool. What I think is I would like ye to do your work and leave here still hale, still alive. For some reason, Donnell doesnae want ye to, weel, pursue me. And Donnell doesnae like it when what he wants is ignored. Men die for that. Men die in great pain."

"Ah, you fear for my safety." He kissed her again. "That is good."

Annora almost laughed, but the very real threat they could both face snuffed out her brief burst of good humor. "Be careful, Rolf. Donnell is a fool at times, but he is also a verra brutal mon. Now, I am off to the great hall to have my meal."

He did not stop her. At the moment he could do no more than steal a few kisses and caresses. It was foolish to keep tormenting himself by reaching for what he could not have yet. All it got him was an ache that would torment him all night long, and the cold bath he was going to have to take now would not do much to cure him of that.

Although she hurried into the great hall very late for the meal, Annora noticed that she received barely a glance from everyone already gathered there. She took her seat and smiled fleetingly at the young boy who hurried over to fill her plate with food and her tankard with ale. Egan cast her one hot glare but then returned to discussing something with Donnell.

Most of the time she liked the way that few of Donnell's men noticed her, but this time it stung. Annora knew it was for the best that she remained almost invisible to them all, that it was the best way to avoid becoming the target of Donnell's anger, but tonight it made her feel angry. She might be a bastard, but she was a person who cared for the laird's child. That had to matter, yet to so many of Donnell's people she was no more than some ghostie. It might have been what she had wanted to happen, but it should not be so easy.

Telling herself not to be so foolish and allow pride to rule her, Annora concentrated on her meal. Donnell and Egan talked in low voices and occasionally glanced her way, but she tried to ignore them. It was blessing enough that she did not have Egan seated next to her. She had to make some plan to find out what they had in store for her. If she could do so without being obvious, she would listen to what they were so intensely discussing in whispers right now, but the last thing she wanted was to be caught out in the act of eavesdropping.

When Egan and Donnell suddenly left the room, she inwardly cursed. She knew they were going to discuss the matter, whatever it was, somewhere where they felt they could do so more freely, and that was probably in Donnell's ledger room. If she bolted down her food and left now, it might be too obvious to someone that she was following them, and that someone could mention it to Donnell. It was a chance she could not afford to take. Despite

the tension caused within her by the need to try and find out
what they discussed, she ate her meal at her usual pace. It sat in
her stomach like a rock by the time she felt it was safe enough
to leave the room.

Once in the hallway, she kept an eye out for anyone who might
see where she was going and made her way very cautiously to
Donnell's ledger room. Master Lavengeance might know about
the secret room in there, but she also knew a good place to hide
and listen to anything being said behind the thick door of the
room. Hurrying as fast as she dared, Annora slipped into the
tiny room just to the right of the ledger room.

There was very little in the room besides a small bed and a
chest, just enough to allow Donnell to have a brief moment with
some maid, she thought with a grimace as she tiptoed up to the
wall between the two rooms. Donnell had had it built shortly
after he had arrived to rule over Dunncraig, thinking he would
be hiring a man to keep his records for him. He had quickly
decided that he would do it all himself and she knew it was
not because he liked the work or felt he could do it better than
anyone else. He simply did not want anyone seeing his ledger
books.

Donnell probably did not trust his own mother, she thought
as she pressed her ear against a small knothole in the wood of the
wall between the rooms. The door between the rooms was thin
and worked just as well, but after nearly being caught because it
had creaked softly as she had leaned against it, she had searched
out a new spy hole. She never again wanted to suffer the fear
she had felt then. For days afterward she had been terrified that
Donnell had guessed it was she trying to listen to him speak to
the sheriff, and it had been weeks before she had finally believed
that she had been so lucky as to avoid detection.

Annora rolled her eyes in disgust as the first thing she heard
was a loud belch. She was certain it was Donnell, for the man ate
far too much food and ate it so quickly, she was not surprised
that his belly protested. There were times when she watched
him eat and wondered how he kept from popping open like an
overripe berry.

"I dinnae see why we had to scurry into this room," complained Egan.

"I didnae want to chance Annora hearing what we had to say," replied Donnell.

"She needs to be told soon. That cursed Frenchmen is sniffing round her skirts far too often for my taste. And he turns down all the maids."

"Mayhap he is a monk in disguise," drawled Donnell and chuckled at his own humor.

"Laugh if ye will, but I begin to think there is something nay right with the mon."

"Why? Because he doesnae rut himself blind with all the maids? Some men dinnae, ye ken. Odd as it seems. I have kenned a few in my time. Too choosy, I am thinking."

"Weel, if he thinks to choose Annora, he had best think again. She is mine."

"So ye have told me from the first day she came here," drawled Donnell.

There was a chill in Donnell's voice that told Annora her cousin felt Egan was pushing too hard. Donnell did not like to be pushed.

"I ken it and I ken I wanted her to choose me. I meant to woo her but she makes it near to impossible. So now she will wed me whether she wishes to or nay. I am certain I can change her mind. The lass just needs a few good ruttings to see the advantage of having a mon in her bed."

The food that had sat like a heavy rock in her stomach now began to churn. Annora did not want to even think about Egan climbing into her bed, and worse, climbing onto her. Rutting was a good word for it, she supposed. Annora had no intention of allowing him to vent his desires on her. She certainly did not wish to become the wife and chattel of a man as brutal as Egan. In a few of the homes she had been taken into she had seen how that sort of life could slowly destroy a woman.

"And that mon must be ye, of course," said Donnell.

"I think I have been verra patient."

"Aye, on that we agree. Verra patient until the wood-carver had to knock ye on your arse."

The amusement in Donnell's voice was clear to hear even through the wall. Annora winced, knowing how that would anger Egan. Not only did being defeated by a man Egan probably thought of as far beneath him infuriate him, but having Donnell constantly rub his face in that defeat could soon put Egan in a killing rage—one aimed directly at Rolf. Annora had to fight the urge to rush off and warn Rolf of the danger he was in. It was selfish, but she needed to stay and try to find out what sort of danger *she* was in first. Once she had heard all she could, however, she would hunt down Master Lavengeance and tell him about the storm that was brewing over his head. She smothered the little sneering voice in her head that said she would be looking for him for another kiss as much as she would be trying to warn him.

"So when will I be allowed to marry Annora?" asked Egan.

"Soon."

"That is what ye always say. Aye, I was willing to wait. As I have always said, I wanted her to be willing. Now I dinnae care; I will make her so."

"As ye wish. It would be far more peaceful if she was willing, but, as ye say, she seems slow to favor ye o'er being a spinster. Twill work for me as weel, for she will have to stay at Dunncraig once she is your wife."

"Ye will expect Annora to act as nurse to that child e'en after we are wed and she is my wife?"

"Why shouldnae she continue to care for Margaret?"

"She will be *my* wife, nay some servant. It may nay look good if my wife is working as a nursemaid."

Donnell made a very rude noise. "Being the nurse to the child of a laird is nay a poor position for any woman to hold, and weel ye ken it. If ye mean to deprive me of a good nurse for Margaret, then mayhap we should rethink this marriage ye are whining for."

"Nay, nay," Egan said hurriedly. "Ye are right. Many a lady born and bred, when widowed or left a spinster, has been the nursemaid to the children of a kinsmon. It will be fine."

"Glad ye feel inclined to see reason."

"Shall we now discuss when this marriage shall take place?"

"Soon."

"Soon isnae a date, Donnell."

"I ken it but there are a few things I must need sort through ere I wed my wee cousin to ye. A few weeks, nay more, but there is nay much sense in planning something until we can agree on an exact date. And I want all the proper steps taken. I willnae have it said that I did wrong by her whilst she was in my care."

That was all Annora could bear to listen to. She managed to keep her thoughts clear enough to slip away with caution and quiet until she was in the hallway, and then she began to move faster and with less thought as to the amount of noise she was making. By the time she had reached the top of the stairs she was running. All she could think of was that she needed someone to help her, and the only someone she could think of was Rolf.

She was nearly blind with a panic she could not control when she reached the battered door to his little room. Without even thinking to knock she opened his door and stumbled into his room. A small part of her mind wondered why his door was unlocked, but she paid it no heed. Instead she glanced around the small room to find him and nearly stopped breathing when she did.

Master Lavengeance was naked, completely and beautifully naked. Annora slowly looked him over, admiring every taut muscle and lean limb. She had caught a few glimpses at naked men, as privacy was hard to maintain at a keep, but she had never seen a man as beautiful as Master Lavengeance. He stood there gaping at her in stunned surprise, an expression she suspected she shared. Annora took full advantage of that and looked her fill of his manly form.

Broad shoulders still gleamed slightly with the damp from the bath he had obviously just taken. His chest was broad and neatly muscled with only a faint V of hair. Slowly she let her gaze slip down his tall, lean form. His stomach was taut and lightly rippled with muscle. Feeling suddenly shy, she blinked to avoid looking at his groin as she looked at his long, well-shaped legs. The sight of him was making her feel very warm.

Then suddenly shock and a growing arousal began to fade into confusion. It took Annora a moment to realize what was puzzling her. Master Lavengeance had long, strong legs lightly coated with hair. Red hair. Her eyes widening as the meaning of that penetrated her mind, Annora forgot her shyness and looked straight at his groin. He was very impressive there as well, proud and erect. The size of him might have startled, even alarmed her, but she was too stunned by the thick curls that manhood rose out of. Those curls were red. Men with dark brown hair should not have red curls anywhere; Annora was sure of it.

Master Lavengeance was not the man he claimed to be.

Chapter Eight

"Who are ye?" Annora asked, not surprised to hear that her voice sounded weakened and hoarse from the shock she still felt.

She suddenly decided that she would not wait for an answer. He had lied to everyone, but what hurt the most was that he had lied to her. Annora turned to leave, but never got the chance to even reach for the door before it was slammed shut and securely latched. She stared wide-eyed at this man she no longer felt she knew and suddenly wondered if she was in real danger. Her gift had never failed her before, but she found herself doubting its accuracy now. The naked man holding her in his room certainly looked dangerous.

James saw the fear in her eyes and cursed. The very last thing he wished was to frighten Annora; he felt she had enough to fear in her life as it was. Nevertheless, he could not let her run away.

He grabbed her by the arm and led her over to his bed. Keeping his gaze fixed on her the whole time, he yanked on his braies. His secret was out and he was not yet sure he could trust Annora to keep it. He wanted to, his heart told him that he could, but this was a matter of life and death and he had to be cautious. There was really no way he could avoid telling her the truth now, but he had to make sure that she did not escape him until he was absolutely certain that she had become his ally.

"I am Sir James Drummond," he said and was not surprised when she paled a little, for he knew the tales told of him had gotten wilder and more frightening with each year he had spent in hiding.

"The mon who killed his wife?" she whispered, unable to stop herself from glancing toward the door, her only route of escape.

"I didnae kill Mary," he snapped.

He took a deep breath and let it out slowly, striving for calm. Yelling out his innocence was not the way to win her over to his side. It was hard, however, for he was weary beyond bearing of hearing himself named a killer of women. To hear Annora say it cut him far too deeply to ignore, as did the way she looked so ready to bolt.

"But ye were cried an outlaw because of it," she said tentatively. There must have been some proof."

Annora realized that she just could not believe it. Although James had lied and fooled everyone with his disguise, she again felt that she knew the man he was now that she was beginning to calm down. It was impossible to even think him capable of killing his wife, Mary. And a false accusation, followed by the loss of everything he owned or loved, would certainly explain all that barely leashed rage she had felt in him from the start.

"Donnell MacKay saw to it that I was blamed," James said. "I am nay sure how he accomplished it, but I intend to find out."

She sat down on the bed and tried to think. So many questions stirred in her mind, she could not decide which one to ask first. It still hurt to know that he had lied to her, but she was beginning to understand why he had done it. He was a man condemned as an outlaw and that meant that everyone had the right to kill him. He was, in many ways, a dead man; he was just awaiting the final, killing blow.

"Who else kens who ye really are?" she finally asked, surprising herself with the question.

"Big Marta. She has kenned me for too many years to be fooled for long by any disguise I put on. I doubt it fooled her for more than a few minutes."

James watched as Annora thought that over for a moment. There was no sign of the fear she had first shown when she had guessed that he was not who he had told her he was. Nor did she look shocked any longer or ready to run from him. There had been a look of hurt upon her face for a brief moment and he supposed he could understand that. He had the sensation he would have felt the same if she had fooled him in a similar way. Such trickery could make her think that everything he had said or done was also a lie, and that was the last thing he wanted her to believe.

"And she has kept your secret all this time?" Annora suspected Big Marta would like nothing more than to have Donnell and his men banished from Dunncraig.

"Aye, she has and she will." Moving cautiously, he sat down beside her, pleased when she made no move to flee or even move away. "She kens that I am innocent."

"Wheesht, I ken that ye are innocent, too, but I am nay sure I ought to." She tensed only briefly when he put his arm around her shoulders and tugged her closer to his side. "I just cannae feel that ye would e'en hurt Mary or any woman, so 'tis verra hard to believe that ye killed her. Yet, weel, I cannae see how Donnell could have blamed ye and then gained all ye had." She looked up at him. "E'en Meggie?"

"E'en Meggie although I doubt she recalls me at all."

"I think she does in a way. She insists that Donnell is nay her father, that her father was a mon who laughed and smiled and loved her. Donnell does none of these things."

James nodded. "I have heard her say the same."

"Do ye mean to take Meggie away from here?"

"Nay. I mean to reclaim her and Dunncraig. I fled here to stay alive, but it hasnae been any life at all. When spring came this year and I crawled out of the cave I had wintered in, I decided I was done with hiding."

Annora thought of this warm, vital man hiding in a cave like an animal and felt so sad she almost started weeping. She replaced that with a fury at Donnell. Her cousin had even stolen this man's dignity. Realizing what she had just thought, she knew she believed him. She had always wondered how Donnell had gained so much, and had always suspected some trickery or crime. What she could not see was how any crime could be proven after three long years had passed.

"It willnae be easy to prove your innocence," she said, finally voicing her fears.

"Nay, I ken that weel enough. I suspicion there was a part of me that thought I could find the truth if I could just get back inside Dunncraig. Weel, I have been here for a wee while, havenae I, and I havenae found anything that will hang that bastard. Of course, a mon clever enough to get an innocent mon declared an outlaw and make a claim on all that mon had wouldnae leave proof of his crimes lying about for all to see. Big Marta has heard a few whispers and rumors and is trying to find out if there is any truth in them. She willnae tell me what those rumors are until she does."

"She wouldnae, nay until she kenned what was the truth and what wasnae. She is a verra honest woman. I dinnae mean to pick at an old pain, but exactly how did Mary die? All I have e'er heard is that ye killed her and she was burned to death in a wee cottage in the wood."

James thought about that day three years ago and only felt a twinge of regret, and one that mostly concerned the death of a young, innocent woman. He felt guilty because Mary should have been loved and her death should have caused him far more pain than it had. Somehow his lack of love for her and the ease with which his grief passed diminished the poor woman in away. Worse, James could think of no one else, save perhaps his daughter, who felt any different than he did. Poor sweet, shy Mary had not left much of a mark upon her world. Her only true legacy was Margaret and in that James felt she had excelled.

"Aye, that is what happened." He shook his head. "I dinnae e'en ken what she was doing there. Mary ne'er went awandering and that cottage is a fair walk from here. She had no need to go there, either. None that I could e'er think of. MacKay convinced a lot of people that I had lured her there and killed her, burning the wee cottage to the ground in the hope of hiding my crime."

"But *why* would anyone think ye would do such a thing?"

"Mary and I had fought that day, loudly and publicly. Mary was a shy, quiet lass, but she had been, weel, nay in a good temper for several weeks." He shrugged. "I thought, mayhap, that she was with child again. 'Tis said that carrying a bairn can change a woman's temperament. I didnae ken why she was so cross or pushed at me until I was, but I couldnae stay to try and soothe her. It was time for the planting and all. There was a great deal of work to do."

He frowned as he thought about how changed Mary had

seemed in those last few weeks before she had died. James could recall feeling confused and irritated. He had had little time to deal with a moody woman. That was one reason he felt guilty and he knew it. Their last moments together had been filled with angry words. Then again, he doubted he would have felt any better if there had been peace between them that day, or, even worse, something that had hinted at a better, more passionate marriage.

"That still isnae enough to get ye, a laird, proclaimed an outlaw and have all your lands given o'er to the verra one who accused ye."

"Weel, as I said, MacKay soon spread that tale that I had lured her to the cottage. There was also talk that I was angry because she had given me a girl child and wasnae hurrying to give me the son I wanted and needed. There was e'en talk that I had another woman at the ready to be my wife, a sturdy and good-for-breeding sort of lass. My mistake was in ignoring it all, in treating it all as no more than the worst sort of gossip that is stirred to life by an unexpected death. And I should have tried harder to find the source of those lies."

"Which was my cousin."

"Aye, I am fair sure it was. What I didnae ken was that he was crying murder to ones who had the power to hurt me with far more than rumor. "James shook his head. "I am nay sure how he did it, if he just talked people into believing his lies and those of the people he bribed or ordered to lie about me, or if he held some dark secret about some of them and used it to force them to help him destroy me. It just seemed as if one moment I am standing o'er my wife's grave and the next I am cried outlaw and running for my life. There wasnae any time for me to search out the truth although I did try. Aye, as did my kinsmen until a few barely escaped death and my pleas to stay out of this trouble halted the more obvious attempts they were making."

"Did ye find anything in Donnell's ledger room?" she asked, resting her head on his shoulder and, despite the dark tale they spoke of, enjoying the feel of his warm skin against her cheek as well as the way he stroked her arm.

"I found the book where the deaths of my men were recorded.

They werenae easy deaths they suffered and too few escaped. MacKay didnae want any mon still loyal to me to remain at Dunncraig and he also tried to make them tell him where I might have gone to hide. I had thought that by coming back here in disguise I would be able to track down the ones who lied against me, mayhap e'en find Mary's killer."

"So ye think she was really murdered, that it wasnae just some tragedy."

"Aye, I do."

Annora sat up straight and finally asked one of the questions that had troubled her for so long. "Are ye verra sure it was Mary who died in that fire?"

James stared at her for a full minute before answering. "Who else could it have been?"

"I dinnae ken. 'Tis just that I heard that, weel, there wasnae much left after the fire, so how could anyone looking at the body be certain it was your wife?"

"No one could be, but the wedding band I had given her was on her finger and there were a few scraps left of the dress she had worn that day. Also, several people said they had seen her go to the cottage."

Annora's questions had stirred up some very disturbing ideas in James' mind and he got up to pace the room. One thing he had never wanted to consider was the possibility that it had not been Mary who died. Since that could mean that she could have helped MacKay destroy him, that possibility had also been the very last thing he would ever have wanted to consider. The last time such thoughts had flickered in his mind he had told himself he should leave no stone unturned in his search for the truth, but he had not followed through. He still did not want to believe it, but he knew he would be an utter fool to completely dismiss the chance that his sweet, shy wife had not been all she had appeared to be, that she had been MacKay's ally. It was time to stop shying away from what might be a very ugly truth.

"Once or twice I have thought that it might not have been her. Thought it in passing and even told myself I should look into that possibility. I havenae done it, fool that I am."

"Ye shouldnae blame yourself for that. No one would want

to even think that their wife or husband could betray them so fully."

"Mayhap not, but it means I ignore some facts that could weel lead me to the truth. I cannae afford to worry about what I might discover. Dunncraig and the welfare of its people depend upon me ending MacKay's rule here."

Annora nodded, feeling a great deal of sympathy for him but guessing that he would not really appreciate her showing it. "Meggie once told me that—"

"She saw MacKay kissing her mother?"

"Aye. She said as much to ye?" Suddenly recalling that fleeting look of guilt on Meggie's face the day she had said she had talked to the wood-carver, Annora almost grimaced. Maybe she should have discussed the matter a little more.

"Aye, but she was just a child of two when her mother died. How could she recall something like that?"

For a moment Annora thought about that and then her eyes widened with surprise. "Mayhap it wasnae so verra long ago."

"What do ye mean?"

"What if it wasnae Mary who burned in that cottage? If it wasnae, that means she was alive while ye were being accused of her murder and e'en when ye lost everything and had to run for your life."

"Which means she was allied with your cousin."

The fury in his voice made her wince, but she did not intend to let that deter her. "Mayhap, or she was being kept prisoner somewhere. Howbeit, it could be that Meggie stumbled across a meeting between Mary and Donnell later, when she was old enough to recall such a thing, and that is when she saw them kissing."

"How could Mary be alive and living close enough to be seen by Meggie yet nay by anyone else at Dunncraig?" James struggled to think of where Mary might have been hiding even as he argued the possibility that she was still alive. "And wouldnae Meggie have said something about seeing her mother?"

Annora gave him a sad smile. "Once Donnell arrived at Dunncraig, Meggie quickly learned that she shouldnae speak much at all and certainly not to Donnell. She learned young to keep secrets. A sad lesson for a child, but I am glad she had the wit to learn it so quickly."

James moved to the small arrow-slot that was his window and, even though he could see nothing, stared out of it. He needed to think about all they had just spoken of. If Mary had been MacKay's lover and ally, it would certainly explain how quickly the man had brought him down. Mary had been a much-needed traitor right inside the walls of Dunncraig. He hated to think he had been such a blind fool as concerned his wife, but it was time to push his pride aside and consider it. If naught else, he could find some comfort in the fact that he had never really loved her. It was sad but it meant he had not been a complete fool.

There had to be someone at Dunncraig who knew, if not the whole tale, at least that Mary may have taken MacKay as her lover. It was the sort of thing that rarely stayed a complete secret. MacKay would have killed nearly everyone who might have known the truth, but there had to be someone, somewhere, that had had enough sense to hold secret what he had learned. He then wondered if that was one of the things Big Marta had heard and was trying to find the truth of.

He inwardly cursed, long and viciously. Instead of uncovering the truth, he was now mired in a web of deceit and betrayal that was becoming more and more entangled. Although he had not been so naïve as to think he could quickly find the truth and be declared innocent, save for a few pleasant dreams about such an event, he had never anticipated that it would all be so complicated. At least he was beginning to gather a few allies. With a few more eyes and ears looking and listening for the truth, he might yet find what he needed.

Annora watched James as he stared out the tiny window, knowing it did not matter that he could probably see nothing even if he wanted to. All of his attention was turned to his own thoughts. It was not just for her own sake that she found herself praying he had not loved his wife too deeply. Every instinct she had told her that Mary, a woman everyone spoke of as being sweet and shy, had been part of the plot that had robbed James of so much. It had to be a bitter potion for such a proud man to swallow.

She studied his broad, smoothly muscular back and idly wondered if she should remind him that he was nearly naked. Selfishly she decided not to. He was too great a pleasure to look at. Considering all the dark, sad things they had to think and talk about, she felt she could be forgiven for stealing a little pleasure for herself.

Letting her gaze move over his fine body with a freedom she would never have allowed herself if he had been looking at her, Annora tried to think of what they had to do to answer some of the many questions they now had. There was also the fact that, if Mary still lived, James Drummond was a married man and she should not be sitting there thinking about how she would love to kiss all that fine smooth skin.

She rolled her eyes. She would not be a woman if she did not enjoy what she was looking at. And Annora doubted any woman could be so cold she was left unstirred by the sight of a nearly naked James Drummond. Then again, if what she was beginning to suspect was true, Mary had been so unmoved as to betray the man with Donnell of all people. That was so hard to believe, yet, over the years, Annora had seen enough proof of how witless some women could be concerning men that she had to believe it was at least possible.

For a moment, Annora closed her eyes and just let her mind wander and her body relax. Occasionally when she did this she would have some insight. It felt foolish even to her, but it never failed to work. If the insight came, it was always a true one, as well. Every instinct she had told her Mary had betrayed James. A moment later, those instincts told her that Mary was dead.

"We need to find where Mary is hiding," James said at last, turning to look at Annora.

"I dinnae think we will succeed," Annora said quietly, blinking rapidly as she came back to her senses.

James walked over to the bed and frowned at her. "Why do ye say that? Have ye just remembered something that might be important?"

"Nay, not remembered. Felt."

"Felt?"

"Aye, felt. Sometimes I can feel things." She quailed at telling

him such things, but there was no other way to explain the
certainty she felt as she told him what she had decided. "I truly
feel that Mary really is dead. She didnae die in that fire, but she
is dead." To her surprise he did not ridicule her or cross himself
to protect himself against evil as some did when they found a
person with her sort of gift.

"Have ye had a vision?"

Annora was so surprised by his calm question and the lack
of fear or scorn in his eyes that she nearly gaped. "Nay, not a
vision exactly," she replied, compelled to tell him the whole
truth. "Sometimes if I clear my head of all thought and relax I
can sense things. I sense that Mary is dead. She knew too much,
didnae she?"

James' expression turned grim as he nodded. "Aye, she did,
and people who ken too much about MacKay and his crimes
have a habit of dying."

"Precisely. He couldnae let her live. Mayhap she e'en pushed
him too hard to act on something before he was ready to. My
cousin reacts verra violently when he is pushed too hard."

"So I have heard. And, aye, if Mary was his ally in what was
done to me, she probably expected him to make her his wife."

"But ye didnae die and so she remained wed to ye."

He nodded slowly, appreciating the way they could help each
other in thinking out all the possibilities. "And so she would
begin to press him to act, to make her a widow so that she could
marry him and return to being the lady of Dunncraig."

"Only he couldnae allow that, for he had had ye condemned
for killing her."

"And her return, alive and hale, would make him a liar. Having
used his deceit to ruin a laird and take his lands, he would hang
for certain. Nay, Mary couldnae live."

Annora shook her head. "I dinnae ken. It all sounds right and
yet 'tis so hard to believe there was such an intricate plot against
ye."

"It had to be intricate and verra clever. I have ne'er done a
thing to bring such a quick harsh judgment down on my head.
What sins I have committed were wee ones, the sort most men
commit, worthy only of some penance meted out by a priest.

MacKay needed to be verra clever to get me cried an outlaw, especially since my family isnae without some power as weel. They were taken by surprise, however, and had no chance to stop the decree of outlawry."

"They could have done that?"

"Oh, aye, I think so. They certainly could have held the final decision in abeyance and given us all time to find out the truth. I suspect MacKay knew that and that is why he moved so secretively. And swiftly."

She nodded. "Aye. My cousin is verra good at kenning who has power, how to use it, or how to get around it"

James stared at her as she sat there frowning, most likely at the perfidy of her cousin. They had talked about his problems enough, at least his body thought so. It was rapidly hardening in a demand he was finding very hard to ignore. She knew his secret now, so there was no longer any reason to be cautious or hide from her, and that loosened the meager restraints he had held on his desire for her. Perhaps it was even the sight of her sitting on his bed where he had so often imagined her, but it could just as easily be the sound of her voice or her soft scent. All he knew for certain was that he wanted her badly and he wanted her now.

Chapter Nine

"I dinnae want to speak of this any longer," James said as he abruptly sat down beside her and pulled her into his arms.

Annora could tell by the look in his eye that he did not wish to talk about anything else, either. She could sense that his desire was rising hot and fierce and it was rapidly feeding her own, making her feel slightly feverish. It was difficult to think of all the reasons why she should leave his bedchamber as quickly as possible. There were a lot of them, but with each soft kiss he placed upon her face, her common sense faded away a little more.

"If I dinnae leave to change and wash, I willnae get to the great hall in time for the evening meal," she said, recognizing that for the weak excuse it was and unable to pull out of his arms.

"Will they miss ye and send someone to search for ye?"

"Nay, I doubt it. They ne'er have before."

"Then stay with me."

"I dinnae think that would be wise." Considering the way he could make her heart pound by simply brushing his fingers over her cheek, she *knew* it would not be wise.

"Ah, my bonnie wee lass, the verra last thing ye stir inside me is the wish to be wise."

Before Annora could say a word, she was on the bed with James moving over her. When he settled his weight on top of her, she felt her whole body welcome him with a shameless abandon. Her mind, however, struggled to cling to a few scraps of common sense. If even a few of their ideas about Mary and Donnell had any true merit, it was a very dangerous time to recklessly indulge their passion for each other. If Egan ever found out she was sure that James would have to run again or suffer a painful death.

She was also a virgin, and although she could think of no one else she would want as a lover as much as she wanted Sir James Drummond, memories of her mother's sad fate flooded her mind. Annora had always vowed that she would not stumble down the same ruinous path her mother had and she would never curse a child of hers with the shame that came from being bastard born. The way she felt as James held her told her how very close she was to breaking every vow she had ever made to herself, and that terrified her.

She pressed her hands against his chest and her good sense took yet another serious battering. His skin was so smooth and warm. The feel of taut muscle beneath that fine skin made her feel dizzy with passion. She ached to touch him all over, to stroke him from head to foot. Annora caught herself tracing a ragged scar that ran from just above his breastbone and over his left shoulder and realized that she was losing her battle with her own desires again. She had never thought it would be so hard to do as she ought to and not as she so badly wanted to.

"Rolf," she began and then blushed. "Nay. 'Tis James, isnae it? 'Tis only now that I e'en ken what your real name is."

James brushed a kiss over her mouth. He could almost feel her conflicting emotions in the way she would tense and then soften. It was easy enough to read them on her slightly flushed face as well. Although he had seen her assume a calm, even meek expression before MacKay or Egan time and time again, she rarely did so with him and he found himself immensely pleased by that fact. Seeing the battle she was waging between what she wanted and what was considered proper made him feel a little guilty. He knew he should immediately pull away, should not push her into an intimacy she was not fully ready and willing to partake of, but he was not sure he was strong enough to do so.

It had been so long since he had enjoyed the soft heat of a woman. In truth, he had not really satisfied that need with his own wife, for Mary had always shied away from any intimacy and had never grown passionate and warm. Or she had been repulsed, he thought, and then he quickly shook that painful, humiliating thought away. All he had as of now was some suspicions. He would not condemn his wife without proof.

Thinking of Mary made him tense for a moment. He might still be married. Although he had every intention of finding a way to end his marriage to Mary if she was still alive and had indeed betrayed him, that could take years and a lot of coin. Then he inwardly shook his head. Mary was dead. She might not have died when everyone thought she had, but he felt sure that Annora was right in feeling that Mary had died. After being raised by the Murrays, a clan riddled with people who possessed all manner of *gifts*, he found it very easy to believe in Annora's *feelings*.

Just as easy as it was to desire her so much that his whole body felt as if it was tied up in knots, hot, aching knots of pure hunger. James knew it was past time to stop trying to explain his fierce need for her by telling himself that it was caused by his lengthy celibacy. So deep and overwhelming was his desire for her that he had continued to cling to his celibacy despite many offers from the maids of Dunncraig to end it. He could have made sure that he and his chosen maid had rutted in the dark so that his disguise was protected. He had simply not wanted to end his celibacy with anyone but Annora MacKay, and unless she strongly, loudly denied him, he fully intended to do so now.

"I have wished to hear my true name upon your lips from the verra moment we met," he said softly as he gently nipped the silken lobe of her ear.

"We really shouldnae do this," she whispered in an unsteady voice, the way he was teasing her ear with his lips and tongue, making her tremble with a need she was rapidly losing all control of. "*I* shouldnae do this."

"Aye, ye should. Ye ken weel that it is what ye want. When was the last time ye grasped what ye wanted or e'en had a chance to do so?"

"It isnae always wise or right to just do as one wants to do. Everything has consequences."

"What consequences can there be to our sharing the passion that we both feel so strongly?"

"I am a consequence of such recklessness," she said softly.

"Ah, lass, ye are no consequence; ye are a gift, a blessing. Ye heed the words of too many fools." He began to unlace her gown, encouraged when she tensed only slightly and made no move to stop him.

"Those fools merely repeat the teachings of the church. Ne'er forget that."

"And the church is ruled by men, lass. Aye, many have a true calling, hold a deep belief, but too many were just sent into the church by their families, nay for serving God, but for a living or e'en for power."

"Heresy," she said and suddenly grinned.

Annora realized that she was ready to throw caution to the wind. She briefly wondered if her mother had felt like this when she had taken a lover, hot and reckless and aching to take a chance on a beautiful man who made her heart beat faster. Unlike her mother, however, Annora knew this man would never turn his back on his own child. That would be enough for her.

"Did ye truly lose your eye?" she asked softly as she lightly touched the edge of the patch he wore.

"Curse it, I forgot that I was still wearing the cursed thing. "James yanked the patch off and tossed it aside. "Nay, I didnae lose it or e'en injure it. I was often told that I had such true green eyes that they were memorable and I dared nay take the chance that my eyes would be enough to ruin my disguise."

"They are verra memorable eyes." She kissed the corner of the eye he had kept covered for so long. "When I first saw ye I was saddened by its loss, for its mate was so verra beautiful."

James actually felt himself blush. It had been many, many years since he had reacted in such a way to a woman's flatteries, and although it felt uncomfortably vain to admit it, he had had quite a few of those. Yet he knew that every word Annora uttered was sincere and not just part of an empty flirtation or a way to make him place an extra coin in the outstretched hand that all too often came after the bed play. The knowledge that she liked his looks had him feeling as proud and satisfied as some strutting cock in the hen yard.

He kissed her before he said something foolish. She made him feel like an untried boy again, too eager and all a-sweat with anticipation. He was not sure what had banished the hesitation she had been so plainly revealing only a moment ago, but he was not about to question that change. If nothing else, it could make her start thinking again, and that was the very last thing he wanted her to do. He wanted her to just feel.

Doing his best to keep her dazed with his kisses, James began to remove her clothing without doing it so quickly that he startled or frightened her. Or worse, he mused, just tore the clothes from her body and threw them aside as he so ached to do. He needed to be flesh to flesh with her, needed to look at her, touch her, and taste her.

When he finally removed the last of her clothing, he could think of nothing else but looking at her. James crouched over her, studying every rise and hollow of her soft body. Annora was a small, slender woman yet she possessed lush, full breasts, a small waist, and nicely rounded hips. She might not weigh all that much, but that weight was placed in all the right places. A small V of dark curls shielded her womanhood, and the hard tips of her full breasts were a deep, tempting pink. For a moment he was so entranced by her soft, creamy skin, he did nothing but stare and try to decide where to taste her first. Then a faint rosy blush crept down from her neck to color the breasts he was admiring.

Glancing up at her face, James could see a blush upon her cheeks so deep he could swear he felt the heat of it. He also saw embarrassment and shyness in her expression and he tensed. It was much like the look he had seen on Mary's face all too often; one that meant that the warmth he sought would yet again be denied him. Afraid that he was losing Annora, that the passion he had felt in her was swiftly fading away, he kissed her, a hard, fierce kiss that he knew revealed some of the desperation he was suddenly feeling. It was not until he felt her respond with a growing passion that he began to lose that fear.

Annora had thought that she would melt from the heat of the embarrassment she had felt as James had stared at her body. She had never been naked in front of a man before, or many women, either, and the longer he had just stared at her, saying and doing nothing, the more she had begun to fear that he was disappointed in what he saw. When he had finally looked into her eyes, she had expected him to say something then. She had even tensed a little, preparing herself for some false compliment used to hide his disappointment and save her from any hurt feelings. Instead he had kissed her—hard.

Even as her desire had begun to flood her with heat again, Annora caught a brief feeling of desperation in James, even a hint of fear. But as she had continued to respond to his fierce kiss with a desire she found difficult to control, it faded away. All she could feel was his desire. When his body settled lightly on top of hers and she felt their skin touching for the first time, she was so caught up in the fierce need that swept over her that she no longer cared about what had been troubling him. She could ask him about it later.

"Ah, Annora mine, I want to go so slowly with ye, to taste every sweet inch of ye, but ye are driving me mad with desire," he muttered against her collarbone.

He wanted to talk? she thought. How could one talk during such a time? Her mind and heart were so filled with the feel of his lips against her skin and the heat of his warm skin beneath her hands, she doubted she could think clearly enough to utter her own name. Then he dragged his tongue over the aching tip of one breast and Annora discovered that she could speak. She gasped out his name as fire raged through her body, spreading out from the place where he now kissed her. When he slowly drew the hard tip of her breast deep into his mouth and suckled her, she made a lot of gasping noises and soft moans that she hoped she would not recall later, for she suspected such a loss of control would embarrass her.

By the time he moved his attentions to her other breast, Annora did not care what noises she made or what he did so long as the pleasure he gave her did not stop. She was aware only of the feel of him, of what he made her feel, and the hard length pressed against her groin. For just a heartbeat she thought she ought to be afraid of that part of him, of the size of it, and then he rubbed it against her and the pleasure that rushed through her drove all such concerns from her mind. She barely even started to gasp in shock when he slid his hand down her stomach and between her legs to stroke her there. With one stroke of his long fingers he gave her such delight that she softened and opened to his caress without hesitation.

"Sweet heavens, love, ye are so beautifully hot and wet," he growled against her stomach, his whole body shaking with the need to be inside her.

"Wet is good?" she said in a trembling whisper, for in some still rational part of her mind, a concern about that growing dampness down there had begun to grow.

"Wet is perfect. Utterly perfect. 'Tis your body welcoming me, inviting me in."

And in was where he had to go—now. James struggled to go slowly, knowing she was a virgin and care had to be taken to ensure that her first time left her with no fears and as little pain as possible. She was a fever in his blood, however, and her whole body signaled its welcome to him. Being slow and gentle was going to be the hardest thing he had ever done. He wanted to thrust into her and keep on thrusting hard until he reached that paradise he craved.

Gently spreading her legs a little farther apart, James began to ease inside her. At the first touch of her heat against his manhood, he had to brace himself against the overwhelming urge to push himself as deep inside her as he could. Little by little he entered her until he felt the barrier of her maidenhead. Leaning down, he brushed a kiss over her mouth.

"This may hurt ye a wee bit, Annora," he whispered against her lips, "but I swear to ye that whate'er pain your breeching brings, it will pass."

That much Annora did know and she wrapped her arms around his neck. "Just do it, James. Get the hurtful part done and then we can return to the joyous part again."

The fact that she used the word *joyous* to describe what they were sharing nearly undid James. He began to kiss her, drawing his body back as he did so, and then rammed his way through that shield. In his arms, her body tensed and she cried out against his mouth. He remained still once he was seated deep within her and kept on kissing and stroking her in an attempt to soothe away the hurt he had had to deal her and bring back the passion she had been gifting him with. He was so concentrated on that that it took him a moment to realize that she was trying to move in the way that he was desperate to.

He lifted his head and looked at her. There was no look of pain or disgust upon her face. The flush of desire was tinting her cheeks and darkening her midnight-blue eyes almost to black. He knew he had hurt her, but she had clearly recovered from it faster than he had anticipated.

"Has the pain passed?" he asked, not surprised to hear that his voice was little more than a growl as he was beginning to feel that he would go mad if he did not get to move inside her soon.

"Aye," she whispered as she tried to move her legs to a position that might enhance the pleasure the feel of him inside her was stirring.

James rested his forehead against hers. "Wrap those bonnie legs around me, love."

Annora did so and gasped, for it settled him even deeper inside her and pure delight flowed through her. "And what do I do next?"

"Enjoy," he said. "Please enjoy this."

She was just thinking that that was a very strange thing for him to say when he slowly pulled almost completely out of her. Before she could protest his retreat, he thrust back inside and she nearly screamed with pleasure. This was what her mother had risked so much for, she thought wildly as he continued to thrust into her, stirring up a heat that threatened to melt her. And the loss of this, she suddenly realized, was why her mother had always looked so sad. Then she thought nothing, only felt.

James fought against the urge to just take his own pleasure. Despite how badly he craved it and knowing he could probably still see that she reached her own pleasure, he controlled himself. He had to grit his teeth and occasionally think of something as dull as possible to stem his need for release, but he wanted them to find that release together, or as closely together as possible. Just as he began to think he would have to forgo that delight, he felt her body start to clench around him. A heartbeat later she cried out his name and her whole body arched and trembled as her release tore through her. The way her heat clutched at him as if trying to secure him even deeper inside her was enough to pull him over that edge as well.

Annora lay sprawled on her back, her whole body feeling as if she had worked feverishly all day. She was just becoming aware of the fact that she was still naked and not making any attempt to hide anything from James, when he slid off the bed and walked to the washbowl. Even as she struggled to make her limp arms work and grabbed the bedcovers to hide her nudity, he returned to the bed carrying a damp rag. Annora was so distracted by the sight of his tall, lean body that she barely flinched when he cleaned her off, despite the intimacy of the act.

It was not until he crawled back into bed and took her into his arms that she began to truly regain her senses. She had just given her innocence to a man who had yet to speak any words of love. Annora knew that ought to send her running from the room and perhaps straight to a priest to confess her sin. She did not feel inclined to do either. She just wanted to stay where she was, in his arms, lightly stroking his broad handsome chest, and enjoying the feeling of lethargic happiness that filled her.

Thoughts of what would happen next began to intrude upon that pleasant oblivion, however. Annora knew she could not ignore all that was wrong with taking a lover, especially this lover. Even if James defeated Donnell and regained all that had been stolen from him, this could only be a passing affair. He was a laird. Lairds did not love and marry poor, bastard women no matter how good the lineage of one of their parents. Lairds found wives who could bring them lands and coins, add to their power or their wealth. Knowing that Donnell had probably spent or wasted most of the wealth of Dunncraig and did little to ensure that its lands were tended correctly, she felt that such things would be even more important to James. She owned nothing but the clothes she wore.

Sadness threatened to overwhelm her but she fought it back. She had chosen this and she would take all the good she could get until the end. There would be plenty of time after it ended to wallow in heartbreak and weep into her pillow.

One thing she did know was that she loved this man and it was a hopeless love. Annora felt the pain of that and then pushed it aside. If he wanted them to remain lovers, she would be his for as long as he would have her and she would not burden him with what she felt. She knew he was a good man and did not intend to hurt her. She also knew that he would have let her leave and hold fast to her innocence if she had offered any real protest. He was not really to blame for the fact that she loved him and would be heartbroken at some time in the future, except perhaps for the fact that he was so easy to love.

When he put his hand beneath her chin and tilted her face up to his, she was able to smile a little. She had had a lot of practice in hiding her hurts and sorrows. Annora refused to allow them to dim this brief time of happiness.

"Ye are verra quiet, lass," James said and brushed a kiss over her mouth.

"I havenae yet regained the strength to have a conversation," she replied.

He smiled and stroked her back with one hand, trailing his fingers up and down her spine. He could see no regret or even a hint of shame in her face, but her silence had begun to make him uneasy. Once James had looked into his wife's face after they had made love and he had tried never to do so again. There had been such unhappiness there, such shame and embarrassment, that he had felt unmanned. In truth, only the lingering hope that he could teach Mary about the pleasure one could find in the marriage bed and a desire for children had given him the strength to return to her bed after that.

When Annora had remained silent for so long, he had begun to fear that she had felt the same things Mary had, and it had taken every bit of willpower he possessed to make himself look into her face. The relief he had felt at seeing only a lingering flush of a well-loved woman and a smile had made him glad he was not standing. James was sure he would have fallen on his face, for his knees had grown so weak.

Annora suddenly thought of the feelings she had sensed in James at one point and then the words he had muttered as he had begun to make love to her. "James, why were ye so, weel, desperate at the beginning?"

It took James a moment to understand what she was referring

to and then he wondered how she could have known what he was feeling. "Ye think I was desperate?"

She grimaced and prayed what she was about to say would not put a rapid end to their affair. "At times I can feel what another person is feeling. I felt the rage in ye when ye first came here, ye ken. Then that time ye insulted Donnell and I had to make up something to say when he asked what ye had said, I felt the loathing ye felt for the mon. Weel, after ye had done looking at me and started to kiss me, I felt what I can only call desperation in ye for just a moment. And, I think, just a hint of fear. I was wondering if it was something I had done to make ye feel that way."

"Ye can feel what others feel? Truly?"

Since she sensed only a keen interest in him, Annora nodded. "'Tis a secret, ye ken. Verra few people ken that I can do that and I prefer it that way. When some have discovered what I can do, they havenae been kind."

"Dinnae fret o'er telling me of your gift, love. I was raised by the Murrays, and that clan has a lot of people with gifts such as yours. My sister Gillyanne has much the same gift as ye do. And, aye, I was feeling desperate and not just because I have wanted ye from the start. I suppose there may have been a wee bit of fear mixed in there, too. As to why? My wife didnae like the loving. She always looked as if it pained her, humiliated her, and shamed her. Naught I could do seemed to change that. When ye were so silent for so long and then I saw that embarrassment upon your face, I feared I had erred again, that somehow I had destroyed the desire I ken weel ye were feeling at the start. I shouldnae have married her, mayhap should have guessed that she was one of those women who wouldnae like the bedding. Ah, but then I wouldnae have my Meggie."

"Verra true." Annora could not conceive of a woman not liking what James had made her feel, but did not say so. Such words could too easily allow him to guess how she felt about him. "Is that why ye find it hard to think she and Donnell were lovers?"

"Weel, aside from the fact that no mon likes to think his woman would desire another, aye, I do. Then again, mayhap my troubles with her were because she really loved MacKay and nay me. She may have been forced by her kinsmen to wed me, for at that time, MacKay had far less to offer her and them."

Annora moved so that she was sprawled on top of his body. For one who had always been very modest, she was a little surprised at how much she enjoyed being naked with this man. She also wanted to banish that look of hurt from his eyes. She knew without asking that he had been a good and faithful husband to Mary and it was not his fault that she had found no pleasure in his arms.

"The fact that Mary might have loved Donnell should tell ye that ye shouldnae take to heart what was wrong between the two of ye. She didnae give ye a chance right from the start. And, of course, she clearly had verra bad taste in men."

James grinned. There is that to consider."

"I, of course, have verra good taste in men."

"Mon. Only one."

"Aye," she said softly. "Only one."

Annora also knew that showing him how good he made her feel, how passionate and greedy, was the surest way to kill the last of those regrets, uncertainties, and fears Mary had left him with. She inwardly smiled as she kissed him. It would not be a huge sacrifice, either, for she was indeed a very greedy woman.

Chapter Ten

James set the mantelpiece he had finished oiling just outside the door of his workroom. It was one of the best pieces he had ever done and he was actually eager to see it displayed in the laird's bedchamber. Soon to be his again, he vowed to himself. Today, however, even the thought of MacKay sleeping in his bed could not completely spoil James' good humor. He felt completely sated after a long night of making love to Annora. It was the first time he had felt so since his marriage. After sending a quick, silent apology to his late wife, James had to admit that he could not recall ever feeling as good as he did right now. Annora satisfied a lot more than just his body.

"Ye are looking to be in a verra good humor," said Big Marta as she walked up to stand beside him.

The sparkle in the older woman's eyes told James that Big Marta knew he had spent the night holding Annora in his arms. He refused to blush, as that might indicate guilt and he felt absolutely none. Annora MacKay was his. Last night he had simply made his claim as clear to Annora as it was to him. He knew that, if he were not trapped in this disguise, he would be making that claim clear to every man at Dunncraig as well.

"Weel, a few more oilings, and this work is finished," he said, pointing to the mantelpiece he had finished, unable to completely hide his pride in his work.

"Aye, tis a wonder what ye can do to wood, laddie, but I dinnae think tis that beauty that has ye smiling at naught but the air. Nay, not when ye havenae smiled for many a year save at our wee Meggie." Big Marta crossed her arms over her chest and nodded. "I kenned she would be good for ye."

James sighed and rolled his eyes. "Just how is it that ye can find out near every little secret at Dunncraig?"

"Wheesht, I wish I could do that. If I had that skill ye would be sitting in the laird's chair where ye belong. Instead we have that vain swine sitting there destroying all he touches whilst trying to surround himself with the fine trappings of a king."

"Aye, he needs killing." He looked at her and asked, "Are ye telling me in your own sweet way that ye havenae found any truth behind all those rumors and whispers ye said ye have heard?" The way Big Marta pressed her lips tightly together and looked away told James that she had discovered something and was afraid he would not like it. "Did ye happen to discover that my wife wasnae the sweet, shy maid I thought her to be?"

When Big Marta spun around to gape at him in surprise, he found himself grinning despite the ugly truth he knew she was about to tell him. Few people could surprise Big Marta. It could be that by talking it all over with Annora and already facing the possibility that Mary had betrayed him, a lot of the sting such a truth could have had was gone. James also suspected that having spent the night in the arms of a woman who gave as much pleasure as she received, one who made no secret of her delight in his touch, gave him a sturdy shield against such hard, painful truths.

"Have *ye* heard something, then?" asked Big Marta.

"Nay, but Annora has a true skill for asking some hard questions and seeing things I didnae but should have. The possibility that Mary helped MacKay, might even have been his lover, has already been presented to me and I couldnae ignore or deny it. Annora also believes that Mary is dead."

"So she did die in that fire, then."

"Mayhap, but mayhap not. As Annora said, how could I be so certain when the body we found wasnae e'en recognizable? Howbeit, she doubted her cousin would have allowed Mary to live much longer as she was a weakness, one who, by simply walking down the road of the village, could plunge MacKay into a great deal of trouble."

True enough. Weel, aye, I fear Mary was unfaithful to ye. That wee cottage where she was supposed to have died was where she would meet MacKay. Weel, sometimes. The maid who actually saw them together saw them inside the keep. Mary slipped into MacKay's bedchamber once whilst he was here a-visiting as he did far too often. The maid also said that she heard more than enough to ken that it wasnae some innocent meeting atween cousins. And, nay, I willnae tell ye what maid. Leastwise, nay as long as MacKay rules here. It took a lot of persuading and vowing to be silent just to get her to tell me anything."

"I understand and ye cannae tell her why she should trust me, either. Nay yet. Did she say exactly when she saw them together?"

"About a month ere Mary died, or we were made to think that she had."

"But ne'er since the day Mary was supposed to have died?"

"She didnae say she had. I could speak to her again. If she did see Mary she is the type of lass who would think it a ghostie and ne'er tell anyone for fear they would think her a witch or something foolish. Why?"

"Because I think Meggie might have seen MacKay and Mary together. She told both Annora and me that she doesnae think MacKay is her father e'en though she saw him and her mother kissing once. I would have thought she was too young to see and remember such a thing if it happened ere the cottage burned down. But after? Aye, a few months or more of aging and Meggie would ken what she was seeing and remember it"

Big Marta shook her head. "The child has ne'er said a word, yet, if she did see her mother after the fire, ye would think she would have spoken of it, wouldnae ye?"

"Annora says my child learned verra quickly to keep secrets. "James sighed. "And, after thinking on the possibility that Mary was allied with MacKay, I thought long and hard on those years I was wed to Mary. A lot was wrong there and she was ne'er much of a mother to Meggie. Try as I would, I cannae e'en recall a time when I saw her holding and loving her own wee bairn. I should have looked more closely ere I married her, but I had taken my place as laird here and I wanted the wife, the bairns, and the family. Instead I got a wife who may weel have been little more than a whore sent to me by MacKay, her lover, and then three years in hell. The only blessing I got from the marriage was Meggie, my bonnie, clever Meggie."

"Aye, the bairn is verra clever. Kenning when to keep quiet and hold fast to a secret at such a young age? Verra clever indeed. 'Tis sad that she had to learn such a thing when she was little more than a bairn, but nay such a bad thing to learn." Looking away, Big Marta said quietly, "I ne'er really took to Mary, ye ken. She was cold."

"Och, aye, she was. I mistook it for shyness or maidenly modesty. I will say that, if 'tis true that she was just playing at being my wife for MacKay's sake, she didnae much like it. She may have been willing to play the whore for him in my bed, but in her heart she ne'er was one." James grimaced. "And I fear she may have been a wee bit witless."

"If she trusted that adder, then aye, she was." Big Marta frowned and rubbed her pointed chin. "Aye, verra much so if she thought she could have ye condemned for her death and then come back here to Dunncraig as MacKay's wife. Think ye that was her plan?"

"Her plan, ne'er his,"James said firmly. "MacKay is too canny to leave such proof of his crimes walking about. If Mary was his ally, she is a dead one now."

"Sad. 'Tis all verra sad. Weel, ye have chosen a good one this time. Just be verra careful, laddie. Egan has wanted her from the start. If he finds out about the two of ye, ye are a dead mon and I dinnae think the lass will be all that safe, either."

James nodded and watched as Big Marta walked away. He did not really need the woman's warning to know that what he shared with Annora was not only precious; it was dangerous. Egan would like to kill him now simply for striking him down. If the man ever found out that James had bedded Annora, he would not be halted in killing James, slowly and painfully. Big Marta was also right to think that Annora could be in the same danger. Egan would be enraged if he knew she had taken a lover. James had the feeling that Annora's good blood and her innocence had a lot to do with Egan's strong interest in her.

As James went back into his workroom to find a piece of the wood he would use for the chairs MacKay wanted, he thought about all the very good reasons he had to stay far away from Annora MacKay. They were all ones he knew he should heed, but he also knew that he would not do so, not too closely. He craved the warmth Annora gave him too much to turn away from it. What he would do, however, is be very, very careful. Big Marta knew about him and Annora, but no one else could ever even glimpse the truth. If he even suspected that someone else had discovered that he and Annora were lovers, he would get Annora and Meggie as far away from Dunncraig as he could, even if it meant he remained an outlaw and never got Dunncraig back.

He found the piece of wood he wanted and decided he would get the required meeting and discussion with MacKay over and done with. Since he had made a point of learning MacKay's habits, James knew that MacKay would soon be headed to the ledger room. Grabbing the scrap of parchment he had sketched out his intended design on, he went to meet with MacKay.

James was only feet away from the ledger room when he saw MacKay approaching with Egan. The two men were so deep into a discussion they had not seen him yet and he looked for a place to hide before they did. Egan was a man badly in need of a beating, but James knew now was not the time for a confrontation. If only for Annora's sake, for her safety, he wanted to avoid meeting Egan as often as possible.

Espying a small door, James quietly slipped into a room right next to the ledger room, one that had never existed when he had been laird of Dunncraig. It only took one quick look around for James to guess at the purpose of the room. It might occasionally be used for a guest of some low rank, but he felt certain that it had been created so that MacKay had a comfortable place to rut on a woman in between working on his ledgers or any other business he was conducting.

Just as he was wondering how long he should linger in the room before slipping away, James heard voices. He set his wood and drawing down on the small bed and moved closer to the wooden wall that had been erected to make two rooms out of one. It took only a moment for him to find the flaw in the wood that allowed anyone in this room to hear what was being said in the ledger room. As James gently pressed his ear against the wall he wondered if MacKay had done it on purpose so that he could listen to what was said when others thought themselves alone in the ledger room.

"The wedding will be held in one month," MacKay said, the creak of wood telling James that MacKay had sat down.

"Have ye told the lass yet?" asked Egan.

"Nay, not yet, and I would prefer it if ye didnae tell her yourself."

"Why not? She and I could spend that month betrothed. T'would give me a good chance to show her that she is in need of a mon in her bed. Might make her more agreeable. Might e'en get her with child and that would quickly end any argument she might make. I suspicion she wouldnae wish to bear a bastard child as her mother did. She has seen how that can hurt a lass."

"Egan, we will do this my way or not at all. Annora really isnae the meek wee lass ye seem to think she is. If we are to avoid a lot of trouble, this must be handled verra carefully. Ye will marry her in a month's time. Be satisfied with that. And spend yourself on one of the maids if ye feel an itch. Forcing yourself on Annora ere ye are married willnae gain ye anything. Unlike some other lasses, she willnae quietly accept her fate or forgo all resistance just because ye robbed her of her maidenhead."

"*I* took her maidenhead," James felt like yelling in some mad gesture of possession and manly pride. He felt both furious and terrified for Annora. It took him a minute to calm himself down and resist the strong urge to charge into the ledger room and tell those two men discussing Annora so coldly that she was no longer free for the taking. She belonged to him. He wanted to use his fists, too, to make sure that both men understood.

Instead he grabbed his wood and his drawing and slipped out of the room. He needed to find Annora and warn her. James knew he needed to do far more than warn her. He could not fully protect her while pretending to be a wood-carver at Dunncraig, a man under MacKay's command yet not one who would be told anything the man had planned. He had to get her away from here, far away where Egan could not get her. With that in mind, he returned his things to his workroom and went in search of her.

By the time he got to her bedchamber unseen, having not found her anywhere else, James was feeling slightly frantic. Now that Egan knew MacKay would let him have Annora, James doubted the man would heed MacKay's advice not to strongarm her. James did not want her to be out of his sight, certain that Egan would grasp any opportunity to force her into his bed.

A soft humming came from within Annora's bedchamber and he recognized the voice as hers. Taking a last careful look around to be sure no one would see him, he rapped softly on her door. He was relieved to hear that she had barred it as he had asked her to, the sound of her unbarring it easy to recognize, and he felt his fear for her ease just a little.

"Are ye alone?" he asked the moment she cracked open the door enough to see him.

"Aye," she replied, "but..."

He gave her no time to say more, pushing past her into the room and then shutting and barring the door behind him. "Ye have to leave Dunncraig now," he said as he looked for something to pack some of her things in, something she could carry.

"Ye want me to leave?" she asked in a very small voice, astonished at how quickly and abruptly their affair had ended.

"I dinnae want ye to leave but ye must and quickly."

"Why?"

James stepped up to her and took her into his arms. He was going to miss her and not simply because his bed would feel cold and empty. Annora had become part of his life, of his hope for a future at Dunncraig. None of his plans for proving MacKay was the one who had committed murder and retaking Dunncraig had changed except that Annora had become a part of all of that.

"I just heard MacKay tell Egan that he can marry ye in one month's time."

"So soon?" she whispered, shocked at how little time she had left to decide what she must do and where she could go.

He leaned back a little and looked at her. "Ye kenned that it would happen?"

"I also heard them speak of it, but Donnell refused to set a date.

He seemed to imply that it would be a while before he did so, but he has obviously changed his mind. When I came bursting into your room last night, it was because I had just heard him and Egan discussing it." She blushed. "I got distracted."

"Ye could have told me when ye werenae distracted." James was not sure if he felt angry that she had not confided in him or if he was just curious as to why she had not.

"There isnae anything ye can do about it, is there? Nay if ye wish to prove your innocence and regain Meggie and Dunncraig. They both need ye to rid this place of Donnell."

"And ye think I can just ignore the fact that ye are being given to another mon?"

"I dinnae intend to be given to another mon. I just cannae leave right yet."

"Ye can and ye will. I will take ye and Meggie to France. Egan willnae be able to follow ye there. If naught else, MacKay willnae allow it."

"James, ye cannae leave."

Annora sighed and watched as he paced the room. It touched her heart that he wanted to protect her so much that he would set aside all he had worked for. She could not allow him to do that, however. Dunncraig was dying beneath Donnell's rule. A lot of people needed James to regain his home, his lands, and his good name. He could not do that if he was in France.

"Donnell is destroying Dunncraig," she said, trying to imbue her words with all the urgency she could. "He raids your neighbors and is making a lot of enemies, ones who will cut down the people of Dunncraig because they see them as naught more than Donnell's people, ones who may e'en have aided Donnell in his raids. In the last raid a laird's eldest son was killed. And it gets worse every day. I willnae let ye trade all of their lives for my safety."

He turned to look at her and almost smiled. MacKay was right. Annora was not the sweet, meek lass Egan thought she was. There was steel in that slender backbone. What touched him was the concern she showed for the people of Dunncraig. It had not taken him long to see that she did not keep herself apart from the people by choice. This show of concern only confirmed his opinion that Annora cared for his people even when she was not allowed to be any part of their lives. She was the sort of lady Dunncraig needed.

"I could send ye to my family," he said.

Annora sat down on her bed. "Mayhap. I must think about it."

James sat down beside her and draped his arm around her shoulders. "What is there to think about? Ye cannae wish to marry Egan."

"Most of the time I cannae abide e'en being in the same room as Egan. He is as brutal and cruel as Donnell; he just doesnae have that cunning that Donnell has. They are the sort of feelings that disturb me the most, sometimes e'en make me physically ill. But I cannae just disappear. Meggie needs me here. Somehow I must find a way to elude Egan yet continue to keep a watch o'er Meggie until ye can rid Dunncraig of Donnell and his men. Any woman Donnell uses to replace me as Meggie's nurse willnae be so careful to keep her out of the reach of Donnell or away from the cruelty that is committed here nearly every day."

He was so moved by her care and concern for his daughter that James had to kiss her. By the time he ended the kiss, they were sprawled on top of the bed and he was hard and aching for her. A little tentatively, recalling how horrified his wife had been when he had once tried to make love to her during the day, he waited for some sign of discomfort or rejection from Annora. His heart soared as he finished unlacing her gown and began to tug it off and she did nothing to stop him.

"We really must be careful," Annora murmured, watching as James sat up to strip off his clothes. He truly was a beautiful man, scars and all.

"I ken it," he said as he tossed aside the last of his clothing and then returned to undressing her. "I kept a close watch as I rushed here to save ye like the gallant knight I am."

Despite being stripped naked by a naked man in the middle of the day, Annora found she could laugh. "Verra gallant, but I dinnae think this is exactly how a gallant knight saves the fair maiden."

"Ye havenae heard the whole truth. This is why gallant

knights risk all to save maidens. The rewards are too sweet to resist." He sighed with pleasure once she was naked and he was sprawled on top of her, savoring the feel of their skin touching. "I dinnae wish ye to leave Dunncraig, but better that than to watch ye given to Egan or, worse, ken that he has caught ye alone somewhere and raped ye, and I couldnae stop it."

Annora reached up and stroked his cheek. "I have kept out of his grasp for three years. I can do so for a little longer. My plan is to leave Dunncraig only when no other choices are left to me. Meggie needs me, and if I have to leave, she will be all alone no matter how many nursemaids Donnell surrounds her with."

"Big Marta and I could help," he began and felt surprised when she stopped his words with a short, hard kiss.

Annora knew she could not hold on to her secret about Donnell's plans for Meggie any longer. James was not yet firm in his decision to stay at Dunncraig and fight for what was his. His fear for her was touching, but he needed to put it aside, to see that there was so much more that needed saving. She just hoped he did not see what she was about to tell him as even more reason to pack up and flee to France.

"Meggie needs to be watched verra carefully o'er the next seven or so years. Donnell is arranging a marriage for her to Sir Ian Chisholm's youngest son." She wrapped her arms around him and held on tightly when his whole body tensed as if he was about to leap from the bed and rush out to kill Donnell immediately.

"Nay," was all James could say, his throat tight with fury. He ached to go hunt down Donnell and kill the man, but despite that fierce need he did not fight Annora's grasp.

"Nay is quite right. It is but another reason why ye must stay and accomplish what ye had set out to do from the start. Donnell has a lot of people thinking Meggie is his child and he would come hunting for her if we took her away. I suspect the Chisholms would also do so as they will undoubtedly gain a lot from tying their family to Donnell's. Meggie's safety and happiness depend on ye defeating Donnell and returning as laird of Dunncraig. S'truth, that is the only solution to all our problems and those of the good people of Dunncraig. Ye cannae let your anger lead ye for it will take ye down the wrong path in the end. Anger always does that."

James rested his forehead against her as he struggled to clear his mind and heart of the fury inside them, a wild fury and a deep fear for the future of his child. It was the latter that finally helped him gain control of himself. Annora was right in all she said. The only way to save them all was to continue to try and get back all Donnell had stolen from him. That his plan left him unable to completely protect his women was a bitter potion to swallow, but he would do it. In the end, it was really the only way to save Annora and Meggie.

Until the threat to Annora grew too great, he silently promised himself. He would not allow Egan to have her, before or after their marriage. Meggie was safe until the day of her first bleeding, and that was years away, but Annora had only a month before she would be dragged before a priest and tied for life to a man who was long overdue for a hanging. For a while, he would allow matters to continue as they had, but if it appeared that Annora was in any real danger, he would get her away from Dunncraig even if he had to tie her up and carry her out in a sack. He had no doubt that Meggie would be his ally once she understood what would happen to Annora if she stayed.

He looked down into Annora's beautiful eyes and saw both the fear and the resolution there. She would argue with his plan and try to talk him out of his vow, so he did not plan to tell her about it. Her concern for the safety of others over her own touched him, but he would not allow her to make any great sacrifices. Running to France with her and Meggie would end his plans for retaking Dunncraig, but not forever. Once the hunt for them eased, and he was sure it would, and he got his women settled somewhere safe, he would return and try again. This plan had worked so far and he was sure he could come up with another that would work as well.

So he would distract her from the whole matter of Egan and Donnell's plans for her and Meggie, he thought and nearly grinned. She was naked and so was he and they were sprawled together on a bed behind a locked door. James would make his plans for her and Meggie's safety later. Right now he intended to reclaim his woman.

Recognizing the gleam in his eye, Annora shivered. "Are we all done discussing the matter?" she asked as she ran her hands up and down his sides, loving the feel of him.

"Aye, talking is done. I mean to distract us both from our worries."

"I believe I approve of that idea."

"Do ye, now?"

"Och, aye, I do. Allow me to show ye just how thoroughly I approve," she said in a voice even she thought sounded very much like a purr.

She did, much to James' delight. As he lay sprawled beside her, his body still humming from the pleasure she had given him, he knew that he would walk away from Dunncraig in a heartbeat if it meant he could keep her by his side. The fact that he planned to try again later to redeem his blackened name and rid Dunncraig of Donnell MacKay made it easier to think that, but James knew he would flee with her and his daughter and never look back if that was what was needed to keep them safe. He could only pray that he did not have to, for Annora deserved to be the lady of Dunncraig and Dunncraig deserved to have her.

Chapter Eleven

As James hurried along the badly rutted road leading into the village, he wondered yet again why Edmund had sent for him. There were too many possibilities, everything from a message from his family to some important information Edmund or Ida had uncovered that could finally end this game and return him to the laird's seat at Dunncraig, a free man again. It was just possible that it was a message from his family, for he had sent them word of his plans. He had still insisted that they stay away, but that did not mean they had heeded him.

Out of the corner of his eye, James caught sight of someone just inside a grouping of trees. For a moment he thought he was being followed. Ever since learning that MacKay meant to give Annora to Egan in a month's time, he had felt as if Egan was watching him all the time. Good sense told James that, if Egan was watching him, it was because he had knocked the man down in front of Annora, but good sense fled him whenever he thought of her trapped in a marriage with Egan. And he had known about that appalling plan for only two days. James hated to think of how he would be feeling as the wedding date drew nearer.

The moment he stopped and stared into the trees, James saw that he had not been imagining things. There was someone in the trees, two someones in fact. Egan had a woman pressed up against a tree and was rutting with her. There really was no other word for it as Egan's breeches were down around his ankles, the woman's skirts were bunched up around her waist, and Egan was thrusting into her so hard and fast that her back was rubbing up against the tree with each move he made. The roughness of the act made James think that the woman could be unwilling, yet another victim of Egan's lust, but just as he took another step toward them, the woman turned her head and looked at James. She saw him and smiled in a way that told James she would willingly allow him to do the same as soon as Egan was done. Shaking his head, James hurried away before Egan lifted his face from the woman's voluptuous breasts and saw him. There would have to be some serious cleaning of the keep once it was his again, as it appeared that Donnell had filled it with whores.

James called out for Edmund even as he entered the man's small shop. Edmund came rushing out from the workroom at the rear of the shop, looked around to be sure that no one else was with James or had followed him, and then dragged him into the back room he had just come out of. All without saying a word. The concern James had begun to feel over his friend's highly secretive actions faded abruptly when he saw the two men seated at a small rough table set in the middle of the workroom. His family had ignored his command to just stand back and allow him to solve the mystery.

Tormand Murray might not be his blood kin, but James knew they were brothers in all the ways that mattered. Eric and Bethia Murray had taken James in when he had been orphaned at the tender age of one, soon after they had fought hard to defeat the man who wanted him dead so that he could claim Dunncraig. He not only owed them his life, but he owed them for the very good life he had had while living with them. Each and every child born to them after they had claimed him as their own had been presented as his sibling and he had been raised as one of them, never once being treated as anything other than one of their own children. If he had not been heir to Dunncraig, a Drummond stronghold, he would have changed his name to Murray, for the whole clan had treated him as one of theirs. And right now he felt as every sibling would when a younger brother completely ignored his wishes. He wanted to pound Tormand Murray into the ground.

"I see that ye still have trouble obeying e'en the simplest of commands, "James said to Tormand.

A wide grin was Tormand's first response to that provocation, but he quickly grew serious again. "This is Sir Simon Innes." He nodded at the other man, who quickly rose to his feet and bowed. "He is a king's mon. A weel-trusted one."

"Ye brought a king's mon here? Did ye just forget that I have been outlawed?"

"Simon has sworn to, weel, forget all about that. And if we cannae discover anything to help ye prove that ye are innocent, he has also sworn to forget that he e'er saw ye."

James knew he was looking at his brother as if he was a complete idiot. "Just forget about all of this, aye?"

"Aye," Simon replied in a voice that was surprisingly deep for such a lean, almost thin, man. "I will forget it all. In truth, I ne'er agreed with the decree. I ken Sir Donnell MacKay, nay weel thank God, but weel enough to doubt his word about anything. Unfortunately, the day the decree was signed, I wasnae at court. 'Tis my feeling that that, too, was weel planned."

"It seems fate was against me at every turning."

"Mayhap fate thought ye needed a wee bit of humbling, brother," drawled Tormand.

James scowled at Tormand. "And mayhap fate sent ye here for a weel-earned pummeling."

"Sit," ordered Edmund as he set out a jug of dark ale and four of James' elegantly carved goblets.

"Ye do fine work, James," Tormand said as they all sat down and he studied the goblet placed in front of him. "Mother was delighted with the pair ye sent her last Michaelmas, although she would have preferred to see ye instead. This has been hard on her, ye ken."

After taking a long drink of the strong ale to drown the sudden painful longing to see his family again, James replied, "I ken it, but death trails me. I couldnae bring it to her door."

"She kens it and often says that she would rather ne'er see ye again if it meant that ye stayed alive." Tormand grinned. "Of course, she often tells our father that she doesnae ken why he doesnae just ride o'er to Dunncraig and cut MacKay into tiny, bloody pieces."

James laughed, easily able to see his tiny mother doing just that and his father calmly agreeing to do it on the morrow, both of his parents knowing full well that he would not do so no matter how much he might wish to.

"So, aside from donning that verra intriguing disguise, what else have ye done thus far?" asked Tormand. "By the way, have ye darkened *all* your hair?"

"Nay as much as I would like to have done by now," replied James, ignoring the second question completely. "I keep telling myself that finding out the truth about a mon who is verra skilled at hiding it is slow work and there is no hurrying it along."

Simon nodded. "The need to be cautious always makes a chore take longer."

Murmuring in agreement, James studied Simon Innes as he had another drink of ale. There was the look of keen intelligence in Simon Innes' gray eyes, and James got the distinct impression that the man had used it well. He was young to be a trusted man of the king. Despite the fact that there was an almost predatory harshness to his features, James also felt he could trust the man just as the king so obviously did. His only question was why the man had chosen to help him, something that could anger the king, for it showed doubt in their liege's decision. James was a little surprised when he heard himself ask that question out loud. He was even more surprised when Simon grinned, an expression that took years off the man's face and softened his harsh looks considerably.

"The king already kens that I dinnae like the decision and why. My doubts stirred some in him as weel, but the deed was done. To suddenly revoke the decree would make the king and those who advise him look weak and easily persuaded. Nay a good thing."

"Ah, nay, of course. "James tried to swallow the resentment he felt over being left to rot in order for the king to look strong and decisive.

"Your kinsmen ne'er let it be, however."

"Nay, they wouldnae. Stubborn, the whole lot of them."

Tormand snorted. "Nay like ye, aye? Sweet, biddable laddie that ye are."

James ignored his brother. "So it was left as it was e'en though it nay longer seemed just. How is it, then, that ye now come to see if ye can find out the truth?"

"As for myself, I but needed an invitation," replied Simon. "The king and his advisers, however, needed much more. The fact that MacKay is raiding the neighboring clans as if they are his own private larder actually helped ye, although I suspicion ye will be struggling to cool tempers and make reparations for quite a while. Howbeit, MacKay has turned a once peaceful corner of our land into a battlefield. That is what now troubles the king and his advisers. I am nay here and I didnae see ye and, of course, I ne'er helped ye, but all of that has been approved by a wee nod and a wink from the king and his advisers."

"The men of the court ne'er do anything simply and directly, do they?"

"They cannae and, after a while, I think most of them actually enjoy playing the games. So, have ye uncovered any truth? Better yet, have ye found any proof that MacKay is guilty of your wife's death?"

James hesitated for only a moment. MacKay's plan to marry Annora to Egan meant he no longer had the luxury of time. Doing it all by himself salved his pride, but it could cost Annora very dearly. His family trusted Simon, and every instinct James had told him that they were right to do so. He briefly wished that he had Annora's gift but decided to just trust in his family's judgment and his own instincts.

"To begin with, there is a verra good chance that not only was my wife MacKay's lover, but she was his ally. Actually, a maid saw Mary enter Donnell's rooms during one of his visits to Dunncraig and says it was soon verra clear that it wasnae an innocent meeting between cousins. I dinnae ken who she is as she spoke to the cook and made that woman swear that she wouldnae tell anyone where she heard the tale. There is also a verra good chance that Mary didnae die that night. "James was rather pleased with the shock on the faces of Edmund and Tormand. Simon just looked intrigued.

"Ye buried her, didnae ye?" asked Simon.

"I buried a charred mess. All there was that was recognizable as Mary were the ring I had given her and a few scorched pieces of the gown she had been wearing when I had last seen her. I assumed it was Mary e'en though I couldnae understand what she had been doing at that cottage. Now, weel, I suspect it is one of the places she met with her lover."

Knowing he had the complete attention of the three men, James told them everything that had happened since he had come to Dunncraig. He also told them all he had discovered and how he had done that Edmund interrupted only once, cursing violently when James told them all about Donnell's plan to wed Annora to Egan and little Meggie to Halbert Chisholm. When he was done, James crossed his arms over his chest and awaited the opinions upon his success, or, as he saw it, his lack thereof.

"I can tell that ye think ye have made a poor showing," said Simon after only a few minutes of thought, "but ye have actually done verra weel. Having Big Marta and Annora MacKay as allies has aided ye a lot. Too many men ignore the women as sources of information, or heed only the ones they can seduce into telling them things. As to the latter, I am ne'er sure such women can be trusted. Too many good men have been brought low by heeding what a mistress or a lover has said only to discover that she was working for his enemies. The mon thought he was the one doing the seducing when, in truth, he was the one seduced."

"Annora is not doing that, "James said firmly, hearing the warning mixed with the accusation in Simon's voice yet trying not to get too angry about it.

"She *is* a MacKay and is living upon MacKay's charity."

"She loathes him and hates what he is doing to Dunncraig. She has always questioned his claim upon Meggie and on Dunncraig. Big Marta trusts her."

"As do I and me Ida," said Edmund. "Being an orphaned bastard, but born of good blood, the lass has had little choice in where she was sent. If naught else, she will do all she can to help Lady Margaret stay safe and happy."

Simon nodded slowly. "That reason for her aid is one I can accept"

"But nay that she will help me because she believes I am innocent? She was a maiden, ye ken, no weel-trained harlot who could blind a mon with her skills in the bedchamber." James hoped Annora never discovered how he had spoken so bluntly about her.

"Yet she stays at Dunncraig e'en though her cousin intends to marry her to a brutish swine of a mon?"

"As Edmund said, she stays for Meggie. It will be many years ere MacKay can marry Meggie to Halbert Chisholm, but Annora doesnae intend to allow that to happen. She lingers here because she needs to make a good plan, one that will keep her safe yet close enough to hand to help Meggie when help is needed."

"Then we shall trust her."

James was not sure he believed Simon's assurance of that, but he said no more about Annora. "Are ye planning to stay in the village?"

"Aye," replied Tormand. "None here ken who Simon is and I will do my best to keep out of sight as much as possible although Donnell has ne'er met me and I dinnae look too much like either of our parents."

"Ye have Mother's mismatched eyes."

"Nay exactly. They are far closer in color than hers."

James did not think Tormand's light green eye and light blue eye were close in color at all, but, deciding it was not something he felt inclined to argue about right at the moment, he just nodded. For a little while longer they all discussed what Simon and Tormand might do to help find a few truths to match all the suppositions they had. Simon did not say much, but what he did say made James feel confident that the man was well practiced in the ferreting out of secrets. It was probably a skill that had helped make him close to the king at such a young age.

By the time he began to leave Edmund's, James was feeling hopeful that his trials would soon end. He was not surprised when Tormand followed him out of the shop and hastily pulled him back into the shadowed alley between Edmund's place and the alewife's. Tormand might be good at hiding his feelings from others, but his family could almost always sense what he was feeling. James had sensed that Tormand was troubled by the fact that Annora was kin to Donnell and he could not really blame him for that unease. He just hoped his brother did not cling to it too tightly.

"Ye have something ye need to say to me?" James asked his brother.

"About this lass Annora," began Tormand.

"She is the one, Tormand. That perfect match, that mate we are all told awaits us."

Tormand swore. "Are ye sure? Didnae ye think that Mary was the one?"

"Nay, I ne'er did, but I was weary of waiting and I liked and desired Mary. I thought she would make a good wife and give me the bairns I craved. I should have heeded what so many of the Murrays say and kept on waiting. 'Tis just a hard thing to accept, though. I dinnae think any mon really likes the idea of being bound too tightly to any woman nay matter what pleasure there is in it."

Tormand nodded. "And finding her has made ye e'en more anxious to clear your name and get Dunncraig back."

"Aye, e'en though I would ne'er have thought I could want that more than I already did. What she does do is make me cease thinking so much on avenging myself against MacKay and more on just trying to redeem my name and regain my lands so that I can set her at my side. I think more on simply making a safe and good life for her and Meggie."

"Then we shall see that ye get that verra soon. Simon is the best, James. He has few equals in his ability to ferret out the truth, and when 'tis an innocent mon who has been wronged, he is e'en more tenacious. He has a deep sense of justice. We will end this and set MacKay at the end of a rope where he belongs."

When James nodded and started to make his way back to Dunncraig, Tormand leaned against the wall of Edmund's shop and watched him. It startled him a little when Simon suddenly stood at his side, for he had not heard the man approach. Tormand idly thought that Simon could make someone a verra dangerous enemy.

"Do ye think he is right to trust the woman?" asked Simon.

"'Tis nay just James who trusts her. Edmund and Ida do as weel," replied Tormand.

Simon slowly nodded but he frowned. "I am reluctant to trust a woman who has shared his bed. A mon can be so easily fooled and blinded by soft words and passion."

Tormand wondered what had happened to Simon to make him so reluctant to trust a woman, but he did not ask the man. "James firmly believes that Annora MacKay is his mate, his match, the perfect woman for him. The one that shall complete his life and put his soul at ease. Ye best nay question her honor again, for he willnae tolerate it."

"His mate?"

"Aye." Tormand grinned. "'Tis a hard thing for a mon to understand and I cannae say I like the idea of it, but many of our clan feel strongly that there is such a thing as a mate, a match for each of us that is just right. Some e'en claim they can tell the right one from little more than a moment's look and a few words. James may nay be a Murray by blood, none of my family is as my father was a fostered son as weel, but we seem to share that instinct." He shrugged. "When men like James foil so miserably in a marriage with a woman all would say was perfect for a laird, one has to wonder if there is some truth in the opinions of so many others—Mary wasnae the right match."

"Annora MacKay is?"

That is what James believes."

Then let us pray he is right, for if he feels as ye say he does, then he will soon be telling her all about us."

Annora was almost asleep when the soft, rhythmic rapping James used sounded at her door. She stumbled out of bed and went to open the door. In the dark it took her a moment to unlatch it, but James was quick to slip inside, shut it, and latch it again. She ignored the soft scolding voice in her head telling her that this was all wrong. There was no denying that it was, for it went against every lesson and warning a maid was given as she neared womanhood, but she wanted to spend every moment she could with James. She would pay her penances later.

"What? No lit candles and wine to greet your mon?" he teased as he picked her up in his arms and carried her to her bed.

She smiled as he shed his clothes with a speed she began to think was his custom and crawled into bed beside her. A moment later her night shift went fluttering to the floor. James had little respect for her modesty. Only the fact that it felt so good to be skin to skin with him kept her from complaining about the way he so rapidly got her naked.

"Ye seem to be in a verra cheerful mood," she murmured, squirming a little in a rising pleasure as he stroked her legs.

"Verra cheerful and I have fairly been chewing wood in my eagerness to get to ye so that I could tell ye my news. My brother and a king's mon are in the village."

Annora did not find the news that a king's man now knew where James was to be very good news at all. "A king's mon? Isnae that dangerous for ye? He cannae just ignore the fact that ye have been declared an outlaw."

"Ah, but he can. He ne'er agreed with the decree and he thinks your cousin kenned that he wouldnae, e'en kenned that Simon might have talked the king and his advisers out of naming me an outlaw. But it seems Simon wasnae at court that day."

"Oh, and ye think Donnell kenned that and that was why he was so quick to get in to see the king and demand ye pay for the murder of your wife?"

"I do and so does Sir Simon Innes, the king's mon. My brother Tormand and he will stay in the village and try to find out a few things that may help us prove that MacKay is the one who should be running and hiding."

Annora had a lot of questions she wished to ask about these new allies of theirs, but James began to kiss her breasts and all her ability to think dearly vanished. When she tried to participate in their lovemaking, he captured her wrists in his hand and held her arms down at her sides. She lay helpless beneath him but had no complaint as he covered her breasts with kisses, teased her hardened nipples with his tongue, and suckled at each breast until she thought she would scream from the pleasure of it.

When he began to trail kisses down her stomach, she was almost relieved, for the madness he stirred within her, that desperate craving, faded just a little. Then, suddenly, his mouth was there, right where she ached for him. She tensed for a moment, such an intimacy startling and discomforting her, but then he began to kiss her and caress her with his tongue. With each intimate caress the tension born of her embarrassment and modesty fled and was rapidly replaced with a blinding need. Desire filled her whole body and the hunger she had for him grew so strong she trembled with it.

Realizing she was close to that moment of blind delight, she called out his name, needing him to be inside her when she was swept away to that place of bliss where only he could take her. He slowly kissed his way up her body. The moment his mouth covered hers, he thrust inside her and she screamed into his mouth as she broke apart. Each hard thrust of his body only intensified the pleasure as wave after wave of a fierce release ripped through her. She was only vaguely aware of him reaching his own completion and groaning her name against her mouth before she sank into a warm oblivion.

James grinned at the way Annora barely twitched when he washed her clean. She was still so limp with sated pleasure she was nearly unconscious. He climbed back into her bed and pulled her up against him, her firm, well-rounded backside fitting perfectly against his groin. He never would have believed that the quiet, sweet Annora he had met when first coming back to Dunncraig would turn out to be such a passionate lover. The fact that his lovemaking could send her into a near swoon soothed every wound inflicted by Mary's coldness.

He kissed her shoulder and she murmured her pleasure at the touch. "I had best nay stay the full night," he said.

"Nay, I suspicion that wouldnae be wise." Annora could not hide her regret over that necessity. She loved having his big, warm body curled around her, and her bed would feel very cold and empty when he left it.

"I ken I should stay away completely but I cannae. So I will do what little my weak will allows to protect ye."

"From Egan?"

"I dinnae think your cousin would be too pleased about this, either, do ye?"

She shivered at the mere thought of Donnell discovering that she had taken a lover. "Nay. He feels it his right to rut with any maid who catches his eye, but he would be enraged if he thought I was nay longer a maid. I dinnae think that would be just because he felt I had spoiled myself for Egan, either. From all I have observed Donnell wants all women he desires to be whores, but his kinswomen have to be as pure as newly fallen snow. He takes it as a personal insult if they are not."

"Weel, a lot of men think that, but I suspicion Donnell's reaction to ye allowing me into your bed could be deadly."

She turned in his arms to face him. "Aye, but I think it would be ye he would be eager to see killed more than me. I am nay so sure that Egan would feel the same, though."

"Hush, lass," he said and kissed her. "The danger was there from the start. We will just be verra careful. The fact that ye are seen as a sweet, innocent maid will protect us some. No one would suspect that ye are a passionate woman who can drive a mon to madness in the bedchamber."

"I believe the madness is shared," she said quietly and then asked, "So, what did ye, your brother, and this Simon Innes fellow talk about?"

"About how I may get my good name, my lands, and my daughter back and how they might help me do it. I think Simon may be feeling a wee bit guilty that he wasnae there to try to stop the decree of outlawry from being issued. My brother Tormand also says that Simon is a mon with a verra strong sense of justice, and justice has been severely abused in this matter. So I told them all we had found out and they mean to find out more. I also told them of those possibilities we discussed, including the fact that my wife betrayed me."

"I am sorry ye had to expose that hurt to those men."

"A little embarrassment o'er being seen as a blind fool is a small price to pay if those two find me the proof I need to be free again."

"If it helps to ease your sense of embarrassment, many of us were fooled by Mary. I didnae ken her verra weel, but everyone always spoke of her as being sweet, shy, and quiet. A perfect lady who knew her place and fulfilled all her duties with skill and patience." Annora could recall having Mary MacKay held up to her as an example she could follow all too often.

"Do ye ken? E'en though 'tis what I thought I wished for in a wife, when ye speak of how she was seen by others, she sounds a verra boring sort of woman." He grinned at her. "Now, ye are a verra exciting woman. Aye, and a verra warm one."

When he began to kiss her neck, Annora began to feel even warmer. "I thought ye said ye couldnae stay the night."

"I cannae but the night is still verra young."

It was only a few hours until dawn, but since his skillful hands were turning her blood to fire, Annora decided she would be a great fool to argue with him.

Chapter Twelve

"An—nor—a!"

Annora started in surprise as that clear childish voice echoed through the wood. She looked around and realized that Meggie was no longer close at hand helping her to collect moss. For a moment Annora was terrified for any number of horrible things could have happened to the child, but even as she leapt to her feet, she realized that there had been no hint of fear or pain in Meggie's voice.

"An—nor—a!"

"Where are ye, Meggie?" Annora yelled.

"O'er here!"

Turning toward the sound of the child's voice, Annora finally caught sight of Meggie and was relieved that she was not as far away as she had feared. The child was standing by a huge tree that had almost as many dead limbs as live ones. Annora idly thought that she should tell someone about that, for it would provide some much needed firewood. Inwardly shaking her head over the tendency of her mind to wander lately, she scowled at Meggie.

"Margaret Anne Drummond, ye ken verra weel that ye shouldnae wander about alone," she said, struggling to sound as stern as possible even though the relief she had felt when she had realized the child was not in trouble still softened her voice.

"I have found something. Come see."

With every step she took toward the child, Annora carefully planned the lecture she would give Meggie. Most of the time Meggie was a good, obedient child who gave her little trouble, but Meggie also had a wide streak of curiosity that often led her astray. It was more important now than it had ever been before that Meggie stay close at hand. Donnell had made it clear that he knew he could use the child against Annora, and that meant that Egan probably knew it too or soon would. The raids Donnell and the Chisholms had led against their neighbors also promised that there were a lot of angry men surrounding Dunncraig lands who would like nothing better than to inflict some pain upon the laird who had done them so much harm.

"Look, Annora, I found a book in the tree," Meggie said when Annora reached her side.

Annora looked at the leather-bound book Meggie held out to her, and the lecture she had meant to give the child fled her mind. She recognized what it was. It was the sort of book ladies liked to use to write down their thoughts or all the things that happened during the day. Not many women knew how to write well, so the little books were still a rare luxury. A luxury a woman like Mary might have had and thoroughly enjoyed. Annora was not surprised to see a slight tremor in her hand as she took the book from Meggie. She hastily thanked God that her guards, bored by watching her and Meggie collect moss, had wandered out of sight, for she sensed that this was a discovery that Donnell could not know about.

"It was all wrapped up in this cloth and stuck inside this tree. I was running and I tripped and I fell down right near the tree hole and I looked into the hole and there it was. Can ye read it to me?"

Glancing at the heavy oiled leather cloth the book had been wrapped in, Annora was not surprised at what a good condition it was in. Whoever had hidden it had wanted to be certain it survived. That implied that it held some information the woman felt would be important to someone. As far as Annora knew, there was really only one thing that had happened at Dunncraig in the last few years that was worth writing about. Hiding the book in which the truth had been written might be *the* worst crime that had been committed against James.

Carefully opening the book, Annora read the few words written on the very first page and felt her heart stop only to quickly start again, its pace so rapid that she felt a little light-headed. The book was a gift from Mary's mother, given to Mary on her wedding day, or, as her mother wrote, *the first day of your life as a lady, a wife, and, praise be to God, a mother.*

"I am nay sure any of this will be of interest to ye, Meggie," Annora finally replied, amazed at how light and calm her voice was, for inside she was shaking with hope and the intense need to get someplace private and read the book. "'Tis a lady's book in which she lists all the things she does every day." *And since that lady was your mother who may well have betrayed your father, what is written in here is most definitely not for your tender ears,* Annora thought.

"Oh." Mary made a face indicating her disgust. "Why would a lady bother to write all that down? Everyone kens what a lady does." Meggie picked up the oiled leather cloth and stuck it in the small sack she carried. "Ye would think she would write about interesting things."

"Weel, if I find anything interesting in the book I will be certain to tell ye all about it. And, Meggie, m'love, I think it might be best if ye dinnae tell anyone about this book until I ken whose it is and what it says. It was hidden away in that tree for a reason and I think I need to find out what that reason is before we let anyone ken what ye found."

Meggie frowned and then nodded. "Aye, it might have some secrets in it."

"It might indeed, for that would certainly explain why it was hidden."

"I willnae say anything. Can I keep the cloth if I say I found it in the woods?"

"Aye, that isnae truly a lie, is it? Ye did find it in the wood. Just dinnae tell anyone what ye found wrapped inside it. Come, let us return to collecting the moss we need and then we can return to Dunncraig to clean up."

It was difficult to remain calm as she and Meggie returned to the tedious chore of collecting plants needed for healing. However, since Donnell had begun raiding his neighbors, there were a lot more wounds to tend to. What Annora ached to do was read the journal she slipped into her bag. She had not looked at any more than the first page, but she could swear she felt Mary in the book. She hoped it was not her imagination, that Mary had indeed written a lot in the little book, and that there would be some answers to all the questions she and James had. They certainly needed a few. Annora just hoped that the answers did not cause James even more pain than he had already suffered.

"I cannae let him see this," Annora told the purring cat sprawled on her lap.

Annora stared at the book in her hands and wondered about what she should do now. The journal only hinted at Donnell's plans, for Mary was obviously not interested in how she got what she wanted, but the woman made it very clear over and over again that she had married James only because Donnell had wanted her to. It was difficult for Annora to see Donnell as a lover who could enthrall a woman so completely that she would do the sort of things Mary had done for him. Annora saw him very clearly for the vain brute that he was. Mary had also made her distaste for sharing James' bed viciously clear in several entries, and Annora did not want James to read those cruel words.

"Ah, Mungo, I just dinnae ken what to do. Aye, this confirms that Donnell and Mary were lovers e'en before she married James. 'Tis clear that James didnae notice his bride's lack of innocence, but mayhap there is some trick Mary played. Yet, this book doesnae say verra much about the plot to be rid of James. A hint, nay more. And the writings end months before Mary was supposed to have died in that fire. Do ye ken, I think there must be another one of these little books hidden somewhere."

Mungo butted his head against her hand in a silent demand and she started to scratch his ears. "I think I shall hide this one and begin a search for the other. There *has* to be another. From all I have just read, Mary was a woman who truly enjoyed writing down all her woes, real or imagined. She filled every tiny scrap of space on these pages."

And a lot of it was nothing more than the whining of a spoiled child who did not get all she wanted, Annora thought crossly. Most women were married to men chosen by their families. Mary had at least been given a husband who was young, and handsome. Even more remarkable, she had had a husband who

had believed in his vows and honored them, remaining faithful
to her despite her often-expressed disgust over his lovemaking.
Someone should have shaken some common sense into the
woman, Annora decided. Instead, Mary had thought Donnell
was her true love, the best of all men. The woman's error in
judgment had gotten her killed. Annora had absolutely no doubt
about that.

Gently moving her softly snoring cat onto her bed, Annora
decided to begin her search for the other journal. She was certain
there was another one and she was equally as certain that it
was hidden in some place Mary often went. Annora did want
to think much about just why Mary might have gone into the
woods a lot, often enough so that she would have found that
rather clever hiding place. If the woman also went to the cottage
a lot, there could be something hidden there, too. The fact that
the cottage had burned to the ground did not necessarily mean
a hidden journal had met the same fate.

She sighed as she left her bedchamber, pleased to see that her
guards were gone, but worried about how long it might take to
find the other journal and how often she would be free to look
for it. For a moment her certainty faltered, but she quickly shook
her head. Every instinct she had told her that there was another
journal and that it held the sort of truths that could be used to
free James. She had learned long ago to trust her instincts.

Suddenly Annora knew just who to ask about Mary's favorite
places, and she hurried down the stairs intending to get to the
kitchen. She nearly cursed aloud when she turned a corner at the
bottom of the steps and came face-to-face with Egan. As quickly
as she could, she moved so that there was no wall close at hand.
Annora did not want to be pinned against a wall or any other
hard surface by Egan ever again. Where she now stood was also
very public, the chance of someone coming by very high, and
she hoped that would be enough to make Egan hesitate in trying
to force himself on her.

"Where are your guards?" Egan demanded.

"I am only going to the kitchens," she said calmly. "Why
would I need guards there?" Annora suddenly feared that her
guards would suffer dearly for allowing her to roam free, and

that would make them far more vigilant just when she needed them to be increasingly lax.

She watched Egan's eyes narrow as he struggled to give her an answer that would not reveal the true reason for having her constantly watched. Annora knew it was to keep her from hearing anything that might make her question Donnell's right to be laird of Dunncraig. Men with secrets always found it necessary to watch all those around them for some sign that their secrets were slipping free of their cage. She also knew that it was not something Donnell or Egan wished her to know. Although she was deeply insulted that they would think her too witless to guess why she was guarded so carefully, she also had to be glad of it. The less those two men thought she knew, the less danger she would be in.

"Ye need to be protected from the other men," Egan said. "There may be some who dinnae ken that ye are mine."

"I am nay yours," she snapped.

"Aye, ye are. E'en Donnell says—"

"Egan, if I might speak to ye for a moment?" Donnell said in a cold, hard voice as he walked up to them. He looked at Annora in a way that made her inwardly shiver, as if he was blaming her for Egan's too-free tongue. "Dinnae ye have something ye need to do?" he asked her in a voice so cold she nearly shivered.

Annora nodded and nearly ran to the kitchen. From what James had said, Egan was not supposed to tell her that she was now promised to Egan and it sounded like Donnell felt Egan had been about to disobey him. She doubted Egan would suffer too much for disobedience, for he and Donnell had been together ever since they were boys and knew far too many of each other's secrets. However, the next few minutes would be very unpleasant for Egan. Annora knew she would have to be satisfied with that.

It took several moments after reaching the kitchens to find Big Marta. It took even longer to convince the woman to move to some place where they could talk privately. Big Marta's curiosity finally got the best of her, however, and she led Annora to a tiny room at the rear of the kitchens where the more expensive food stores were kept, things such as spices and good wine.

"Now, what do ye wish to speak about?" asked Big Marta as she lit some candles and then shut the door to the room. "I was about to seek my bed, ye ken." She nodded toward the back of the room.

Annora's eyes widened when she saw the small bed. "Ye sleep in here?"

Big Marta shrugged her narrow shoulders. "Easier than walking back to town, trying to sleep in my son's verra crowded home, and then walking all the way back here ere the sun has e'en risen. Smells better here, too. So, what did ye need to tell me that no one else could be hearing?"

"Actually, I need to ask ye a few questions about Mary," Annora said.

"Why?"

"Because I think she was a verra big part of the plots and schemes which put my cousin's arse in the laird's chair here."

"Oh? And just why would ye be thinking that?"

Annora could sense that the woman was fighting hard to keep something secret, to be cautious before she spoke. Big Marta knew something about Mary that she did not believe she ought to tell anyone, except perhaps James. Information would have to be shared with the woman before she would feel that she could trust Annora enough to tell her what she knew.

"Meggie found a wee book hidden in the hollow of an old tree," Annora finally said.

"What kind of book?"

"One of those little ones ladies like to write in, to hide their secrets in, and to talk about their lives and all of its trials and joys."

"A waste of expensive parchment, I am thinking," grumbled Big Marta. "If the fool woman has secrets, it seems to me that the surest way to make verra certain everyone and his brother kens what the secrets are is to write them down in a wee book. Did ye read it, then?"

"Aye, I did, and the book belonged to Mary." She nodded when Big Marta's eyes widened more with anticipation than surprise. "Mary and Donnell were lovers. 'Tis made painfully clear in the journal."

"Aye, they were lovers, and probably ere she married the laird."

"A long time before."

Big Marta shook her head and cursed softly. "Foolish, foolish woman. Aye, and a completely witless fool to write down all of her sins."

"On that we are agreed. How did ye ken that Donnell and Mary were lovers?"

"One of the maids saw Mary enter Donnell's bedchamber and heard enough to ken that the woman wasnae there to ask what he wanted for a meal."

"Oh dear. Do ye think she would tell anyone else what she saw?" Annora asked, wondering if she and James could get the woman to James' brother and the king's man.

"Nay. I fair had to pull it out of her word-by-word and only after I had sworn meself to silence about it all. Weel, all but the truth about what she saw and heard."

"So, were ye but wishing me to confirm what ye have read in that wee book?" asked Marta.

"Nay, I need ye to tell me if Mary had any places she favored, places she would go to be private."

"Ye mean like the laird's own bedchamber?" Big Marta drawled.

"Weel, aye, although I pray what I seek hasnae been hidden in there, as it will be nigh on impossible to get in there without being seen. Donnell keeps his bedchamber verra weel guarded."

"Such is the way with a mon who holds a lot of secrets, especially the sort that can get him hanged."

"Aye, true enough. Donnell has a great many secrets, I think."

"Why do ye wish to ken if Lady Mary had some wee secret places so that she could commit adultery without being caught?"

"Because I think she may have hidden a second journal. The one Meggie found only goes to a few months before she was killed."

Big Marta tensed and studied Annora closely before she said, "Aye, there were a few places where Lady Mary went. Now that I ken a wee bit more about her, I suspicion they were places where she could meet her lover without fear of being caught."

When Big Marta said nothing more, just stood there scowling down at her feet, Annora gently asked, "Are there none ye can think of?"

"Och, aye, there are some. I was just trying to think of the ones that might offer her the chance to bury something or just hide it. Down by the burn. Lady Mary often slipped away to go there. Ye cannae be seen down there because of all the wondrous big trees. I saw her slip away to go there many a time, and now that I think on it, it was mostly when that bastard was visiting. She could also have crept to the place from where'er she was hiding after the fire and no one would have seen her."

Annora thought about that for a while, trying to picture the various places along the burn where someone could hide, or at least be out of sight of anyone at Dunncraig. There were several that she could think of although she rarely went near the water. She was somewhat afraid of burns and lochs and had been ever since her mother had drowned herself in a burn. Yet, to find some proof that would help James regain his land, she would go and search that burn for miles along either bank if she had to.

"Then I shall go and find Mary's secret place as soon as I can," she murmured.

"Do ye really think the fool wrote another journal?"

"I do, because Mary verra clearly liked to write in the wee book. Since she was alive for months after the other one ended, I cannae believe she stopped writing. If it is hidden somewhere near the burn, I will find it. It might weel hold all that is needed to make Donnell pay for his crimes and set James back in the laird's chair where he belongs."

"Ye dinnae intend to give him the other one, do ye?"

Big Marta could be annoyingly perceptive, Annora mused and then sighed. "Nay. There isnae anything in there which will save him, but there is a lot of things in there that will hurt him. Mary may have appeared sweet and shy to many people, but those writings reveal a verra strong dose of cruelty hid beneath that sweetness. I assume ye told James about what that maid said?"

Big Marta nodded. "Aye, I did although I didnae want to, for he was a good husband to the lass, better than she deserved e'en if she hadnae been betraying him with MacKay."

"On that we are agreed. He already kens that she broke her vows with Donnell and feels as certain as I do, that his wife helped dangle a rope around his neck by letting everyone think he killed her. I dinnae think he needs to ken that she thought him less than a mon and a verra poor lover as weel."

"Nay, the lad doesnae deserve that. But are ye absolutely sure that nothing in that wee book can help him?"

"As sure as I can be. If naught else can be found, then I will give it to him so that he might try to use it to get the decree of outlawry set aside."

"Fair enough. If ye need any help slipping away to look round the burn, just ask me. I will help as I can."

Thank ye. Now I had best try to slip away to my bedchamber ere Egan comes sniffing round again."

The moment Big Marta let her out of the tiny room, Annora fled to the safety of her own bedchamber, watching closely for any sight of Egan every step of the way. Even as she reached for the latch on her door, she changed her mind. Egan might well try to come to her room and, securely latched or not, she was not sure her door was enough to keep him out if he was determined. He was, after all, going to be angry to have been reprimanded by Donnell, and it would be just like Egan to blame her for that. Taking a very careful look around, she hurried toward James' bedchamber. Annora knew that it was an easy choice to make and not only because she would feel safe from Egan if she was with James. She may have been his lover for only a short time, but she already missed him when he was not in her bed.

She had barely finished one quick rap on James' door before it was opened and James yanked her into the room. Annora waited as he closed the door and barred it before he turned to her. For a moment, she had feared she had stepped far beyond her bounds, but his wide smile told her that was a foolish concern. James' ear-to-ear grin told her that she was welcome. Annora suspected the hint of unease she could feel in him was because she had risked a lot to come to his room.

"This wasnae verra wise, but I am too pleased to see ye to complain too much," he said.

"I was a wee bit afraid I had o'erstepped," she began, still uncertain of her welcome.

"Och, nay, love, ne'er that. If the threat of discovery didnae lurk round every corner, there wouldnae e'en be the hint of secrecy about what we share." He pulled her into his arms and kissed her. "I would be strutting about like the fittest cock in the hen yard and letting every mon within leagues ken that ye are mine."

"And letting every woman ken that ye are mine?" she could not resist asking.

"Nay a woman from here to London, cursed city that it is, would e'er doubt it." He leaned back a little and looked at her. "But I get the feeling that there was more than my charming and verra handsome self that brought ye here this night."

"I needed to feel safe," she whispered.

James felt his anger stir for a moment even as her words touched him deeply. His anger was born of the fact that she had felt afraid and he suspected Egan had been hard at her heels. He ached to kill the man, or at least beat him into the ground, but that justice had to wait, for there was too much at risk to give into the need. That she would think to come to him to feel safe, despite the fact that he was as tightly bound as she by the need to play the waiting game when it came to Egan and Donnell, touched him in ways he would be hard put to explain.

"Then stay, love, and let us both pretend for just a wee while that all is right and weel in our world."

"It soon will be, James," she said as he tugged her closer to his bed even as he began to unlace her gown.

"From your beautiful lips to God's ear."

Annora gave herself over to his lovemaking. Her love made her want him so badly she ached, but she too knew that the need to feel happy, safe, and content also drew her into his arms. James made her feel wanted and welcome. It was a feeling she had enjoyed far too few times in her life. As he finished undressing her, then looked her all over as he shed his clothes, she realized that James made her feel as if she had truly found a home.

Pain tore through her heart and she hastily banished it. She did not fool herself into thinking that was true. When he became the laird of Dunncraig again, she would have to leave. Annora would not stand in his way of making a complete life here for himself and Meggie, and that would eventually require a wife, a proper wife and not a poor, landless bastard. But, for now, she could afford the luxury of pretending she was home and simply enjoy the feeling.

As passion swept over her body, stirred into fierce life by James' touch, the feel of his big, warm body, and his heated kisses, Annora had to wonder how any woman could have been as stupid as Mary. Or as blind. Or so cold and confused that she could not see what a wondrous lover James was, what a fortunate woman she had been to be given such a kind, generous, and honorable man as a husband. The idiocy Mary had shown in her choice of lovers and the heartless cruelty she had revealed in how she had treated her husband and child, acting without a care for their safety and happiness if nothing else, would never make sense to Annora.

For as long as she could Annora knew she would hide the little book filled from cover to cover with far too many unkind words about the man she now held in her arms, hoping that she might even be able to destroy it because it was not needed to prove James' innocence. On the day she had to leave James so that he could begin his new life at Dunncraig, Annora wanted to be able to toss that small book of poisonous words into a fire and watch it burn to ashes. Mary had hurt James enough. Although she felt a little sad for her ill-fated cousin, she knew Mary had brought her sad end upon herself and forgave the woman all of her sins save for two. Annora did not think she could forgive Mary for being such a poor mother to Meggie and she would never forgive the woman for trying to destroy James.

Chapter Thirteen

It was not easy to lose her guards, for they had indeed become far more diligent in watching her, but Annora finally managed it Two long days had passed before she had been able to find the time and a safe way to get to the burn, and she intended to search every possible hiding place along the banks. There was no way to guess when she might get another chance, and the very last thing she needed was two hulking men watching her search. Her guards would have reported such actions to Donnell the moment they returned to Dunncraig. Annora shivered just thinking about the trouble that could have brought down on her shoulders.

With yet another glance around to make certain that no one was watching her, she clutched the front of the old hooded cloak Big Marta had loaned her and hurried toward the burn. When she finally reached it, she stared at the water. It ran noisily over the rocky riverbed and it looked cold, but it was not deep enough to be any real threat Annora felt she would be able to do what she had to do without becoming so afraid that she became too upset and frightened to do it. She even wondered if such a fear could eventually be grown out of, but shook aside that puzzle, for it was not the time to worry and wonder over all her little fears and sad childhood memories.

It was when she reached a shady copse that she knew she had found Mary's special place. It was several yards away from where the narrow path from the keep met the burn. Annora felt her body fill with the excitement of an imminent discovery. She knew it was foolish to let her hopes rise too high, but instinct told her that she was but a step or two away from the truth about what had happened to Mary. Annora actually wondered if she had yet another *gift*, one that allowed her to find things. She *had* always been good at that, but never had it been so important to her to find something.

The shady copse where Mary had often come was a beautiful place, prettily enclosed with tall, aging trees so that not even a person standing in the highest tower of Dunncraig would have been able to see her. It was indeed a perfect place to meet a lover, she mused, especially if the woman was one who was supposed to be dead. If Mary had dressed the right way, anyone who might have seen her would have assumed she was just some maid who had come to the banks of the burn to meet her lover. A few people would fear they were seeing a ghost.

First Annora carefully checked every tree to see if there was a hollow in the trunk similar to the one where Meggie had found the first journal. To her complete disappointment there was none, but she told herself she should not have expected it to be so easy. She then began to study the roots of the trees in the hope of finding some odd rise or hollow around them where a small book might be hidden, but that too proved fruitless.

Annora was about to give up when her gaze settled on two large flat stones embedded in the ground near the bank of the burn. They formed a seat of sorts where one could sit and watch the river tumble by. She was just thinking that Mary had gone to a lot of work, or made someone else do so, to make sure that her skirts did not get damp or dirty when her whole body tensed with the certainty of discovery. Annora felt a little like a dog must when it caught the scent of its prey, but she still knelt down by the stones to study them more closely.

Surprising herself with her own strength, she tugged up one of the stones. All she found beneath it was dirt and a vast array of bugs. Quickly dropping it back down, she moved to lift the other stone. Once she pried that up out of the ground she was so surprised by what she saw, she dropped it. It was a struggle to lift it again just enough to push it aside. There, partly buried in the dirt, was a lump of oiled leather just like the one that had been wrapped around the other journal.

After carefully taking it out of the ground, she settled the rock back into place. As gently as she could, fearing that this one might not have been as protected from the damp and other ravages of time and weather, Annora spread open the oiled cloth. When she saw that the little book she had been looking for was wrapped inside and that it was in nearly as good a condition as the other, she said a little prayer of thanks. Before touching the journal she washed her hands in the icy water of the burn and then dried them completely on her skirts. Annora sat down on the rocks that had sheltered the little book for so long and began to read.

When she finished reading what Mary had written, Annora set the book down on her lap. She wiped tears from her cheeks even as she wondered why she wept. Amidst all of Mary's complaints and long rambling accounts filled with self-pity was a tale of betrayal. Mary had betrayed James and Donnell had betrayed Mary. Annora supposed that was enough to make anyone cry.

"Foolish, stupid woman," she whispered. "Ye gave up all that was good for a mon who ne'er loved ye and were rewarded with an unmarked, unconsecrated grave."

A chill breeze swirled around Annora and she shivered. Everyone always said one should never speak ill of the dead. For just a moment, she feared Mary's spirit was trying to reach her, but then she looked up at the sky. Big, dark clouds were rapidly eating up the blue sky and promising a fierce storm. She stood up, tucked the little book into a hidden pocket in her skirts, and started on her way back to the keep. To give herself a good excuse in case someone caught her outside alone, she paused now and again to gather a few plants that might prove useful. It was so easy to find such plants that she began to think she needed to overcome her fear of water enough to come near the burn regularly and find out just how big its bounty of healing plants was.

With each step she took toward Dunncraig, she worried more and more about what to tell James. She would not hide this book from him as she had the other. It held the full ugly truth about all of Donnell's deceits and treacheries. It was also proof that James had not killed Mary. She had lived for nearly a year after James had been condemned for her murder and cried an outlaw. Since James had been hiding and running for his life during that time, it might be difficult for him to prove that he was nowhere near Dunncraig at about the time Mary wrote her last entry in her journal, the one where she had starkly stated her fear that the man she had loved for so many years was going to kill her. From all James had told her about his talk with his brother and the king's man, however, Annora suspected that would not cause James all that much trouble. The ones in power, the men who could end James' exile, had already begun to doubt Donnell's word. There was only Mary's increasing fear to point the finger of guilt in Donnell's direction, but Annora was sure there was more than enough in the journal to push Donnell out of Dunncraig.

She was so deep in thoughts about how the journal might help James that she nearly walked into Donnell as she hurried into the keep. Annora could not completely hide the flush of guilt upon her face and hoped Donnell would think she was just flushed from the cold wind that had sprung up outside. Not only had she been creeping about, avoiding her guards again, but in her pocket was a little book that could possibly see Donnell hanged. It was not easy to look a man in the eye when one was working so diligently to get him hanged, Annora thought, even if he did well deserve the punishment.

"Where have ye been?" he demanded and then he grimaced with distaste as he looked over the cloak she wore. "And why are ye wearing that tattered rag?"

"I was wandering about in the wood again," she replied, ignoring his criticism of her attire.

"Without your guards. Again."

The suspicion she could hear in his voice and see reflected in his narrow-eyed expression made Annora very uneasy, but she forced herself to act and speak as if she was as calm as a loch on a windless day. "I cannae always remember to tell your men where I am going."

"Weel, I strongly suggest that ye try. Now, come with me to my ledger room. We need to talk."

Ominous words, she thought as she followed him. With each move she took the little book in her pocket bumped against her thigh, reminding her that she had a powerful secret to keep. It was more difficult than she liked to hide the growing fear inside her, for Annora knew that if Donnell found the book in her pocket, her life would be in immediate danger. James would also lose one of the first good sources of the truth he was seeking that had been uncovered at Dunncraig.

Once inside Donnell's ledger room she stood quietly in front of his big worktable while he seated himself behind it. He clasped his large-knuckled hands on top of the table and stared at her silently. It was something he always did and Annora was certain it was meant to make her nervous or afraid. It was working, although not as well as it had in the first few months of her time at Dunncraig. She met his steady look with an outward calm.

"Ye are now four and twenty, aye?" he finally said.

"As of two months ago," she replied.

"'Tis far past time ye were married, dinnae ye think?"

"I have naught to offer a husband. No lands, no dowry at all, nay even a wee chest of linens."

Donnell shrugged. "That doesnae matter to some men."

Some men being Egan, she thought. A cold knot formed inside her stomach and for the first time since meeting up with Donnell she forgot about the book in her pocket and all the danger it put her in. She realized that some foolish part of her, the one that did not like to look at any unpleasant truths, had hoped that Donnell would not order her to marry Egan.

"I have yet to meet one," she murmured, knowing full well that, although Egan expected no lands or coin, he was also not marrying her because he loved her. He expected some gain from taking her as his wife; she was just not sure what that was.

"Weel, ye have met one and I think ye ken it weel. Egan has asked to marry ye and I have said aye."

"He has ne'er asked me and I wouldnae have said aye if he had." Despite her effort to speak softly and calmly, Annora knew there had been a bite to her words because Donnell began to look angry.

"Ye *will* say aye, Cousin."

"Why? Why must I marry that mon?" Although she could tell by the angry flush growing on Donnell's face that he thought she was being impertinent, Annora truly wanted to know why he was forcing her to marry Egan.

"Mayhap I am but weary of having the care of ye, as are many of our kinsmen. Egan wishes to relieve me of that burden and I intend to let him. Do ye truly think ye can do better than my first? Do ye forget who ye are? Allow me to remind ye. Ye are naught but a poor, landless bastard. S'truth, I think Egan could do far better in a wife but 'tis ye he wants and he will have ye."

Annora knew Donnell was being purposefully cruel, trying to quell her resistance with hard words, but knowing that did not lessen the hurt very much. "As ye wish, Cousin," she said, knowing that there was nothing she could say or do that would change his mind. "If ye will excuse me now? I have much work to do." She did not even wait for his permission to leave but turned and walked toward the door.

"Dinnae dare disobey me in this, Annora. Believe me when I say that ye will be verra sorry if ye do. And try to come to the great hall for meals more often. It would do the people of Dunncraig good to see ye and Egan together a few times before your wedding."

She did not look at him, just nodded as she hurried out of the room. It undoubtedly looked like the retreat it was but she did not care. Annora was not sure what Donnell could do to her that would make her any sorrier than if she married Egan, either. As for going to the great hall to share a meal with the man she was about to be given to, playing the smiling betrothed couple for the sake of Egan's pride, Donnell would wait a long time for that to happen. Avoiding that torment was even worth risking a beating.

After returning the cloak to a blatantly curious Big Marta and making certain that Meggie was safe and happy with Annie in the nursery, Annora hurried up to her bedchamber. She needed to wash up and change her gown before she confronted James with what she had found. It was not a chore she was looking forward to. The last thing she wished to do was hurt him, but handing him the little book full of Mary's poisonous little comments about him would do just that even though it might also free him.

As she started to leave her bedchamber, she paused and looked at the chest beside her bed where she had hidden the first journal. Annora wondered if she really should take that one to James as well. Hiding it from James was much the same as lying to him, and that was not something she liked to do. A moment later she shook her head and hurried out of her room. There was all the proof James needed in the second journal. It spoke of how Mary and Donnell had been lovers for years as well as all about how they had planned to fool the world into thinking James had killed his wife. All it lacked in comparison to the first one was page after page of Mary complaining about how she had to endure James as her husband, her disgust over his lovemaking, and her many wishes for Donnell to hurry and free her from her marriage. James did not need to read such hurtful words. In truth, he would undoubtedly find more than enough pain in the words Mary had written in her second journal, including the ones that revealed her utter distaste for motherhood.

It was almost time to go down to the great hall before Annora finally found James. She was beginning to fear that she might be seen and escorted there to share a meal with Egan if she did not get out of sight quickly. When she returned to James' bedchamber for a second time and he answered her rap upon his door, she nearly cursed. They had obviously passed each other at some time during her search for him, probably several times. The fact that he greeted her wearing only a big smile did a lot to ease her growing temper, one born mostly of frustration.

"What if it wasnae me?" she asked, laughing softly when he tugged her inside the room, then quickly shut and barred the door.

"Oh, I kenned it was ye, love," he said as he picked her up in his arms and carried her to the bed.

Annora gasped with surprise when he dropped her onto his bed and began to tug off her clothes. "James! I came here to talk to ye!" she protested, laughter making her voice unsteady and stealing all command from her words.

"We can talk later."

She opened her mouth to protest and quickly shut it again. What she had to tell him and show him would hurt him even if only in his pride. Annora might not be certain of what his true feelings were for her, but she was certain that he desired her and that she could stir his passion to such a strength that he could not even talk coherently. Making love before she gave him the bad news would not make him accept it with a smile, but it might well lessen the sting of it. Their lovemaking would still be fresh in his mind when he read all of Mary's unkind words.

"Aye, we can talk later."

Annora pushed him onto his back, straddled his body, and stared down at him. She intended to make love to James in a way that had him feeling like the handsomest, most enticing male that had ever donned a sword. Tossing all of her modesty aside, for it would have no place in what was to happen next, she kissed him. He murmured his encouragement against her lips, but she did not need any prodding. She was on a mission. By the time James was lying sprawled at her side, his body would be weak from the pleasure she had given him but his pride would be strong enough to withstand the blows Mary's poisonous words would deliver.

When she ended the kiss he made a move to take control of the lovemaking, but she easily resisted him. As she had hoped, his curiosity about what she planned to do was stirred and he remained unresisting in her hold. A tickle of excitement began to grow inside her as she kissed her way down his body, lingering on all her favorite spots like his broad chest and his taut, smooth stomach. He tasted so good and the way he began to nearly purr beneath her caresses, his big body shifting with the force of his growing arousal, excited her and made her feel incredibly bold and daring.

The groan that escaped him as she neatly avoided the proudly erect manhood demanding her attention and began to kiss her way down his long, strong legs made her smile. It was a sound of both frustration and delight. Instinct told her that making him wait for what he so obviously hoped she would do would only make the pleasure more fierce. A soft curse of surprised pleasure escaped him when she kissed his feet, teasing his toes with little nips and sucks before kissing her way up his other leg.

When she reached his groin his whole body tensed with

anticipation again and this time Annora did not tease him. She slowly ran her tongue up the length of him and around the faintly glistening top. His hips lifted slightly off the bed with the force of the shudder that went through his body. Annora did not really need her special gift to know that what she was doing was giving him a pleasure so great it was almost painful and she turned all of her attention to trying to make him crazed with delight and need.

James threaded his fingers through Annora's thick, soft hair and held her close to him and she created magic with her tongue. For a woman who had been a virgin only a few days ago, she was proving to be the best lover he had ever had and he knew it was not all because of how he felt about her. Softly urging her to take him into her mouth, he nearly shouted out his pleasure when she slowly drew him deep into the damp heat of her mouth.

For as long as he could, he reveled in the gift of her passion, his body tightening in a way that was nearly painful as he fought the urge for release. Finally, knowing he was but one stroke of her clever little tongue from losing all control, he urged her to mount him. As she did so, he saw the flush of desire on her face and the way her midnight-blue eyes had turned black. The fact that she had stirred her own need and desire to such heights simply by loving him almost undid him. The moment her tight heat enclosed him, he grabbed her by her soft, rounded hips and helped her ride him as hard as she wanted to, as he so desperately needed her to. His release came far sooner than he would have liked, tearing through him with a force he had never experienced before, but she was right beside him, her body tightening around him and seeming to drink heartily of the seed he spilled deep into her womb. The possibility that that seed might take root only added to his pleasure even though he knew it was a reckless wish. James barely found the sense and strength to catch her in his arms when she collapsed upon his chest.

It was a long time before James returned to his senses. He was still on his back with Annora sprawled on top of him and he was idly stroking her back. James suspected the fact that she had moved just enough to separate their bodies had been what had roused him from his stupor, but he noticed that she had not found the strength to move to his side, curling up against him as she usually did.

No other woman had ever made love to him like that. He had once paid for a woman to love him with her mouth, something a lot of women refused to do or thought was a sin far more grievous than any of the other bedplay they indulged in. James was suddenly glad that he had never really made love to a woman with his mouth, not in the way he had done with Annora, for now they had each shared something with each other that they had never shared with another. For the first time he was glad that his experience with women had never been as extensive as that of some of his brothers or cousins. He could never be untouched for Annora as she had been untouched for him, but at least he had not spent his unwed years leaping gaily from one bed right into another.

Feeling a faint tension entering Annora's body, he asked, "Are ye ready to talk now?"

Annora grimaced and slowly sat up. It amazed her that she was only a little embarrassed about what she had just done, but she would puzzle over that later. The very last thing she wished to do was spoil this beautiful time with Mary's journal, but it was time he saw what she had found.

He must have sensed her unease, for he slowly sat up and frowned as she moved off him. Clutching the bed linen around her, she scrambled off the bed to find where he had tossed her gown. She picked it up, shook it out, and idly thought on how hard James was on her clothing. Then she took the journal from her pocket and handed it to him.

"What is this?" asked James, for it gave him a very uneasy feeling as he held it in his hands. He had none of the gifts that were rampant amongst the Murrays, but he did have very good instincts and all of them were telling him that he was not going to like what was inside this little book.

"A journal written by Mary. It starts a few months ere ye were declared an outlaw and had to flee for your life," Annora replied and was not surprised when he paled slightly even though the glint of anticipation began to lighten his eyes.

"Have ye read it?"

"Aye, and sad to say it just may help ye. That it will help ye is good but 'tis sad that your own wife was part of all that happened to ye." She took a deep breath and began to get dressed as she said, "It willnae be an enjoyable read for ye nay matter how it might help ye."

It took James only a few minutes of reading to understand what Annora meant. All he could think of was how could he have been so blind as to not see that his own wife despised him? The surprisingly crude remarks demeaning his manhood and his prowess as a lover made him wince, but with his body still feeling the pleasure of making love with Annora they lost some of their sting. By the time he finished the little book, however, he was furious, but not just at Mary and Donnell. He was furious at himself for being such a blind idiot. James looked up from the book to see a fully dressed Annora sitting at the foot of his bed watching him warily.

"How could I nay see that Mary was such a—" He faltered, the hard lessons of courtesy taught in his youth making it difficult to say what he truly wanted to.

"Bitch?" Annora finished and blushed only slightly. It was a curse and unkind, but she could think of no better word for the woman at the moment as she saw the pain and confusion in James' beautiful eyes.

"Aye, a traitorous"—he glanced down at the little book and then met Annora's worried gaze again—"whining little bitch. How could I nay see that?"

"Because she didnae want ye to. James, verra few of her own kinsmen ken the Mary ye read in that book. She was always sweet, somewhat shy, and verra, verra dutiful. She may nay have been the smartest woman in the world, but she did have a cunning that allowed her to be as all thought she ought to be and thus gain the rewards of such fine behavior. Behind the backs of all those who thought her such a perfect lady she probably laughed at our stupidity. What do ye mean to do with the book?"

James got out of bed and began to dress, his anger growing as he tugged on his clothes. He knew what he had to do with the book but he did not want to do it. It was something Tormand

and Simon needed to see if only because there had been some names mentioned in it of people they might be able to find. People who would be far better witnesses to the crimes Donnell had committed than the words of a woman who had clearly never known much happiness. Worse, Mary's misery was all of her own making, born mostly out of wanting things and not always getting what she wanted.

He felt a light touch on his arm and looked down at Annora. "I need to go to the village and speak to Tormand and Simon," he said.

"'Tis late."

"They need to see the book as quickly as possible, Annora, e'en though it will humiliate me to have them see the things my own wife said about me."

Annora just nodded. She could feel a great deal of new anger in James. He undoubtedly thought himself an utter fool and now had to let others see that he was. She also wondered if he had loved his wife and if this proof of her betrayal and dislike cut him far deeper than he wanted anyone to know.

"Take care," she murmured as he started for the door acting almost as if he had forgotten she was even in the room.

James halted, turned back, and gave her a hard kiss before he started to leave again. "Ye be careful as ye leave here. It seems my wee wife did one good thing and that was write down far more than she ought to have. We may soon be rid of Donnell."

As the door shut behind him, Annora sighed. They might soon be rid of Donnell, but she had to wonder if James would ever be rid of the ghost of his wife. He may or may not have loved her, but he had respected her as his wife and the mother of his child. He had also trusted her. Annora did not know how discovering that Mary had deserved none of that would leave James feeling once he sorted through all of the confused emotion she had sensed in him. He was fully over anger over Mary's betrayal and his inability to see what Mary truly was, but anger could swiftly turn into bitterness. And with bitterness came a lack of trust in one's self and in others.

As Annora crept away from James' bedchamber, she thought it would be just her luck if by bringing James the proof that his wife and Donnell had planned everything that had forced James to live as a hunted man for three years, she had lost what little good there was between them. That was something that would have delighted Mary, Annora decided as she slipped into her own bedchamber and hoped she would be able to cease worrying about what might happen between her and James now and get some much needed sleep. Somehow that seemed like yet another injustice.

Chapter Fourteen

"Weel, this is interesting."

James glared at Simon. He had left a warm bed and an equally warm Annora to bring Mary's rantings to Simon and Tormand. Creeping through a few dark passages and tunnels to get out of Dunncraig unseen had not been very enjoyable, either. He loathed small, dark places. Dragging Simon and Tormand away from their women and out of their warm beds at the inn without being seen and bringing them through the dark to the back room of Edmund's shop had given James some pleasurable moments. Yet, waiting so long while Simon very carefully read the journal, Tormand reading it over the man's shoulder, had stolen most of that mild enjoyment. It seemed what was written there deserved far more than a simple *this is interesting*.

"'Tis a confession, isnae it?"James demanded. "It makes it clear that she was hand-in-fist with MacKay, that she was alive when I was decried as her murderer, and that Donnell killed her because she was too great a threat to him."

"Ah, weel, it does make it clear that she was Donnell's lover and that she was plotting with him to get rid of ye so that Donnell might claim Dunncraig as reparation for her murder. Demanding that reparation was clever, I will admit that. And I will agree that 'tis strong proof that your wee wife was alive months after ye were declared an outlaw for killing her. But—"

"I hate that word," muttered James.

"But," continued Simon, "there isnae any proof in here that Donnell killed her. Plenty of reason for him to do so, aye. If only to shut her up," he muttered softly and then quickly shook off that odd mood. "Proof, nay. Mary was certainly increasingly afraid that he would kill her. Howbeit, after one reads this wee book, one realizes that Mary MacKay Drummond was a woman who, weel, felt all should forever be right in her world, that she deserved to get all she wanted simply because she lived and breathed, and if things went wrong for her, she ne'er felt it was her fault. In truth, after reading all of this, I believe your late wife was little more than a horribly spoiled child. Her suspicions about Donnell wanting her dead may nay carry much weight simply because she had them."

James cursed and dragged his hands through his hair. He was still reeling from what Mary had written. For a moment or two he had actually considered throwing the cursed little book filled with his late wife's complaints and ramblings straight into the fire. He had not really wanted anyone else to read what Mary had said about him. James inwardly cringed as he recalled how Mary had unfavorably compared the width and size of his manhood to that of her *beloved* Donnell. The fact that she had felt Donnell had won that contest really stung James' pride.

If his body did not still immediately grow warm and hard at the memory of how thoroughly Annora had made love to him, James knew he would have been more hurt than angry now. He had no doubt that that was why Annora had so readily and eagerly made love to him even though she had at first said she needed to talk to him. Although he was embarrassed by the fact that she had read all of Mary's cruel words and complaints, the fact that Annora had left him sated and grinning like a fool before she gave him the journal had actually lessened the sting of his late wife's rantings. How could he take to heart any of the demeaning things Mary had said about his manliness and his lovemaking after hearing Annora cry out his name, the passion he stirred in her making her lovely body tremble as she rode him? A man made love to by Annora MacKay would never question his manhood, James thought, actually feeling quite pleased with himself despite having to share Mary's complaints about him with Simon and Tormand.

"Ye find this amusing?" asked Tormand.

Abruptly pulled from his thoughts, James found his brother staring at him as if he was either lack-witted or slipping into madness. James was glad for the shelter of the heavy table they sat at in the rear of Edmund's shop as well as his long, linen shirt, for he had had his usual reaction to thoughts of Annora. He had a lot of lonely nights to make up for, he told himself, then turned his gaze onto the book Simon still held and forced his thoughts back to what was a very disappointing reaction from the king's man.

"Nay, I was but thinking about the day when I can watch Donnell hang," James said. "So, Simon, are ye saying that the wee book is utterly useless, that I have let ye read how dearly my wife cared for me for naught? Did I resist tossing it into the fire and watching it burn into ashes for naught?"

James was not surprised to hear the strong taint of bitterness in his voice, for even though Mary's words could no longer hurt him, her betrayal had been completely undeserved. He may not have loved her, but he had been willing to try and, unlike her, he had remained true to his vows. It was a great deal more than many another man offered his wife. James sincerely doubted that Donnell had ever been faithful to her.

"I wouldnae say it is useless," Simon replied. "'Tis just that it is only her word and ye must concede that, once one has read what she has written in here, one's confidence in her veracity, indeed, e'en in the soundness of her wits, is sorely tried."

"Aye, I ken it." James scratched his chin. "It truly astounds me that I ne'er saw what a silly child she really was. It wasnae until I was hurrying o'er here to show ye that that I began to think long and hard on my marriage and my wife." Deciding there was little use in hiding anything from Simon now that the man had read the journal, James continued, "What I always thought was a natural modesty and shyness, if mayhaps a little extreme e'en for a weel-sheltered lass, was actually distaste, even loathing. Mary makes that verra clear on near to every page. She also makes me sound like a mon who beat her all the time. Will that nay make anyone who reads it think that Donnell was actually right? Aye, I ken it doesnae accuse me directly, but the implication that I was a brutish mon is behind every complaint Mary made. Odd, though, I believe it does say that Donnell was, too, and that he conspired against me," he drawled, his bitterness becoming harder to control. "I cannae believe that ye didnae see that in there."

"I can see it and ye can see it because we already ken that it is the truth."

James cursed. "So it was a waste of time for me to bring this to ye."

"Nay, not at all. It will be a large part of a plea concerning your innocence, the pleas made to clear your name and return your lands, and in gaining MacKay's conviction. But I think it can only be a part, nay the whole. Tormand and I will hunt down a few of the people Mary makes mention of in the book and see if we can gather a few living, sensible witnesses. Someone standing in front of the men who can free you and repeating even a few of the accusations Mary makes in her journal will carry much more weight than her writings."

Nodding slowly and knowing he was not doing a very good job of hiding his disappointment, James finished his ale, retrieved the journal, and stood up. "Ye ken where to find me if ye have aught to tell me. Annora and I will continue to try and dig up something more useful at Dunncraig."

Leaving with James, Tormand and Simon then slipped into the shadows to make their way back to the inn. It was not until they were nearing the door of the inn that Tormand asked, "Is that journal truly useless?"

Just because I said it wasnae all that would be needed to get James free of the trap Donnell set him in doesnae mean it is useless," said Simon. "It just isnae enough. Any mon who reads that woman's writings is going to question every accusation she made. S'truth, some would think it but a good reason for James to have killed her."

"'Tis hard to believe that any woman would think so unkindly about James."

"I didnae see ye read it, so how do ye ken what she said?"

"I am verra good at reading o'er a person's shoulder. Ye werenae trying to hide the book, so I read o'er yours."

"And what did ye think of it all?"

"Aside from the wish that the wench was still alive so that one could throttle her, it did seem to me that it held enough to raise a lot of questions about MacKay's charges against James."

Simon nodded as they entered the inn and started up the narrow stairs to their beds, always glancing around to make certain no one was near enough to hear what they were saying.

"It does and now we are going to do our best to answer some of those questions. There are people here who ken enough to lead us to the truth if nay all the truth. MacKay isnae weel liked and his part in the raids in this area has made him verra unpopular. We dinnae need a lot to end his reign here."

"Weel then, best we get some rest and start searching for some of those people Mary mentioned."

Simon cursed softly. "I should have kept the journal so as to be sure of the exact names of all the people she mentioned."

"Dinnae worry. I remember them all."

Simon stared at Tormand. "Truly?"

"Truly. I read something and the cursed words are seared into my brain whether I wish them to stay there or not."

"Have ye e'er considered becoming a mon of the court, one who aids the king in keeping order?"

"Why? Because I have such a good memory?" Tormand laughed and shook his head. "I dinnae think I would be verra good at all the secrecy and wee games played. Court is like a huge chess game and I have ne'er been verra skilled at chess." He opened the door to his bedchamber, saw the woman he had left behind sit up in his bed and smile at him, and said, "I believe I will stay with the games I do ken and ones that dinnae get me killed."

"Bedding women has sent more men to their deaths than a plague," grumbled Simon as Tormand closed the door on him. "Weel, we shall see how ye feel at some other time," he said as he went into his room only to note that the woman he had been enjoying before James had interrupted them had fallen asleep.

James was severely disappointed that Annora had not chosen to stay in his room and wait for him. He briefly considered going to her bedchamber and then decided that it might be best if he left her to sleep. His greed for her caused him to put them both at far too much risk. Tossing the journal onto his bed, he stripped off all his clothes save for his braies, and went to clean up.

Creeping out of Dunncraig through long-unused passages had been filthy work, and coming back into the keep the same way had only worsened his state. James would really have liked to have a long, hot bath, but he knew that was a luxury he would have to forget about for now. Men carving the laird's chairs did not have hot baths brought up to their bedchambers on their whim. Most men with such skills did not usually even get a private bedchamber. Using the chilly water from the bowl and pitcher set on a small table would have to suffice.

He was just drying off his arms when the door to his room creaked open and James tensed. In his distraction, his mind fixed too firmly on what he might look for to add to the ravings in his late wife's journals and bring MacKay down, he had obviously forgotten to lock the door. Even as he turned he knew it was not Annora who had tiptoed into his bedchamber if only because she would have remarked upon the unlocked door. He was not really surprised to see Mab standing there, staring at him, but he was extremely annoyed at his own idiocy.

While Mab stood there gaping, James wasted no time on trying to think of some explanation for why he had brown hair from the waist up and red hair from the waist down. He leapt toward her and wrapped his arm around her to pull her away from the door. Even as she began to struggle he shut and latched the door tightly. Mab proved to be a fierce and somewhat dirty fighter, but James managed to get her onto the bed and tied up without too many bruises.

When it appeared that she had gathered her wits enough to start screaming, he covered her mouth with one hand, and, clasping the other into a tight fist, he held it threateningly before her face. James could tell by the look on her face that she believed he would not hesitate to beat her. There was both anger and fear in her face. It was clear that she expected such harsh treatment from men, and for one fleeting moment he felt some sympathy for her, but he quickly smothered it. She could, and undoubtedly would, use the information she had just stumbled into to better her place at Dunncraig without a single thought to the consequences.

"Why are ye here?" he demanded. "Did Egan send ye?" He lifted his hand just enough for her to reply yet remain able and ready to smother any attempt she made to scream.

"I just came to see if ye had changed your mind about a wee bit of bed play," Mab replied. "Thought mayhap that after some cold nights abed all alone ye would have changed your mind."

She was a poor liar, he thought, a little surprised at that. Most women in her position in life learned to be very good liars. "Egan sent ye here, didnae ye? I have refused your offered favors far too often for ye to just decide to try again. E'en ye have some pride. Why did he send ye here? What interest is it of his if I am kept busy or not?" James had a sinking feeling Egan had begun to suspect that Annora was showing a distinct interest in a man and that that man was not him. With a man like Egan such suspicions could get someone killed.

"Now, why would a mon like Egan care what ye are doing at night, eh?"

"Best ye answer my questions, Mab. I am nay kenned for my patience or kindness. 'Tis nay to my liking to hit or hurt a woman, but dinnae think that means I willnae do it. I will and it will hurt. Now tell me the truth about why ye are here."

"He will beat me if I do that, mayhap e'en kill me!"

"And ye think I willnae do the same if ye dinnae tell me what I want to ken?"

James watched the woman think that over for a moment. A knot of panic was beginning to twist in his stomach. Every instinct he had was telling him that Mab's ill-timed visit to his bedchamber had something to do with Annora and he feared his lover, his mate, was in real danger. It took all of his willpower not to just shake the truth out of Mab, for he had the strongest feeling that he was running out of time to save Annora and to get them safely out of Dunncraig. The fact that Mab had seen that he was a man in disguise and thus ruined his plan of uncovering something that would hang Donnell did not really trouble him all that much. The fact that Egan was behind this visit of Mab did, however.

"Egan thinks ye are trying to woo that foolish nursemaid Annora and he wants ye to be too busy with another woman to do so. He felt sure I had the right touch to keep ye weel occupied."

Mab obviously thought she was a very skilled lover, and she just might be, but James had never once been tempted. "Is Egan planning to try and woo Annora tonight?"

"Weel, aye, I think so. And what harm is there in that, eh? He is going to marry her," Mab grumbled, her bitterness over that all too clear in her voice.

Ignoring her attempts to turn her face away, James quickly gagged Mab with the long piece of linen cloth he used for washing. He then hurriedly got dressed and packed his small sack of belongings. No matter what else happened this night, he had to leave Dunncraig as fast as he could. The first person who untied Mab would undoubtedly hear all about the man who was half brown-haired and half red-haired. It was just too good a secret for a woman like her to keep for very long. Once she began to tell the story of what she had seen, James knew that he would be hunted again. Before that hunt began, however, he had to be certain that Annora and Meggie were put somewhere safe.

Annora stretched and then rubbed at her lower back. She had spent far too long bent over in a chair trying to mend clothing in the poor light of a few tallow candles and waiting to hear some word from James. She finally decided it was foolish to lose so much sleep when he would undoubtedly find a way on the morrow to talk to her. At least she hoped he would. Annora was still afraid that reading the poison in Mary's journal might affect what she and James now shared. She had no delusions that what they shared was forever, but she hated to think it would end too soon because of the cruel words of an unfaithful wife.

Even as she started to take off her gown, she began to worry that something had happened to James. Egan had never ceased to glare angrily at James whenever he saw the man. There was the chance that Egan might grasp the chance to do James harm if he saw him out walking in the dark. She paused in her undressing and decided it would not hurt to just go and see if James had returned safely from his talk with Sir Simon and Sir Tormand.

A small voice in her head said that was not a good idea, but Annora easily ignored it. She relaced her gown just enough to keep it from falling off and unlocked her door. The moment she opened it she heartily wished she had listened to that small voice. Egan stood there and he slowly smiled.

Annora tried to shut the door in the man's face, but he was both fast and strong. He shoved her back into the room, stepped inside, and then slammed her door shut. For a moment, Annora hoped the loud noise would bring someone to see what was going on, but that hope rapidly faded beneath the onslaught of reality. Even if someone did come to see what was happening, she could not expect rescue. No one at Dunncraig would go against Egan.

"Ye must leave now," she said, backing away as he advanced on her. "This is nay right. I am a weel-bred maiden and no mon should be in my bedchamber at this time of the night. And certainly nay alone with me."

"I am your betrothed. I have every right to be here," he replied.

"We arenae wed yet, Egan, and I am nay sure we will e'er be. I dinnae wish to marry you." She cried out in pain when he slapped her across the face so hard she fell back against the bed.

"Ye will marry me, wench, and I am here tonight to ensure that ye will agree with nay more arguing."

"By beating me?"

"Nay, by showing ye what it is like to have a mon in your bed. Ye have held fast to your chastity for far too long."

She almost told him that she had let go of that chastity several nights ago and enjoyed every moment of its loss. Good sense prevailed, however. Annora had the feeling that Egan would beat her as she had never been beaten before if she let him know that she was no longer a virgin. He wanted her pure and there would be hell to pay if he discovered that she was not. And such reckless words would put not only herself in danger but James. All she should be concerned about now was escape, but he stood squarely between her and the door.

Before she could offer up any more arguments against his plan to rape her, he grabbed her and tossed her on the bed. Annora screeched softly in surprise and fear when he threw himself down on top of her and began to rip off her clothes. Each time she tried to stop him or even just cling to the clothes he was so roughly removing from her body, he slapped her and Annora soon doubted that she would remain conscious enough to end the game if she kept fighting. It was difficult to stop, however, as she was more terrified of the rape he planned than of the pain he was inflicting on her now.

Her ears still ringing from Egan's last blow to her head, Annora was unsure of what she heard. It sounded like the door to her bedchamber had just burst open and slammed into the wall, but she was still certain that no one at Dunncraig would try to stop Egan. Then Egan was pulled off her as if he weighed nothing at all. Annora watched the man's body go flying across the room and slam into the wall before she looked up to see who had achieved such a feat of strength.

Chapter Fifteen

"James?" she whispered, fighting with all her strength to overcome the pain Egan had caused and cling to consciousness. "Are ye really here?"

"Aye, lass. Did he succeed?" James kept a close watch on Egan, who was struggling to stand up, even as he very gently touched her already bruising face.

"Nay, but I fear I was losing the battle." She tried to give him a smile of reassurance, but the movement of her mouth caused a pain that made her wince instead.

"Weel, best ye move to a far corner, lass, for I have nay intention of losing this one and I wouldnae want ye to be hurt as I teach this bastard some manners."

Annora really wanted to tell James not to do anything that would get him thrown out of Dunncraig only to realize that he was not speaking in French, or even trying to sound like a Frenchman speaking as a Scot. When she took a quick glance at Egan, who now stood unsteadily facing James, she could see that Egan had heard that as well. For just a moment the two men stared at each other and then Egan cursed and spat on her bedchamber floor.

"Drummond," he said, spitting out the name like a curse. "I cannae believe Donnell didnae see it. Clever of ye to cover one eye like that. Tends to make people avoid looking ye straight in the eye. That and coloring your hair like some woman have probably helped to keep ye free and alive for all these years. Weel, this time ye willnae get away. Nay, this time we will make verra certain ye are dead."

"Come and try, then. Please." James very carefully shut the battered door. "I dinnae think we will be interrupted now."

Annora winced as the fight began. She hated fighting, but this time the only reason she wanted it to stop was that she feared for James. There was an angry part of her that wanted Egan beaten into a bloodied mess for what he had tried to do to her and what he had done to too many other women.

Struggling to stay out of the men's way, she sought out some new clothes to put on, for her gown was so badly torn she was nearly naked. It took some clever feints and swift ducking, but she finally got herself pressed hard into a corner of her room with new, untorn clothing in her hand. Keeping a close eye on the two men so that she would know when to help and when to run, she tossed aside her torn clothes and dressed in the new, clean clothes she had gathered.

She was just lacing up her gown when James delivered a blow to Egan's already badly battered face that sent the man to the floor. It took only one look to know that Egan would not be rising from that floor any time soon. There was a chance that, when the wounds on his face healed, he wouldnae be even faintly handsome. And that, she knew, would make him nearly mad with fury, for Egan had always considered himself a very handsome man. The last thing she and James had needed was to give Egan even more reason to hate James.

Annora stumbled up to James when he bent down to grab Egan by the front of his shirt, a little afraid that James was so angry he meant to keep on beating Egan despite the fact that Egan was unconscious. She was not concerned for Egan, but worried that James would sorely regret such an act once his fury eased. James was a man of honor, of that she had no doubt, and a man of honor would never feel right about beating on a man who was already down, no matter what the man had done or tried to do. In his eyes it would leave a stain that he could never completely be rid of.

"Ye need to flee here, James," she said. "He kens who ye are now."

"So does Mab," James said as he hefted up Egan's body and

put it on Annora's bed, then looked around for something to tie the man up with.

"Mab? "Just the sound of the woman's name was enough to stir the bitter taste of jealousy inside Annora. Ye have seen Mab tonight?"

"Aye, Egan sent her to keep me verra busy. I fear I wasnae dressed when she walked into my bedchamber. I still cannae believe I was so stupid as to leave my door unlocked. So I tied her up as weel. It took a little persuading, but I made Mab think me as big a threat to her life as Egan is and she finally told me what he planned." He yanked the rope ties from the thick drapes over Annora's tiny window and began to tie Egan down. "She saw me with only my braies on, lass, so she kens that I am nay what I claim to be as weel. I kenned that, if she was allowed to go free and talk to MacKay or Egan, they would soon guess who I really am. And now this bastard kens it anyway."

"Then ye have to leave." It hurt Annora to even say the words.

"*We* have to leave. Ye, me, and wee Meggie. I may have to give up the chance of regaining Dunncraig for a while, but I willnae give up ye and my child. Gather some clothes together and then we will get Meggie and leave this place."

"But surely it would be best if Meggie and I stayed here."

"Love, he kens that ye have known my secret for a while, cannae ye see that? He heard ye call me by name."

Annora cursed. James was right. Her game was over as much as James' was. Even if she survived the punishment that would be meted out for not telling Donnell who Master Lavengeance was, she would never be left alone to go anywhere or speak to anyone again. The guards that would be put on her would never waver in their watchfulness. She hurriedly began to throw some clothes into a heavy bag made from blankets.

"Where shall we go?" she asked as he took her packed bag, grabbed her by the arm, and began to hurry her out of her room.

"I am nay sure just yet." He shut her door and then began to walk swiftly in the direction of the nursery. "For now 'tis just important that we get out of here ere either Mab or Egan is discovered. Or we are."

A chill settled deep in Annora's stomach. She had lived with fear since the first day she had stepped through the gates of Dunncraig, but never like this. Death caused by the brutality Donnell and Egan meted out so easily was also no stranger to her, but she realized she had never truly felt she was in mortal danger. Rape and beating were the things she had feared. She had also never really considered fleeing in the night until Donnell had told her that she had to marry Egan. Now she was packed, was about to kidnap Meggie from her home, and was running off into the night with a man who had been wrongly proclaimed a murderer and an outlaw.

Life certainly held a lot of surprises, she thought, feeling a little dazed. She could not help but wonder what this meant for her and James. He made no mention of love or marriage, but it was very clear he intended to keep her with him, at least for a while. With him as an outlaw or a wood-carver, she could actually think that they might have a life together, but James Drummond was a laird. Inwardly, she shrugged aside those concerns. What would be, would be. She would just take each day as it came and hope there was some happiness to be found at the end of what promised to be quite an adventure.

Annie scrambled to her feet when James and Annora entered the nursery. "Mistress Annora? Is something wrong?" she asked in a sleepy voice and rubbed at her eyes like a sleepy child, something she was not far past being.

"Annie," Annora began as James roamed the room collecting some things for Meggie, "we are taking Meggie away from here."

For a moment, Annie just stared at her as if the words had no meaning to her, and then she frowned. "Why?"

"Because she isnae safe here any longer. Did ye hear that MacKay thinks to marry her to Halbert Chisholm?"

The curse that escaped Annie's full lips shocked Annora. She was even more surprised when the girl found a bag and, taking the things from James, began to pack it. James moved to the bed and gently began to rouse Meggie, so Annora turned her full attention on Annie.

"I gather ye dinnae approve of the marriage," she murmured.

"Nay. The mon is a pig," said Annie and then she stared at Annora for a moment. "And so is the mon MacKay is trying to make ye marry. I assume that swine paid ye a visit this night thinking to start his married life a wee bit early."

Annora touched her cheek and faintly winced. "Aye, he did. He thought it was time for me to be taught how good it would be to have a mon in my bed."

"It might be but that bastard isnae the one to have."

Annie sounded a lot older and wiser than her years, and Annora felt a touch of dismay begin to grow in her heart. "Has Egan hurt ye, Annie?"

"He tried but Big Marta stopped him. Egan doesnae dare do anything to Big Marta since MacKay likes her cooking so much. 'Tis she who got me the work here in the nursery. That bastard willnae come after me here. Nay only doesnae he see much of me as I stay close to this room, but MacKay wouldnae like Egan to be hurting one of the ones what care for the wee lass." She glanced toward the bed as she put a little wooden doll into Meggie's bag, one that Annora had not seen before but she was quite sure it had been made by James. "She likes your mon."

"Weel, he isnae really my mon," Annora murmured, but Annie just smiled.

"Are we going on a journey, Annora?" Meggie asked sleepily as James got her dressed.

"Aye, love, we are," Annora replied as she moved to stand beside the bed.

Meggie stared at Annora's face for a moment. "Who hit ye? MacKay or Egan?"

"Egan." Annora saw no reason to lie to the child as Meggie was all too aware of the brutality of the man who claimed to be her father as well as that of MacKay's first. "Master Lavengeance stopped him."

"Are we leaving because Master Lavengeance killed Egan?"

"Nay, but he did beat him rather badly and that could get him killed. It also puts us in danger, for we have shown ourselves to be his friend."

"And because Sir MacKay wants me to marry that smelly Halbert Chisholm?"

Annora was not able to fully hide a gaping sense of surprise. "How do ye ken that?"

"I listen. People talk. I think they thought it was verra big news."

"Come," said James, picking Meggie up in his arms. "We need to leave."

"Annie," said Annora, "ye best find a place to hide once Meggie's disappearance is discovered."

"Soon as I hear that Egan has started a roar I will cry out that the lass has gone missing," Annie said. "There will be a lot of confusion then and I will slip away. I think they will be so busy trying to get out of here to hunt ye down that they willnae think about a wee nursemaid."

"A good plan, lass," said James. "Do nay more than that, howbeit, for ye could draw their attention to ye. If ye think ye are in danger at any time, seek out two men staying at the inn. Their names are Sir Simon Innes and Sir Tormand Murray. They will see that ye are protected from any punishment for this."

Annie nodded and hastily gave Meggie a kiss on the cheek. "Take care, all of ye."

Carrying her bag as well as Meggie's, Annora followed James out of the room. The way he weaved through the shadowy passages of Dunncraig revealed that he knew the keep very well. She had always believed his tale of being Sir James Drummond, but Annora had to admit that it was comforting to see such hard proof of the fact.

When he led them into a very dark, narrow passage, she hesitated. It was not going to be easy to set aside her deep fear of such places. Foolish as it seemed to be to her, she had never been able to rid herself of all the scars of her past. She even considered just letting James leave with Meggie since it would mean she did not have to travel through the passage. Such cowardice shamed her, but even that did not do much to ease the fear.

"There is nay other way?" she asked in a whisper.

James set Meggie down and lit a small torch before taking the child's hand in his. "Does that help?"

"A little," Annora said and then stiffened her backbone. James might not need her, but Meggie did. "These passages will get us out of Dunncraig unseen, will they?" she asked.

"Aye, love. I fear there is no other choice, nay if we wish to leave here safely and unseen. It willnae be so bad, for ye arenae alone, are ye?"

Meggie reached out to take Annora by the hand. "I will be with ye, Annora."

Annora felt tears sting her eyes. Meggie was a child with a very big heart and it was hard not to be touched by the little girl's kindness. "Thank ye, Meggie. Best we get going. I think it best if we get as far away as we can tonight."

"That is my plan," said James as he began to lead them through the passage.

When they finally reached the outside, Annora nearly fell to her knees to kiss the ground. She had clung to her sanity by a thread as they had traveled through one narrow passage to another. They had gotten out of Dunncraig unseen, but if they had to come back, she intended to do so by riding through the front gates. Annora did not want to wander through those passages again.

They hurried into the wood and started walking. At some point, James picked up and carried a sleepy Meggie. Annora wished he could carry her, too. She was tired and her body ached from the fight with Egan. She knew her increasingly unsteady pace was slowing James down, but she could not make herself go any faster. When they entered a small clearing where a tiny cottage with no door stood, Annora almost collapsed with relief. She hoped that James meant to stop and rest at this cottage, for she was not sure she could walk another step.

"We havenae gone so verra far," she felt compelled to say, knowing that putting a lot of distance between them and Dunncraig was very important.

"Far enough for now and this cottage is verra near the border between Dunncraig and the MacLaren lands," James said as he walked toward the cottage. "It was the eldest son of their laird who was killed in MacKay's last raid."

"Wouldnae that make this a verra unsafe place to be?" she asked as she hastily spread a blanket on the dirt floor of the cottage so that James could put a now sleeping Meggie down.

"A little, but more so for MacKay and his men," replied James. "We will be safe enough for a few hours of rest, however, and then we shall have to move on."

"What about your brother and Sir Simon? They willnae ken what has happened to ye, will they?"

"They will understand that I have fled for my life. I mean to get word to them about exactly what happened as soon as I feel it is safe enough to try and can find a trustworthy mon to take them my message. Howbeit, the moment they hear what has happened at Dunncraig, they will ken it is me."

"Will it be safe enough for them in the village?" she asked. "We dinnae get many strangers staying around and they must be easily spotted."

"E'en MacKay will balk at killing a king's man and he will ken exactly who Simon is. Simon said he had met the mon a few times and I suspect MacKay will remember each one of those meetings. Nay, they will be safe enough as long as they keep one eye open when they sleep."

Annora sat down on the blanket he spread next to Meggie. "I havenae been verra good at this," she said quietly.

"Lass." James sat down beside her, draped his arm around her shoulder and very gently kissed her bruised cheek. "Ye have done verra weel for a woman who was fighting off a big, hardened warrior only a few hours ago."

She smiled her gratitude for his kind words even though she did not really believe them. "What will we do, James?" she asked in a very soft, slightly unsteady voice as she realized more fully what they had done.

"Run and hide until I can get ye and Meggie to a safe place. No one will care if MacKay and Egan hunt me to the ends of the earth and murder me. Until I am rid of the taint of being named an outlaw, anyone can kill me and many would help MacKay in his search. Ye and Meggie dinnae carry that burden.

Aye, MacKay has claimed Meggie as his, but she was born to my wife and so his claim carries no weight. He was only allowed to get away with it because I was as good as dead. Ye are naught but his cousin, and although kinsmen are considered the rulers of the women in their care and family, no one will help him hunt ye down, either. In truth, who ye are will be your best protection now."

"Ye mean being a poor, landless bastard whose own kinsmen dinnae want her?"

"Sad to say, aye. Rest, Annora," he said as he gently pushed her down onto the blanket.

She stared up at the starry sky she could see through the big holes in the thatched roof. James spread a blanket over her and then crawled beneath it to curl up around her body. She held herself very still and just allowed the warmth of his body to soothe her aches and the chill of the night air. This was exactly where she wanted to be, but she could not completely stop her weary mind from chewing over all the difficulties they now faced.

"I am such a coward," she whispered even as she pressed her body hard up against his.

"Nay, lass, ye are no coward. Ye didnae hesitate to come with me. There is no cowardice in seeing all the problems we now face. Do ye think I dinnae worry o'er how we can elude MacKay and the men he will send to hunt us? I am nay alone now. It will be verra difficult to get away and find a refuge with a woman and a child with me nay matter how fit and willing they are. There just wasnae the time to make a good plan."

"Nay, I ken it and I had only just begun to make a few myself in case I had to flee a marriage to Egan."

"I will take ye to my kinsmen. Ye will be safe there; ye and Meggie."

"It willnae bring any trouble to the doors of your kinsmen?"

"It might but nay anything they cannae handle. They have had to deal with many a danger o'er the years from lasses taken for ransom to sons accused of near any crime ye can think of. But they can hold Meggie in their care without much trouble. After all, they are seen as Meggie's blood kin by the law and the church. MacKay willnae have any power to wield if he tries to take ye or Meggie back."

James touched a kiss to the back of her neck and then held her close, trying to warm the chill in her body. He still ached to kill Egan and the feeling swelled up each time he saw the bruises on Annora's face. After the pain his family had suffered when his sister Sorcha had been raped and beaten, James knew his rage was easily stirred beyond reason by the rape of a woman. Any man who did such a thing, or tried to do it, deserved to be killed, but he had had to let Egan live. One just did not kill an unconscious man. He certainly would have had an even more difficult time clearing his name if he had done that.

When he felt Annora's body go limp in his hold, he smiled and kissed the top of her head. He would have liked to travel even farther but she had been staggering by the time they had reached the cottage. Considering how many miles they had to travel before he could hand her and Meggie over to his family's care, James had known that they had to stop for a rest.

James glanced over at a sleeping Meggie and smiled. She had not argued or whined at all. He suspected it was because the child would go anywhere just to stay with Annora, but it still made him proud. After reading Mary's journal and realizing that MacKay's claim to Meggie might have some merit, James had expected to feel differently about Meggie, but he had not. He might never be sure whose seed had fathered her, but she was his sweet wee Meggie and no one else's.

This was his family, his future. James knew they were all in danger, but he could not help but feel a sort of peace come over him. This was what he fought for and he would not give up. Donnell MacKay had stolen three years of his life, his good name, and his land. James now knew that Donnell had also held full control of his wife, Mary. He would not allow the man to take this from him. The warm woman he held so close and the sweet child murmuring in her sleep were his and he meant to keep them, to have a life with them. James knew that if he lost them, it would make his previous losses seem small and unimportant.

Chapter Sixteen

James looked down at Annora and Meggie, the child curled up in the woman's arms. At some time while he and Annora had slept, the child had woken up enough to seek out Annora for warmth or for comfort or even for both. He knew they had had little choice but to flee Dunncraig as swiftly as possible, but he felt a little guilty for the way the child had had to be dragged away in the middle of the night.

What he had to do was make a definite plan about what to do next. He could not expect a little girl and a slender woman to live the same life he had led for the past three years. Nor could they stay too close to Dunncraig and still try to find the proof needed to remove the threat of MacKay from their lives. MacKay would be searching high and low for them, pushing all his men to do the same. He had to take his women far away from here, and he no longer felt that France was a good idea, even if it would allow him to live with them. That left taking them to his kinsmen and asking their help in keeping Meggie and Annora safe.

His women, he mused, and grinned as he grabbed a wineskin and headed to the burn to fill it with water. He really liked the sound of that. And they would soon be his to claim openly and to take care of. James knew that he was very close to defeating MacKay. The need to run and hide now was only a brief stumbling point on the road to success in the long battle to regain all he had lost. James knew he had to believe that or the battle was already lost.

Just as he finished filling the wineskin, James heard a twig snap from a few feet behind him. He turned swiftly, his dagger in his hand before he even completed the move, and then he cursed, more from a sense of relief than of anger. A wide-eyed Annora stood only a few feet away from him dressed only in her shift. Eyeing him warily, she moved to the edge of the burn to wash her face and hands.

"Ye startled me, lass, and with enemies at every turning, I acted accordingly but I didnae mean to frighten ye," he said as he sheathed his dagger.

"I am sorry. It will take me a while to fully understand that we are, weel, running and hiding from a dangerous mon and to act accordingly." She patted her face and hands dry with the skirt of her shift. "I didnae think I was being verra quiet as I approached ye. S'truth, I stumbled along quite noisily, more asleep than awake."

"Weel, I was deep in my thoughts, which isnae a good thing to be right now. Mayhap spending time at Dunncraig has taken the edge off all the skills I learned whilst being an outlaw. Meggie?"

"Still sleeping, and considering how early in the morning it is, I suspicion she will be sleeping soundly for a few more hours. She had a busy night, aye?" Annora suddenly smiled. "And wee Meggie likes to sleep and sleep verra deeply, too. I was most surprised that ye were able to rouse her so quickly when we went to the nursery to fetch her. If by some chance she does wake ere I return, she will wait for me or e'en call for me."

"Good, I wouldnae wish her to wake alone and be afraid."

"'Tis so verra difficult to believe that it has come to this. We were so close to finding out the truth, to wiping the false stain from your name and getting back all ye have lost. And all this because some whore of a maid couldnae abide the fact that ye told her nay. I hope she is still tied to the bed."

James smiled and pulled her into his arms. She looked so beautifully angry on his behalf despite the violence she had suffered herself last night. He was afraid that he had become increasingly resigned to a life of running and hiding. Annora's outrage reminded him that it was unfair, unjust, and that he deserved a better life. It was enough to keep him from changing from a man who was only declared an outlaw into a true outlaw. The step needed to cross that line was a small one and he knew

he had been very close to making that step before he had come
to Dunncraig.

"S'truth, I am glad that Mab tried yet again to seduce me." He
kissed her scowling mouth, pleased with that hint of jealousy.
"It was what sent me to your bedchamber and allowed me to
save ye from Egan." James lightly brushed a kiss over her badly
bruised cheek and wished he could beat Egan senseless all over
again. "Does it pain ye?" he asked as he tentatively stroked his
fingers over her bruises.

"Nay, not truly. The only thing that does pain me is that ye
are having to run away again and now ye must try to do so with
me and Meggie. Mayhap she and I should go back to Dunncraig,
or e'en stay right here."

"Nay, that isnae a verra good idea, love. I was nearly too late
to save ye from Egan this time. I willnae, cannae, leave ye in his
reach."

"But Sir Innes and your brother—" she began.

"Will soon ken what has happened to me. Big Marta has been
told to go and tell them if anything has caused me a problem.
Having to flee Dunncraig in the middle of the night is definitely
a problem. As soon as it is discovered that all three of us are
gone, Big Marta will be on her way to the village to tell Simon
and Tormand all she kens about the matter including everything
she has seen and every word she has overheard. 'Tis a verra
good thing that there appears to be no pursuit, at least nay yet. If
there had been, Simon and Tormand would have been told about
us a great deal sooner than they have been. Aye, sooner would
have been better, but so long as they *are* told, I am satisfied."

Annora nodded and then realized that James was slowly
moving her back toward a small, sheltering circle of trees. "What
are ye doing, James?" she asked, although the gleam in his eyes
gave her a very good idea.

"I was thinking how difficult it will be now for us to be alone
since we will have Meggie with us. Then I realized that we are
verra alone right now."

"Meggie," she began to protest as he pushed her up against a
tree.

"Ye said she would sleep awhile longer and bellow for ye if she wakes and is afraid or in need of help."

"Weel, aye, I did say that."

James kissed her and the way his tongue teased and stroked the inside of her mouth robbed Annora of any urge to protest further. She wrapped her arms around his neck and kissed him back, as hungry for him as he appeared to be for her. She knew she should say a very strong no and rush away to be with Meggie, for it was full day and they were outside, things she felt a true lady should protest against. The way he was wrapping her legs around his waist and rubbing himself against her made Annora suspect that this would be no slow, genteel lovemaking, either. She had seen a man take a woman in this manner a time or two and had always thought it looked rough and crude. It did not feel that way to her now. Mayhap it was just because it was James and she could not think of anything he did to give them both pleasure as being rough or crude.

"Lovely, sweet Annora, I am verra eager to have ye, right now, right here," James said. "Say me aye."

Not only was her blood running hot from the magic of his swift but very thorough caresses and his kisses, but Annora admitted to herself that she was intrigued by the idea of making love this way. "Aye," she said.

"Ah, love, ye are a fine, agreeable lass."

"I do try to be."

He laughed even as he thrust himself inside her. Annora clung to him and hung on tightly during what proved to be a wild gallop toward bliss. There was no real tenderness, no soft stirring kisses over her heated skin, and very few soft words spoken. It was fast and furious and Annora found it intensely arousing. The release that tore through her made her cry out his name and she had the fleeting thought that it sounded so freeing to hear that cry echo in the air. A moment later he joined her in that sublime fall.

When he caught his breath, James slowly eased free of her body and set her down on her feet. He smiled when she slumped against him, her arms tight around his waist. Annora was not only passionate; she was adventurous. He desperately wanted the trouble with MacKay gone so that he could enjoy the happiness she gave him in more than brief moments snatched between troubles. He also wanted the freedom to make love to her as often as he wanted and in any way he could. Having an adventurous partner could give a man ideas, he mused, and moved away from her before she could feel the interest some of the ideas flickering through his mind were stirring in his greedy body.

He kept his hands on her shoulders, however, not wanting to give her the impression that now that he had had his body sated, he was done with her. Such rushed, eager lovemaking could be exciting, but it left no time for all the caresses and soft words that told a woman she was more than some easily gained release to a man. Moving away from Annora too quickly now would be much akin to rolling off a woman, getting out of bed, getting dressed, and going home. The very last thing he wanted Annora to feel was used or, worse, have her questioning her own behavior, deciding she was some wanton, and working to beat down her passionate nature. He had a lot of plans for that passionate nature.

"Ye are a verra welcome sweetness in the midst of all the bitterness that has been my life for too long," he said and kissed the top of her head when she pressed her blush-stained face against his chest.

"I am a terrible wanton," she whispered, terrified when she realized that she felt little or no shame for how she had just behaved.

"Ah, nay, lass, ye arenae. If ye were ye wouldnae have still been a nearly unkissed virgin at the great age of four and twenty." He had to bite the inside of his cheek to keep from grinning when she immediately lifted her head to glare at him.

"Great age?" she said, a little astonished at how her voice sounded very much like her cat Mungo's did when it met another cat it did not know well walking on its land.

"I didnae really mean ye were old, just that most women have had a mon or two ere they reach that age." He moved away from her to pick up the wineskin, for he had the distinct impression, that tickle of a warning up the back of his neck, that she wanted to kick him.

"Of course they have. Most lasses of my age have been wed, some for quite a while."

"Wheesht, Annora, do ye really believe that they all dutifully wait for the priest to bless them?" He shook his head. "Nay, the moment a couple is officially betrothed, if they have any liking for each other at all, they are trying to get themselves into a bed as fast as they possibly can. And the poorer lasses can often have several lovers ere they settle on a mon for a husband. S'truth, 'tis often only the verra young, the verra godly, or the verra rich maidens who cling tightly to their maidenheads."

"I am none of those."

"Nay, ye are a lady, and though ye are nay rich, ye have e'er lived amongst them, aye? Always within the walls of the keep or the manor, and always related in some way to the one who rules all the others. The poor work from dawn to dark all the week long. They have more of a greed for those few moments of bliss. Just where do ye think all those hungry young men get their experience, eh?"

Annora had absolutely no intention of answering that question. She certainly did not wish to hear the fool relate a tale or two about his undoubtedly extensive romantic past. The faint smirk on his handsome face told her that he knew it, too. She was really not so naive that she thought all women who never took a lover were saints or all women who did were sinners doomed to burn for eternity in the fiery pits of hell. On the other hand, women who allowed their lovers to have them while pressed up against a tree in the bright morning light on a riverbank had to be teetering precariously on some ledge that overlooked some part of the underworld.

Despite all her good intentions she had actually opened her mouth to say just that when she heard Meggie yell out for her. Answering that call was a perfect disguise for the retreat she had been considering. Annora bolted for the cottage.

"I need to look round, "James called after her rapidly retreating figure. "Stay close to the cottage."

James knew it was foolish to be yelling in the woods when they were supposed to be trying to slip silently away from an enemy. It was too late to mend that mistake, however. He would just have to speak to Meggie and Annora about the need for silence when he got back to the cottage. He would talk sternly to himself about the danger of getting distracted by his own lust, another dangerous thing to do. When he was making love to Annora he was aware of only her and how she made him feel. MacKay could have gotten close enough to skewer them to the tree they were making love against and he was not sure he would ever have heard.

Although he was not sure what was pulling him in the direction he was headed, James decided to just follow his instincts. Someone had to have found Egan or Mab by now, so he could not waste too much time on a whim, but there was no real harm in giving in to it for a moment or two. Many of his cousins would insist that he do so, he thought with a smile as he edged into the shelter of the trees and began to walk back in the direction of Dunncraig. They were not his blood kin, however, so it was impossible to have the same skills so many of them did. He would concede, though, that he had very good instincts and they had been honed to a very sharp edge during his years of exile. Right now they were urging him to hurry along and study whatever it was that had caught their interest. James feared it might be a sign that he, Annora, and Meggie were already being tracked by MacKay and his men.

He was about to turn around and get back to the cottage, disgusted with himself for wasting time looking for nothing, when he heard voices. Slipping even farther into the shadow of the trees, he moved toward the voices until he saw five men watering their horses. James eased himself down until he was sprawled on his stomach on the ground and studied the men. He was a little too far away to see the badges they wore on their muddied clothing, but he suspected they were from the MacLaren clan, the one MacKay had recently raided. The one where the laird's eldest son was killed, he thought and was suddenly alarmed that what was obviously a scouting party was roaming on Dunncraig lands.

"I think we need to find out what has that bastard in such a frenzy," said a huge, rather hairy man, his dark hair and beard nearly obscuring his whole face. "It could be useful."

"And I agree with ye, but with so many of his men riding all o'er the place and in every direction, 'tis too dangerous," said a shorter, much thinner man. "Ye saw how they are grabbing hold of every mon, woman, and bairn they find and demanding answers, Ellar. They wouldn't just ride by if they caught a wee peek at us. There is nay hiding amongst the shepherds or the like this time."

Ellar scratched his long thick beard. "Weel, Robbie, from what little I heard whilst they beat on that poor mon doing naught but relieving himself outside his own wee cottage, they are looking for someone named Annora."

"I think that is the lass who is the nursemaid to the bastard's child."

"A wee lass with blond curls?"

"I think that may be right although I always thought she was Drummond's get."

"My cousin Will says she is and he doesnae care what that bastard MacKay claims," said a short, brown-haired man standing to Ellar's left. "And I am thinking our laird made a mistake in nay getting to ken all about that bastard MacKay. 'Tis sure that is why we werenae prepared for a raid from Dunncraig and that got poor David killed."

"I think ye are right in saying that, Ian, but I am nay about to tell the laird that," said Ellar. "Are ye?"

"Nay," grunted Ian. "So, what do we do now if we cannae keep trying to gather some information?"

"We got some information for the laird. We ken that the child, her nursemaid, and some wood-carver have fled Dunncraig Keep and MacKay is willing to beat near to death everyone he meets to try and find out which way the three of them went."

"And that he and near all his men are riding about leaving the keep lightly protected," added Robbie.

"Are ye sure we ought to be telling the laird that?" asked Ian. "He is near mad with grief as David was his favorite son. He will be calling us to arms and riding for Dunncraig without hesitating."

Ellar nodded. "I ken it and that is a good fast way to send many of us to our maker, but we have to tell him. The way these fools are conducting their search it willnae be a secret for much longer."

James had the urge to hail the men even as they mounted their horses and rode away. They might be convinced to join him in his fight against MacKay, but there was too great a chance they would see him as a source of a reward and Annora and Meggie as weapons to use against MacKay. From what he could recall the laird of the MacLarens had never been sharp-witted and he was now maddened with grief. Tempting as it was to try and gain a few allies, James knew he could not risk Annora's and Meggie's safety on a chance he did not feel was so good it was guaranteed.

The moment the MacLaren men were out of sight, James began to make his way back to the cottage as fast as he could. He felt a growing urgency as he ran. Although he had gained a little useful information, James started to fear that his instincts had tricked him into leaving Annora and Meggie just when it was most important that they stay together and get away.

Annora finished packing what few belongings they had and then sat down on the threshold stone to watch Meggie skipping around the clearing the cottage sat in. She idly wondered what had happened to the people who had once lived here. A moment later she decided that might not be a safe thing to think about. Donnell had driven away, hanged, and imprisoned a lot of people at Dunncraig simply because he felt they were too loyal to James. After a brief prayer for whoever had lived in the cottage, she turned her thoughts to what lay ahead.

It was probably a good idea for James to take her and Meggie to his family instead of fleeing to France, but the thought of meeting all his kinsmen made Annora very nervous. He had told her that many of them had gifts similar to hers, and that meant it might prove impossible to keep a secret from them and she had a big one she wanted to keep. Annora did not think his family would want the woman he had made his leman to be the same one who took care of his child.

"Annora, do ye hear something?" asked Meggie as she ran up

to stand beside the stone where Annora sat. "I hear something. I think someone is coming."

A moment after the child spoke, Annora could hear something as well. From the direction of the burn she could hear someone or something crashing through the trees and undergrowth as if he or it was running without a care for the need of a silent approach. It could be either a panicked animal or a panicked James, and neither of those possibilities helped calm her rapidly rising fear.

From behind the cottage and to the north of it, she could hear horses approaching. Annora knew that sound could only mean that she and Meggie were standing right in the midst of a rapidly approaching danger. One rider could simply be someone passing by on their way to somewhere, a simple traveler or one of the people of Dunncraig. There was far more than one rider coming their way, however. That could mean that a raid was headed for Dunncraig or it could be that Donnell and his men were just about to find the very people they were searching for. Raiders would see her and Meggie as a wondrous prize and Donnell would see them as someone who needed to be taught exactly who ruled their lives. Neither circumstance boded well for her and the child in her care.

Annora grabbed up their belongings and then grabbed a wide-eyed Meggie by the hand. She had barely gone a few feet in the only direction where there did not appear to be danger approaching when the little clearing the cottage stood in was filled with men. Donnell and over a dozen riders broke into the clearing on two sides, reining the horses in hard as they saw her and Meggie. A heartbeat later James burst out of the trees only to come to an abrupt halt to stare at Donnell and his men.

For a moment, Annora just watched the silent confrontation, her heart pounding with fear for James. She wanted to yell at him to run, but just as she opened her mouth, he gave her a brief, hard glower that silenced her. She began to inch her way back from all the men glaring at James, a look of fury and hatred he readily returned. Annora knew that any moment now all the silent tension would snap and she did not want Meggie caught in the middle of a battle even if it would be a short one. James was but one man against over a dozen armed men. Annora knew their chance to escape Donnell was lost. All she could do was pray that James was not lost as well.

Chapter Seventeen

"Have ye come here to die, then, MacKay?" James said as he drew his sword.

Annora blinked. Was the man insane? Then she thought of how he must feel. Not only had he been forced to give up his search for the truth and run from Dunncraig, but being discovered by Donnell here and now meant that he had undoubtedly lost all chance of clearing the stain from his name. He would die with the world believing he had killed his wife. Annora hastily shoved all thought of James dying from her mind because she knew she would never find the strength she would need if she even thought of his fate once he was back in Donnell's hands.

"Ye are a fool, Drummond," Donnell snapped. "Did ye think ye could best me by seducing my cousin?"

"I didnae seduce her. I took her because she cares for the child. I took the child to bring ye to me." He looked at all the men with Donnell. "I should have guessed that ye were too much the coward to come on your own. Nay mon enough to face me? Prefer to do your fighting against poor men chained to the walls?"

"Is something bad going to happen, Annora?" whispered Meggie as she pressed herself hard up against Annora's leg.

"I fear so, love," Annora whispered back as she continued to inch her way to the far edge of the clearing.

"I wanna go home."

"Hush, love. Best if we dinnae draw any attention our way."

It seemed that fate did not want to bless her with any good luck at the moment, Annora thought as she was suddenly grabbed from behind. She did not need to look to know it was Egan who held her. She recognized his rather unpleasant smell.

Meggie screeched and started to kick the man who held Annora, but the child's efforts were abruptly halted when Egan slapped her so hard she seemed to fly backward a foot before hitting the ground. Desperate to get to Meggie to be sure she was not badly hurt, Annora began to struggle in Egan's grasp, kicking and softly cursing.

James stared at his child as she sprawled in the dirt. Only a flicker of relief disturbed the hard grip of his rage when Meggie began to sit up, tears making a muddy trail in the dirt on her face. He looked briefly at Annora, who struggled to get free of Egan and go to Meggie. Then he looked back at Donnell MacKay.

How had everything gone so wrong? James wondered. Inwardly, he shrugged, feeling surprisingly numb except for the need to kill MacKay. Fate was dealing him a very hard hand at the moment and failure was a bitter taste in his mouth. The only glimmer of hope he had was that Tormand and Simon would soon know what had happened to him. They would do their best to get Annora and Meggie away from this bastard. He would not allow himself to think of anything but their safety, for his losses were so great he feared he could go mad if he thought about them.

"I think it is time for ye to surrender, Wolf," said MacKay.

"Why? So ye can kill me slowly as ye did my men?" James saw no reason to deny his identity to the man now.

Donnell cocked his head a little to the right and smiled faintly. "Aye."

A moment later nearly all of Donnell's men rushed James. Annora screamed, certain she was about to see James slaughtered before her eyes. He held his own for a while, revealing a skill with his sword that was nearly awe-inspiring. Several of Donnell's men actually backed away despite Donnell's insults and commands that they continue to fight. Then one unusually clever man got behind James while he was too occupied fending off three men in front of him to do anything to save himself. The man hit James so hard with the hilt of his sword on the back of his head that the sound echoed in the clearing.

A soft moan of despair escaped Annora as James fell to the ground. She stood still in Egan's grasp as Donnell dismounted and walked over to James. When he kicked James hard in the side, she gasped, but then Donnell's attention turned to her. She tensed as he walked up to her and looked her over from head to toe.

"So, Cousin, ye felt the need to betray me with this outlaw?" he asked in a cold, calm voice that sent shivers down her spine.

Deciding to stay with the tale James had told, that she was no more than a woman dragged along to take care of a child, she shook her head. "I had to stay with Meggie."

He stared at her for so long that she feared the truth was somehow marked on her face. "I think there is more," he murmured. "Much more but this is nay the place to find out the truth." He looked at Egan. "Get her and that sniveling child on a horse and let us get this wolfs head to the dungeon where he belongs."

Annora watched out of the corner of her eye as Donnell's men lifted James up and tossed him over the back of a horse. She tried to tell herself that there was still hope, that he was alive and that was all that mattered for now. It did not ease her fear by much as Egan roughly threw her on the back of a horse and then nearly threw a quietly crying Meggie up into her arms.

Relief briefly lightened her grief when Egan did not try to mount behind her, but got back on his own horse. He grabbed her reins and led her back toward Dunncraig. Annora silently tried to soothe Meggie as she fought not to think of what she faced once they were all back at Dunncraig. Donnell did not really believe that she was some innocent victim. Somehow she was going to have to convince him that she was or she, too, might be locked away and then she would be unable to help James.

As subtly as she could she looked toward where James' limp form bounced around on the back of a horse. Blood dripped down his face from the gash on the back of his head. That was not good, but she reminded herself that head wounds often bled freely and her fear for him eased just a little.

What she needed was a plan, she decided. If she was lucky enough not to be so badly beaten she could not move or locked up to face hanging as a traitor, she would need a plan to get help for James. It was hard to think clearly when she was facing

God alone knew what punishment and fearing for the life of her lover, but Annora worked to push all those concerns aside. What chance she might get to help James could be a small one, and the time in which she could grasp it might be fleeting. She could not allow the weakness her feelings stirred within her to cause her to miss any opportunity.

By the time Annora found herself facing Donnell in his ledger room, she was exhausted. Egan had never left her side as she had taken care of a still weeping Meggie. His silence and the way he stared at her were beginning to drive her mad. It was as if he was trying to see some sign that she had let another man touch her. The fact that she had taken James as her lover made it very hard for Annora to act the innocent confused virgin. She did not feel guilty for loving James, but she did feel that there might be something she would do or say that would give her away.

"Ye wish me to believe that ye went with Drummond because he had taken Meggie?" Donnell asked as he sprawled in the chair behind his worktable, his eyes fixed unblinkingly on her.

"Ye put her in my care, Donnell. I felt it was my duty to stay with her and try to protect her."

"Ah, and the fact that Drummond came to your bedchamber and beat Egan senseless was nay because ye and Drummond are lovers?"

"I may be bastard born, Cousin, but if naught else I learned from my mother's mistakes," she said coldly. "Egan was trying to rape me. He came to my bedchamber uninvited. I didnae lure him there for Master Lavengeance to find, if that is what ye are implying."

"That mon is nay Master Lavengeance. He is Sir James Drummond, the mon who killed our Cousin Mary."

"Are ye sure of that?"

Donnell sat up straight and glared at her. "Of course I am sure. Didnae it puzzle ye that he has two good eyes yet wore that patch?"

Annora had forgotten that James had discarded the patch during their flight from Dunncraig in the night. "Weel, a wee bit, but there are many reasons to wear such a thing. An injury, a weakness in the eye, an infection."

"Aye, aye." Donnell waved away the rest of her words. "Weel, I will be kind and pretend that I am believing all of your explanations and excuses for being with the mon who is my greatest enemy. James Drummond wants me dead, Cousin. He disguised himself and wormed his way into Dunncraig and my confidence in order to murder me. The fact that ye seem to have become verra friendly with the mon doesnae make me feel that ye are one who can be trusted."

"He was a wood-carver, Cousin. That is all I e'er thought he was."

"Did ye think a wood-carver could do this to me?" hissed Egan, grabbing her by the arm and turning her to face him.

Egan's face was a mess, Annora thought. She had not taken the opportunity to really look at him since he had grabbed her by the cottage. His eyes were so blackened and swollen she was surprised he had been able to see clearly enough to ride a horse.

"Ye were trying to rape me, Egan, and ye were beating on me." She lightly touched her bruised cheek. "All I saw when Master Lavengeance burst in was a mon who was about to save me." She looked back at Donnell. "I admit I was suspicious and verra disappointed when the mon I thought my rescuer dragged me to the nursery and took Meggie. But, as I keep saying, I felt it was my duty to stay with Meggie."

"How did ye get out of the keep without being seen?" demanded Donnell.

This was going to be a difficult question to answer, she thought. Annora was heartily glad that she had thought over all her possible answers and excuses as she had been taken back to Dunncraig. She was not a particularly good liar, but she could tell a very good story. Having planned ahead for this question, she began to tell her story.

As Annora told an elaborate tale of slipping through the shadows with a knife-wielding man and a sleeping child, she watched Donnell closely. He frowned as she spoke but she could not tell if that was a frown of thought or one of disbelief and, worse, she could sense nothing in him to tell her, either. Since Donnell already had plenty of proof that his men did not always make the most vigilant of guards, she felt no shame in implying that their lax guard was why she and Meggie were so easily slipped out of the keep.

"The mon is more clever than I thought," murmured Donnell.

"Do ye really believe all that?" said Egan.

"Most of it. I but wonder if my dear Cousin isnae really the complete victim she claims, however."

A tiny trickle of sweat went down Annora's spine but she kept her expression one of calm innocence. "I ne'er saw any evil in the mon, Cousin. Ye trusted him so I felt I could as weel. And since he twice saved me from Egan's attempts to steal my virtue, how could I not think him a good mon, one I could trust?"

"Ye are mine, woman, and I have the right to take ye anywhere and any way I please," said Egan, and then he backhanded her.

Annora hit the floor so hard she was dazed for a moment. She noticed that Donnell said and did nothing to stop Egan, and that silent approval of what the man had done made her very uneasy. It told her that, although Donnell could not see where her lies were, he suspected she was telling him some.

Egan yanked her to her feet and shook her. "Look at her mouth!" he yelled at Donnell. "'Tis verra clear that she has been thoroughly kissed."

"It does appear that way, Cousin," Donnell said. "Are ye sure ye didnae allow that bastard to seduce ye to his cause?"

"Ye think me some whore?" she demanded, acting completely outraged at the mere suggestion that she had taken a lover. "Do ye nay think I at least have enough wit to tell when I am being seduced? I am nay my mother."

"But ye carry her blood."

"I carry that of my grandsire as weel and he was no mon's fool."

"Ah, verra true. Still, I fear I dinnae completely believe your tale, Cousin."

"I cannae change it, for 'tis but the truth."

"As ye say but I think I will allow Egan to ease some of that fury that has him so tense and try to convince ye that ye just might have a wee bit more to tell us."

Even as Annora realized what Donnell was saying, Egan hit her in the face with his fist. The only reason she kept standing was that he had a painful grip on her arm. He smiled and she knew she was in for a very long, extremely painful time of questioning. She prayed she had the strength to remain firm and stay with the story she had told them.

It seemed like hours of pain and brutality, interspersed with the same questions over and over again, before Donnell said, "Enough, Egan. She is either telling us the truth or she will die ere she changes her story."

Annora stayed where she had fallen the last time Egan had hit her. She did not think there was a single part of her that was not shouting in pain. Turning her head upon the cold stone floor just enough to look at the two men standing there looking down at her, she wondered how they could still be free and alive while a good man like James was chained in their dungeon awaiting what would undoubtedly be a long, cruel death.

Just as she was thinking she might at least try to sit up, a man burst into the ledger room crying, "The MacLarens are raiding us!"

"'Tis nay e'en dark yet," muttered Donnell. "What do the fools think they are doing?"

"Avenging the death of the laird's son?" Annora said as she eased herself up onto her hands and knees.

A hard kick to her side sent her sprawling again, and Donnell snapped, "That was a death caused during a raid. It happens all the time. And only an utter fool raids a weel-manned keep in the full light of day."

"Mayhap someone let him ken that we arenae fully manned at the moment," said Egan as he roughly dragged Annora to her feet and then nearly threw her into a chair.

Fighting unconsciousness, she listened to Donnell question the man who had brought the news. From what was being said, she gathered that the MacLarens had come very close to taking Dunncraig Keep. It was only the sudden return of the rest of Donnell's men from their hunt for her and James that had saved Dunncraig. Those men had come up behind the MacLarens and the battle that had ensued had quickly become a rout. That so enraged Donnell that he punched the man who had delivered the news right in the nose, breaking it. Out of the corner of her rapidly swelling eye she watched that man slip away as Donnell turned all of his attention to making plans with Egan, plans that included chasing down the MacLarens and slaughtering them to a man.

When both men strode toward the door, Annora thought they had completely forgotten her. Then Donnell turned as he opened the door. He looked her over and his face twisted in an expression of distaste. Annora decided she must look very bad indeed if it was enough to trouble Donnell.

"Dinnae try to leave Dunncraig again, Annora," he said. "We arenae through asking ye questions."

She stared at the door for a long time after it closed behind Donnell and Egan. As she sat in the chair and tried to fight back the pain she was in, Annora wondered what she could do next. At the moment, she was not even sure she had the strength to get out of the chair.

The door slowly opened, and Annora frowned. It could not be Donnell or Egan, for they had no reason to enter the room in a secretive manner. The person who slipped into the room looked familiar, but her vision was so blurred by pain that the person was within a few steps of her before Annora recognized Big Marta. The woman was right by Annora's side before Annora saw that the strange lump to the right of the woman was a bowl of water and a little sack full of what she assumed were supplies to help heal all the wounds throbbing on Annora's body.

"Do ye think they broke any bones, child?" Big Marta asked in a voice that was surprisingly gentle for her.

"Nay, but I dinnae think there is one tiny spot upon my body that isnae bruised," Annora replied and decided her own voice sounded odd because her lips were swollen. "What is happening?"

"Meggie is in the nursery and Annie has finally managed to get the child to sleep," Big Marta said as she began to clean Annora's face. "I fear the true laird is hanging in chains in the dungeon, just where too many other good men died when that bastard cousin of yours took o'er Dunncraig. And MacKay and his men are haring off across the countryside trying to catch and kill MacLarens."

This was an opportunity to do something, but Annora found all of her thoughts and strength consumed by Big Marta's care of her many bruises and scrapes. She was fighting hard to stay conscious by the time the woman had spread salve on her bruises and wrapped her badly bruised ribs. Simply loosening her gown and dropping it to her waist, then putting it back on again had been pure torture.

"I must go find Tormand Murray and Sir Simon Innes," she said as she struggled to sit up straight.

"Lass, ye are so badly beaten I doubt ye can get to a piss pot without help," said Big Marta.

"I have to go to the village. Has the fight with the MacLarens gone beyond there?"

"Aye," Big Marta replied as she helped Annora stand up and then steadied her when she swayed on her feet, "the fools are chasing them all the way back to MacLaren lands."

"I pray the MacLarens win that race if only because they have given me the chance I have been hoping for."

"The chance to do what? Kill yourself by trying to do too much when ye should be lying abed?"

"I *must* go find Simon Innes and Tormand Murray. I can get them into the keep without being seen."

"Ah, of course. The lad took ye out through the secret ways, didnae he?"

"He did and I mean to bring some help back through the same way. Will ye watch Meggie for me?"

"Of course I will. I will make certain that she isnae caught up in any fight that happens."

"Thank ye. I believe she has seen enough of that for now, aye."

As Big Marta walked her to the door, Annora tried to push aside all her pain and steady herself. She would do no one any good if she fell facedown in the dirt before she even reached the village. She took each step very carefully and by the time she reached the door leading to the outside, she felt she could walk without any assistance.

"Mayhap I should help ye get to the village," Big Marta said as she looked around at the nearly deserted bailey. "I dinnae think MacKay realizes that he has left this place so empty."

"Good. He was in a rage and rages make him stupid. James is being guarded, though, isnae he?"

"Och, aye, by six burly fellows who wouldnae let me near the lad e'en though I told them I was to see that he didnae die of the bleeding from his head. Told them the laird would be most unhappy if the mon died, for then he wouldnae be able to torture him, would he?"

"And that didnae work?"

"Nay, they said they already kenned that the mon wouldnae die so why didnae I get my skinny arse back to the kitchens where I belonged? I will play the game again later and it may work then."

Those men would be lucky if they were not poisoned at the very next meal they sat down to, Annora thought. "Watch Meggie, Big Marta. She will be scared and Donnell might e'en try to hurt her if he sees that he is about to lose everything."

"I swear to ye, lass, that child will be safe. Just ye worry about yourself."

Annora almost nodded but then feared that moving her aching head like that could be just enough to send her into the unconsciousness that was beckoning at the edges of her mind. Instead she concentrated on putting one foot in front of the other. She grew a little more steady on her feet as she moved along, but her pace was slow. Annora suspected she looked much like a bent old woman as she walked, but her appearance was the least of her worries.

As she reached the edge of the village, she felt someone take her by the arm and looked up at the person now walking by her side. "Ida, it isnae safe to be seen with me right now."

"It isnae safe to be living in Dunncraig right now," Ida said. "I dinnae ken where ye think ye are going but I couldnae abide watching ye hobble along looking as if ye were going to fall into the dirt for one minute more. Where are ye going?"

To the inn. To James' brother and that Sir Simon Innes."

"Weel, ye are in luck for they but just returned to their rooms. They heard what had happened and I think they are trying to make some plans. Dinnae ken what they think they can do. E'en now, with most of the fighting men riding o'er the countryside screaming for the blood of the MacLarens, it wouldnae be easy to get the laird out of those chains."

"Nay, for Big Marta told me that there are six verra big men watching him and there is nay telling when Donnell and his dogs will return. A plan more clever than just running o'er there now and trying to free James has to be made. I but hope this Simon and James' brother are clever men."

"Och, aye, lass. They are verra clever. Havenae they been sitting here right under MacKay's big nose for days now and doing so without MacKay catching wind of it?"

That gave Annora hope as she looked at the stairs inside the inn and felt every ache in her body cry out in protest at the mere thought of going up them. Then Ida slipped one strong arm around her waist and Annora started up the stairs. With each step she took her bruised ribs sent pain throbbing through her body. Annora knew she never would have made it up the stairs without Ida's help and suspected poor Ida was nearly carrying her by the time they reached the top. Ida kept a firm grasp on her as she rapped on a door at the top of the stairs.

A tall man opened the door and asked, "What is the trouble, Ida?" A harsh curse escaped the man and Annora felt a strong arm encircle her shoulders. "Who is this woman and why have ye brought her here?"

This is Annora MacKay, Sir Innes," replied Ida.

Another tall man appeared in the doorway and Annora asked, "Tormand Murray?"

"Aye. Jesu, what happened to you?"

"I was asked a few questions about your brother's attempt to flee Dunncraig."

"Why have ye dragged yourself here? Ye should be abed."

"Later. Is the king's mon ready to help James in more ways than just gathering information?"

"Aye, he is," said the shadowy form that Ida had addressed as Sir Innes.

"Oh, good, for I can get ye into Dunncraig so that ye can get him out ere Donnell cuts him into small pieces just for the joy it would bring him." She felt as if her knees had turned to water. "Although I think that may have to wait just a moment."

The last thing Annora heard was a deep voice curse and then say, "Catch her. She doesnae need any other bruises."

Chapter Eighteen

Pain was the first thing Annora was aware of as consciousness returned. Then a cool wet cloth moved over her aching face soothing some of the pain there. Cautiously, she opened her eyes. They did not open very much but, recalling why she was in such pain, she was surprised they opened at all. A handsome face with mismatched but very beautiful eyes appeared in her narrow field of vision.

"Tormand Murray?" she asked, remembering what James had said about his brother's eyes. There could not be another man at the village inn with one green eye and one blue eye.

"Aye, and ye are James' Annora," he said.

"Oh, that sounds nice." She blushed when he grinned, for it had been a foolish thing to say. "How long was I unconscious?" she asked.

"Five hours."

"Nay!" she cried, terrified that they had lost the chance to help James. "Why couldnae ye have woken me up?"

"We did try from time to time but then we decided we could make some preparations while ye rested for a wee while." He slid his arm around her and helped her sit up. "We are ready now for ye to lead us into the place where they are holding James. S'truth, without that wee rest ye took I dinnae think ye would have been able to do it."

"I am astounded that ye made it to the village," said the man standing at the other side of her bed, drawing her attention, and then he bowed slightly. "Sir Simon Innes, mistress. At your service."

"Only the two of ye?" she asked as Ida nudged Tormand out of the way and helped Annora drink some mead.

"Nay. As ye rested we gathered some men," replied Simon. "It wasnae hard to find ones eager to rid Dunncraig of your cousin. Was he the one who beat ye so badly?"

It obviously troubled Sir Innes a great deal to see a woman beaten so badly, and Annora felt that was a good sign. James had said that the man could be trusted, but she was feeling very wary of everyone at the moment. Unfortunately, James did not have the time to wait while she decided who she could trust.

"Nay, he had his mon Egan do the honors," she replied. "Egan was most eager to do so as James had beaten him rather badly just before we fled Dunncraig. Did Donnell slaughter any MacLarens? That was what he intended to do when he left me."

Tormand shook his head. "Nay, they got away. A few have slipped back, though. Simon felt they might prove a good source of trained fighting men. We will need such men to take Dunncraig back from MacKay."

"Of course ye will and the MacLarens will be more than eager to help ye. Donnell did a verra thorough job of ridding Dunncraig of all the men loyal to James. So, when do ye wish me to lead ye inside Dunncraig?"

"In one hour."

Annora slumped against the pillows Ida had placed at her back. "Then give me a cold wet cloth again so that I might put it o'er my eyes. It will help me to see more clearly where I am going when it is time to leave."

"Do ye think an hour will be long enough?" asked Tormand as he gathered what she had asked for.

"Aye, though dinnae expect me to do any more than slump in a corner somewhere once I get ye inside."

"I will see ye safely set into one myself."

She placed the cloth over her eyes, nearly sighing with pleasure over how good it felt, and then she heard the door to the room shut softly. "Ida?"

"Still here. Rest, lass. Ye will be in sore need of all the strength ye can muster to just get through the next few hours."

"We will win this time, willnae we, Ida?"

"Och, aye, I dinnae doubt that for a moment."

"I cannae believe she was able to e'en stand up let alone walk all the way here in search of us," said Tormand the minute they entered Simon's bedchamber.

Simon poured them each a goblet of ale and handed Tormand his. "She doesnae look as if she would have such strength, yet it took a great deal to do what she did. E'en her ribs are wrapped tightly, meaning they were badly bruised or worse. And I can tell ye that e'en breathing with such wounds can be an agony."

"So, ye are nay longer afraid that she cannae be trusted."

"Nay, but it really isnae because she came here all battered. Aye, that actually moves me to think she is a good woman, but nay, it was that look she got when ye called her James' Annora. Despite all the swelling and the bruises, ye could see that that delighted her and then she said oh, *that sounds nice.*" He grinned briefly when Tormand laughed at Simon's attempt to imitate Armora's voice. "It held that almost too sweet note of a woman who believes she is in love."

Tormand shook his head. "Ye are a cynic, Simon. A hard mon. Mayhap someday ye will tell me what has made ye so sour on such things as love and marriage and put that soul deep distrust of women inside ye."

"Mayhap. Right now what I think of it all doesnae matter. I do believe that she feels she is a woman in love and she has done something extraordinary because of that. I just wish that James had told ye of the secret way in and out of Dunncraig and then that poor woman could have crawled into a bed where she belonged and had some maid tend to all her bruises."

"Weel, James had intended to tell me, e'en draw me a map, but then everything went wrong at Dunncraig and he had to try and escape."

"'Tis good the lass kens it, then, or your brother would have no chance of surviving this, and we both ken that MacKay willnae gift him with a swift, clean death."

Tormand took a deep drink and then studied the wooden goblet he held. This is one of James'. One of his more simple designs. The innkeeper must have bought them for these, his best bedchambers." He sighed and looked at Simon. "I ken weel what MacKay is. I ken that the moment MacKay rode back through the gates of Dunncraig my brother would soon be suffering a lot of pain. James will abide it if he must. He will wait for me to come to his aid but will ne'er fault me if I fail to save him. I dinnae think I need to say that I wish to save him any pain and save his life, but right now e'en that doesnae consume my mind the most. Nay, I wish to reach James before MacKay's torture goes too far, before he ruins James' hands."

"His hands?" Simon looked at the goblet he held, a perfect match to the one Tormand held. "He does do verra fine work."

"Ye dinnae understand. This isnae work to James. Aye, he can make money with his skill, but he does this because he *has* to. James has always carved wood, e'en before our mother wanted him to be within yards of a sharp edge. He can stand before a piece of wood, stare at it for a while, and then abruptly start working on it. Sometimes he just sees a picture in the wood. Sometimes he scratches it out on a piece of parchment so that he can show someone else what he sees or just be certain that what he sees will work perfectly. It always does."

"I fear I have ne'er really understood such things, yet 'tis all around me, from the weaver of a tapestry to the maker of jewelry. Yet, your brother is a laird."

"It doesnae matter. If he was a king, ye would still be certain to catch him carving something out of wood e'en on the throne. Truly, he *has* to do it. If MacKay crushes that skill in James by hurting his hands beyond repair, it will destroy something in my brother, something I am nay sure e'en his Annora will be able to mend. I think it is the way of it for many people with such gifts."

"Then we shall get him free of MacKay ere that can happen. If 'tis any comfort, for all of his cunning and brutality, I dinnae think MacKay is all that quickwitted. I dinnae think he will ken what your brother's weakest point is."

"I pray ye are right, for if MacKay does ken how important James' work with wood is to my brother, those hands are what he will go for first."

Cold water hit his face hard and James abruptly woke up. He felt as if his head was going to split apart. His body felt as if he had been thrown from a cliff onto the rocks—several times. MacKay had come back from trying to catch MacLarens, if James recalled what he had heard correctly, and he had been in a rage over his failure to kill even one MacLaren. MacKay had felt insulted by the MacLarens' attempt to take Dunncraig and had wanted them to pay for that insult in blood. Instead MacKay had used James' body to soothe his rage. It had been a hard punch to the face that had finally driven him into a very welcome blackness. It appeared that respite was over.

He looked toward where the water had come from and had to blink several times to clear his vision. No faces came into view until he looked down. Big Marta stood there holding a bucket of water, a tankard, and a sack.

"Good, ye are awake now," she said as she set down the bucket of water and opened the sack.

"And ye think I should feel good about that?" If MacKay was soon to return, James thought he might prefer to be insensible.

"Aye and nay." Big Marta looked all around before she started to wash the filth from his body. "MacKay will return soon and he intends to make ye beg for mercy."

"He will be four score years buried and rotted ere that happens."

"I wouldnae be so sure. He has broken many a brave mon."

"My men, ye mean. Good men who wouldnae break their oath to me e'en if it would have saved their lives."

"Aye, the weeks after ye left and MacKay claimed all of Dunncraig as his were verra sad days. But t'will soon all be set aright again."

James stared at the woman standing on her tiptoes so that she could wash down his arms. "Do ye have the sight, then? Ye have seen me taken from this place and nay just as a corpse for the burying?"

Big Marta tsked her impatience over the cross cynicism in his voice. "Ye ken weel that I have no skill or gift or whate'er ye wish to call it. What I do have is a pair of good ears and, at the moment, a wee bit more knowledge than ye do."

"'Tis a wee bit difficult to gather knowledge whilst hanging from a wall and a mon is punching ye senseless." James almost smiled at the creative curses Big Marta spoke. "What do ye ken?" he asked quietly, briefly looking round for any sign of his guards. "Do ye ken how Meggie and Annora fare?"

"Your lasses are fine. Meggie is a wee bit frightened and Annora a wee bit bruised."

"Only a wee bit?"

"Weel, while MacKay was out chasing MacLarens she went to the village to find your brother and his friend, so how bad could she be feeling?"

James was not sure he believed her but decided there was no time to argue. She had said that both Meggie and Annora were alive and he would let that be enough for now. "Weel then, what do ye ken if nay information about their fates?"

"I ken a lot," she said, using a very soft voice again. "Now your guards have left to find food and a garderobe. MacKay thinks I am safe enough in the kitchens although I dinnae think he understood that I wasnae *asking* to see ye, I was *telling* him that I would come and see ye. So I came down here, told those hulking great fools watching o'er ye that I was here to tend to your wounds, and they decided that was just fine with them."

"And they didnae argue with that? I dinnae think MacKay often sends someone down here to tend to the wounds of his prisoners."

A sigh escaped Big Marta. "He has done so in the past. He wanted to keep your men alive as long as possible, didnae he? There are things from those days that I still see in my dreams."

"I am sorry ye had to see that. I shouldnae have left."

"Wheesht, shake away that guilt, laddie. Ye had to leave to save your life and no one could have expected MacKay to treat your men as he did. Most expected he would command them to swear an oath to him or leave Dunncraig. There were some who had heard some verra dark tales about the mon and left as soon as ye did. A few others did swear fealty to him and stayed, although they have ne'er really mixed with the men MacKay brought with him. Their only thought was, and still is, to survive and stay close to their loved ones."

"I hadnae realized that some of my men were still here. I had thought them all dead or gone. How many?"

"Oh, five, I think. They had lovers or family here and didnae want to leave. Edmund didnae ken all of your men weel enough to ken that. But they are ready now," she said in a whisper.

"Ready for what?" James felt better after having been so thoroughly washed down and some of his wounds salved, but his head still throbbed so badly he was beginning to have difficulty following whatever it was Big Marta was talking about.

"For rescue, laddie. For rescue. This time the bastard willnae win."

Before James could ask what Big Marta meant the woman was standing at the door to his prison. It was only a moment later that all of his guards returned. Big Marta was sent away and James felt himself tensing for MacKay's arrival. This time the man would take his time.

A tremor went through his body, but James hid it from the guards by pressing himself hard up against the stone wall at his back. Any sane man would be afraid of what MacKay might do to him, but James refused to let his fear show. He still had his pride, and if this was the time of his death, he wanted to meet it with courage and dignity.

He found his thoughts slipping to Annora and it felt as if his heart broke in his chest. At long last he had found that perfect woman he had always been looking for, his mate, and he was not going to be allowed the future he wanted with her. There would be no black-haired children with wide midnight-blue eyes. His little Meggie would grow to womanhood thinking MacKay was her father and there was a chance Annora would eventually be forced to marry Egan or flee to some relative's home, yet another kinsman who did not care for her at all. James knew Tormand would do his best to protect both Annora and Meggie, but it might not be as easy as they had both thought it would be. MacKay now held both of his women in his grasp, and after their near escape he would be sure to tighten his grip on them.

What he ached to do was see Annora and Meggie just one more time, but he knew that wish would never be granted. It could also prove dangerous for Annora. If she had succeeded in convincing MacKay that she had been no more than an innocent victim of some madman, then she had a good chance of coming out of this adventure alive.

For a moment James feared Annora would be unable to lie so well to her cousin. She was a very honest woman. Then he recalled the time he had insulted MacKay in French and the man had asked Annora to tell him what had been said. She had revealed a very good skill at telling lies to her cousin then. James suspected that when she felt she or someone she cared about was in danger, Annora could tell a complete lie without blinking, not just one of those ones where she just did not tell the whole truth or even failed to actually answer the question.

"Weel, let us just look at the great Laird Drummond hanging up there like freshly dressed meat," drawled a woman's voice James was all too familiar with.

He looked at Mab and nearly gaped. The woman was a mess, her face badly bruised and her hair cut in ragged lengths all over her head. Mab had obviously paid dearly for not holding him in his bedchamber.

"And why has anyone let ye down here?" he asked in a voice that was so sneering and rude, all the guards chuckled. Mab blushed with fury. "There is naught ye can distract me from in here, lass. Get ye gone."

"Ye willnae escape this place, Wolfs head. Nay alive, ye willnae."

James shrugged and then fought to hide the pain the movement caused him. "'Tis verra clear that ye have no intention of aiding me or e'en giving me a wee bit of sympathy. So, as I have asked before, each time ye tried to creep into my bed, why are ye here?"

"Mayhap I just wish to watch MacKay teach ye a little humility ere he hangs ye."

"And mayhap ye need the rest of your hair cut off," drawled a deep voice James immediately recognized as Egan's.

Mab paled and hurried away. James looked at Egan and knew without asking that he was the one who had tried to destroy what claim Mab had to beauty. He was probably the one who had kept sending the foolish woman to James' room. It would be just like Egan to make anyone close at hand suffer for his humiliation.

"Ah, yet another visitor," drawled James. "I am a popular fellow, aye? To what do I owe this honor?"

"I just have a few questions for ye ere Donnell starts to make ye scream," said Egan.

"What questions?"

"Have ye touched Annora MacKay?"

James just stared at him. The man had just revealed that he had done nothing to Annora yet that would have exposed her lack of a maidenhead. The relief James felt was so strong he needed a moment to collect his thoughts.

"As I told MacKay, I needed the woman to care for the child."

"Ye expect me to believe that ye spent a night with her and didnae touch her?"

"Some of us dinnae find throwing an unwilling lass to the ground and taking her to be verra rewarding. So, to answer your question, nay, I didnae take Annora MacKay."

Obviously he could also lie very well under certain circumstances, James thought. He could tell, however, that Egan was of no mind to believe him even if he had been telling the truth. It was impossible for a man like Egan to think any man could stay so long alone with an attractive woman and not have to ease his lust on her body, willing or unwilling. James suspected that Egan preferred the woman to be unwilling, for it would give him the sense of being the one with all the power.

And this was the sort of man who would still be close to Annora after James was gone. It appalled James to even consider what the man might do to Annora. He did not really have to think too hard since twice he had had to pull the man off Annora. It hurt James beyond words to know that there was a very good chance he would no longer be able to protect her from such brutality.

"Egan, I have been looking for ye," snapped MacKay as he approached the prison that held James.

"I had to ask the mon if he had touched Annora," said Egan.

MacKay cursed and pushed Egan out of his way as he walked right up to where James hung from the wall. "So what if Annora is nay longer a virgin?" he asked, staring at James but still speaking to Egan.

"Because that maidenhead was mine to claim. He keeps saying that he didnae touch her, but I think he is lying."

"Are ye, Drummond?" asked MacKay in a soft, almost gentle voice that made chills run down James' spine. "I think Egan may be right. I think ye are lying to me. I think Annora is lying as weel. I shall have the truth beaten out of her soon. She needs to heal a wee bit since Egan questioned her about ye a little too vigorously." MacKay reached for a whip that hung on the wall. "I believe I shall take my time in questioning ye. Ye see, one thing I believe Annora is lying about is the way ye could all get out of Dunncraig without being seen."

"Ye have some verra poor guards on your walls," James said, forcing himself not to look at the whip and anticipate the pain MacKay was about to inflict.

"Och, aye, we do, but nay that poor. Few men could miss seeing a mon, a woman, and a wee child leave Dunncraig. Nay, I think this keep has a few secrets I have yet to uncover and I am going to make ye tell all of them to me."

"Do your worst," James said in a cold voice, his fear hardening into a deep, cold hatred for the man.

"I intend to," said MacKay and he raised the whip.

Chapter Nineteen

It was beginning to feel as if everyone was just waiting for her to fall facedown in the dirt. Annora knew she was but one stumble away from doing just that, but feeling everyone's concern as she was only made it much more difficult to keep on going. That concern coupled with a deep respect coming from the men creeping through shadows alongside her made her want to just sit down and allow them all to coddle her. The only man she felt had any fierce need to keep on going was Tormand and she tried to remain open to his feelings. It was enough to keep her plodding toward the well-hidden opening leading into the secret passages of Dunncraig.

"How close are we?" whispered Tormand.

"But a few yards away," she replied as one by one the men with them slipped deeper into the shadows of the wood they had just entered.

"Sit," he said and gently urged her to rest for a moment, her back against the rough trunk of a large tree.

"This may nay be verra wise. I may nay be able to get moving again." When Simon crouched down in front of her and held out a wineskin, she smiled her gratitude and accepted a drink.

"All ye need to do is stay conscious," said Tormand. "I will carry ye on my back if need be and ye can point the way. S'truth, mayhap I shall do that anyway."

"Kind of ye to offer but I dinnae think it will ease my pain much at all," she said.

"Are ye verra certain ye cannae just tell us the way from here or scratch out a map in the ground here?"

"I dearly wish I could, Tormand, but I have only traveled

this way once. I ken how to get to the opening e'en though this isnae the way James and I traveled when we fled Dunncraig, but only because I have walked about in these woods for three years and ken every tree and bush around here. 'Tis the passage itself which I need to see in order to tell ye the way to go."

"Are ye certain ye will recall the way once ye are inside?"

"Aye. I willnae weary ye with tales from my childhood but I learned verra quickly to always be able to find my way back from whence I came. I can travel a path but the once and return the same way nay matter how long a time has passed. It takes many more times of journeying a path for me to be able to tell people where to go or to draw some map."

"An intriguing skill," murmured Simon.

"I suppose it is." She looked at the MacLarens who crouched in the thick shadows several feet away and asked softly, "Are ye certain 'tis wise to let the MacLarens see the way inside Dunncraig? They have a grievance against Dunncraig, aye?"

"They have a grievance against your cousin," said Simon. "If, when this is all over, James worries about the MacLarens' kenning where this bolt-hole is, he can easily block the entrance."

"True enough." She straightened up and took a few deep, slow breaths. For she knew there would be a lot of pain to deal with when she stood up. "'Tis best if we get moving along again."

The way Simon and Tormand helped her to her feet eased some of her pain, but it still took another round of slow, deep breaths to regain her balance enough to get moving along again. With Tormand remaining close by her side, his strong arm around her waist to steady her, Annora led them through the woods until they reached the opening to the passageways that roamed throughout the underbelly of the keep. The doorway that led to the tunnels was cleverly hidden within the thick roots of an old tree, but Annora had no trouble leading the men right to it.

Tormand entered the tunnel first and then Simon gently lowered her down to him. It still hurt but she found she was getting very good at hiding her pain. Annora simply kept promising herself the comfort of a soft bed, a potion to ease her pain, and a few moments alone to weep and cry out all the hurt she had kept hidden for so long. A few times she even imagined herself tucked up in bed with a handsomely concerned James gently bathing her forehead with cool lavender water. The image was enough to keep her moving even when all she wanted to do was lie down and cry like a bairn.

As she slumped against the rocky wall of the tunnel, slumping being something else she was getting very good at, she mused, Tormand lit a torch. Annora blinked as the sudden light hurt her eyes. Leaving Edmund to assist the others into the tunnel and hand out the occasional torch, Tormand escorted her along the tunnel. She steadily led them past several turnings and then turned down the next one. She had only gone a few steps when Simon stopped her.

"Where does this lead to?" he asked.

"The dungeons," she replied, recalling very clearly how James had paused to point it out to her. "The passage we have just left goes to the kitchens. Ye just keep going straight, watching carefully for a set of wide, uneven steps. Go up the steps and at the top is a door. It leads into the pantry, the one that is always unlocked."

"Wait here."

She rested against Tormand's strong body and muttered, Just where does he think I will go?" She smiled faintly when Tormand laughed so softly that it was little more than a mere whisper of a sound. "What do ye think he is doing?"

"Sending some of the men into the keep through the kitchens."

"I hope he warns them to be wary of Big Marta."

"She is expecting something to happen so I dinnae think she will hurt them. How far down this passage are the dungeons?"

"James said it was a straight walk, taking no turnings off it, and it would take about ten minutes if ye were making your way there cautiously, much less if ye had no fear of being seen or heard. I wasnae particularly interested in how far, just where it went to and how I got there. I am only interested in returning to the place I came from."

"Because ye were left places? Deserted?"

The man had too quick a mind, Annora decided. "Aye. Some of my kin would take me to another kinsmon without making sure that kinsmon was home first or able to take me in. My aunt Agnes did that three times ere a cousin accepted me into her household."

He said nothing, but she felt his arm tighten round her shoulders ever so slightly in a silent gesture of sympathy. Annora expected to find such sympathy humiliating but she did not. The sense of outrage she felt in Tormand and the feeling of comfort he offered made his feeling of sympathy acceptable. It was not pity, something she would have been repelled by.

When Simon returned they continued on their way. The soft sound of voices alerted them that they were rapidly nearing their destination. Tormand doused his torch and Annora waited for the fear she always felt when caught in the dark to overcome her, but it only flickered to life for a moment and faded away. She decided she was simply too occupied with her pain and James' safety to care about the dark. It held nothing as frightening as the possibility that she could not help James get free of her cousin's cruelty. Even as she started to slide down the wall, Tormand returned to her side and pulled her up against him.

"Steady, lass," he whispered against her ear. "I have found ye a safe place to rest as we rescue James," he said even as he began to move her farther down the passageway.

She could feel his growing excitement and decided men were strange creatures. She could not understand how men could find this sort of attack exciting. Tormand and the others were actually anticipating a battle. Annora felt certain that, if there was not a satisfactorily bloody battle, all these men would be disappointed.

A faint glow of light inched into the dark just as Tormand settled her into a niche in the wall of the passageway. Annora could hear voices clearly now and knew she was only feet away from where Donnell had imprisoned James. The sudden sharp crack of a whip nearly made her gasp. Tormand had anticipated the reaction and had gently covered her bruised mouth with his hand.

"Be at ease, lass. Ye have shown great courage to come this far," he whispered against her ear again as he removed his hand. "Dinnae falter now."

"He is hurting James," she whispered back, afraid that she was about to burst into tears.

"He willnae be doing so much longer."

Even though he was still whispering, Annora could hear the cold, hard resolve in his attractive voice. There was also a fierce anger bubbling up inside the man. Anger such as that usually made her very uneasy, but this time she found comfort in it. Tormand Murray would make her cousin pay dearly for every twinge of pain he had inflicted upon James. She nodded and he slipped away. Annora sat with her back pressed hard against the cool, damp stone hoping the chill that entered her body from the stone would keep her alert. She listened to Tormand's men slip past her one by one. The silent way they moved and the grim resolve she felt in each man eased her fear for James. Donnell's cruel reign at Dunncraig was about to come to a bloody end.

James feared he would have no teeth left if he was not saved from this torture soon as they would all be ground to dust. He could do little to stop himself from sweating, however, but MacKay could think that was caused by many things other than fear. James wished he did not have any fear, but knowing this man would stop at nothing in order to inflict the most pain he could made it difficult to hold fear back.

"Ye are a stubborn mon, James Drummond," MacKay said calmly.

That calm was one of the things that made MacKay seem far more intimidating than he actually was. James doubted the man would be standing there bravely, all calmness and soft, cold smiles, if he was faced with a man freed of his chains. Most brutal men of MacKay's ilk were actually cowards beneath the skin. Once his own life was threatened MacKay would be running for his life. James was sure of it.

"And ye are a cowardly swine who struts before a chained mon acting brave and in command. Release me to fight ye fair and we shall see how brave ye are." He was not surprised when those words earned him another lash of the whip.

"Ye dinnae rule here anymore, Drummond," MacKay

hissed, revealing the anger and envy that hid behind his cold ruthlessness. "I rule now."

"Your rule here is based on lies and treachery. How long do ye think it can last?"

"As long as I wish. The only ones with any legal claim to this place are either dead, like your wee wife, Mary, or on the run."

"I suppose ye got some great joy out of cuckolding me."

"Mary was mine first."

"Then why didnae ye keep her?"

"Because she had a verra large dowry and her felt she could find a match better than me. But I wanted it. I had earned it."

"Earned it, how so?"

MacKay stood up very straight, a posture that thrust his rounded chest out until he looked very much like a strutting cock. James decided that he wanted to hear this man tell the truth of his crimes. If he was going to die, then James wanted to do so with all of his questions answered and all of his suppositions confirmed or replaced with the full ugly truth.

"By making the stupid cow fall in love with me." MacKay shook his head as if amazed all over again at how easy it had been to win Mary's affections. "Do ye ken why she hated you? Why she did anything I wanted and betrayed ye again and again?"

"Weel, I will admit that I am curious as to why she would want a brutal wee swine like ye and nay a laird with a full purse, one nay too ugly or too old." He gritted his teeth again as MacKay struck him with the whip but inches from his groin.

"Fool. Ye ne'er really kenned the woman ye had married. She wasnae the sweet shy maid she let everyone, e'en her parents, believe she was. She was a whore. I wager ye thought she was a virgin but that was just some trick she learned from a woman in a tavern whilst she was on a pilgrimage with her mother."

James had wondered how he had been so fooled. The fact that he had never bedded a virgin had probably aided Mary in her deceit. Since bedding Annora, he had occasionally pondered the mysteries of his wedding night with Mary. The confessions in her journal that revealed she had been a well-experienced woman had not come as a complete surprise.

"Yet ye were willing to murder the woman ye had cared about for so verra long."

"Wheesht, who said I cared for the cow? She was a lover who enjoyed the rougher side of passion and when she was chosen as your bride I saw the chance of gaining something. But ye didnae offer me any position or e'en to help me find one worthy of my wit and guile." The tone of outrage in MacKay's voice told James that that insult still stung. "So, I decided I would have your position. I had learned of a mon who had gained all another mon possessed by proving that the mon had murdered one of his kinswomen. He claimed it all as reparations for the loss of the woman. That is when I realized Mary might be useful. I urged her to marry you and swore to her that she would be a widow verra soon."

"Ye took your sweet time executing your plan."

A shadow moved in the far corner of the dungeons near where the guards sat drinking and listening to their laird confess all his crimes. Even as James wondered why the men did not leave, did not seem to understand that it was mortally dangerous to hear any of MacKay's secrets, he saw another slight movement in the shadows. His heart pounding with the hope that what he saw was not just some trick of the light or a false vision brought on by pain, James tried to keep his gaze fixed upon MacKay. If there was something happening in the far corner of the dungeon, he did not want to alert MacKay to it.

"A good plan takes time to perfect," MacKay said a little pompously. "I needed to collect up allies, men in power who could see to it that I got the reparations when ye were convicted of the crime of murdering your wife—my kinswoman. Then Mary bad Margaret and I saw that as even more opportunity. I had witnesses to the fact that she and I were lovers and could claim the child was mine by blood if nay by law. That would help and it would present a verra good reason for why ye murdered her."

"But she wasnae murdered, was she? It wasnae Mary's body we found in that burned-out cottage."

"Nay, it was a maid from the next village. She and I were lovers and Mary found us. She joined in our play for a while but then grew jealous and killed the woman. Since I had all I needed to get ye charged, convicted, and grab hold of Dunncraig, I decided we would just let the world think it was Mary and set my plan into motion."

Resting his chin against his chest for a moment, James peeked over at the guards and nearly cursed aloud in surprise. They were gone. Since he was sure no one but him and Annora knew the secrets of Dunncraig, he knew they had not slipped away down one of the passages. Just as he was about to return to making MacKay confess all of his clever plans, the whip struck him across his belly and he gasped, surprise making it impossible to hide all signs of the pain he felt.

"Growing weary of listening to my triumphs?" sneered MacKay.

"Mayhap ye shouldnae be telling him so much," said Egan.

"Why not? Who is he going to tell? He will be feeding the worms verra soon and dead men can tell no tales, eh?"

Egan grimaced. "I have always felt that the fewer who ken one's secrets the better."

"The fewer living, breathing people, Egan. This fool is a dead mon; he just hasnae had the sense to stop breathing."

"Just where did Mary hide, then?" James asked as soon as he felt he could talk in a calm voice that revealed none of his pain.

"Here and there," replied MacKay. "I made her move from place to place so that no one would discover her. But she wouldnae do as she was told. She kept coming round and then she began to demand I marry her. The stupid woman did not seem to understand that she could ne'er come back to Dunncraig. She had gotten it into her foolish head that once I held Dunncraig, she could be the lady of it again, be my wife. I tried to get her to leave the area for months and then she told me she carried my child. Weel, ye dinnae need to ken why I was sure it wasnae mine, but it wasnae. It was then verra obvious to me that she was taking lovers and running the risk of being recognized. If she was e'er caught I kenned full weel that she wouldnae protect me. That is when I killed her, nearly a year after ye had run away accused of her murder."

"Where is she buried, MacKay?"

"Why do ye care where her bones are?"

"I am nay sure I care but Mary was Meggie's mother and thus she deserves the respect of a proper burial. And I am surprised that ye didnae make sure she had a proper grave so that ye could visit her now and then."

"Why should I wish to do that?"

"Because if she hadnae been such a foolish, blind woman, ye would ne'er have gotten your fat arse into my great hall."

"Ye just dinnae have the sense to be quiet, do ye?" MacKay hit him with the whip across his right hip.

James ignored the sting and the feel of warm blood running down his thigh and kept his gaze fixed upon MacKay. "Where is she buried?"

"*Why* do ye care?" demanded MacKay again.

"Someday Meggie might ask and I would like to show her where her blood mother is buried."

"Show Margaret? Are ye sure ye arenae mad? How can ye show the child anything when ye will be dead? I ought to bury ye right next to Mary and let her whine ye into hell. Ye are a dead mon, fool. Ye. Are. A. Dead. Mon."

A fleeting glimpse of his brother Tormand told James that the loss of the guards was only the beginning. He wondered if it was Annora who had brought someone to get him out of the dungeons. Knowing that any moment the attack would begin, James looked at MacKay and smiled.

"Nay, actually, I believe ye are."

Chapter Twenty

The attack began so quickly, Annora nearly missed it. She had been sitting right where Tormand had put her, feeling stunned by all the confessions pouring out of Donnell. As the truth had rolled out of the man, pauses in his ramblings coming only when he felt James needed to be humiliated a little more, she had tried to find Simon in the shadows. The moment she saw him crouched against the opposite wall of the passage and closer to James than she was, he briefly turned his head and winked at her as if he had felt her looking for him. Relieved that the king's man was hearing every foul word Donnell said, she returned to listening to her cousin dig his own grave.

Even though she had a fierce greed for the answers Donnell was so blithely giving her, Annora soon found it difficult to stay awake. Her body was demanding that she rest so that it could begin to heal. Annora snapped herself out of one of those half sleeps just in time to see Edmund carrying away the body of one of the guards. Wide-awake again, she looked toward where the guards had been sitting and realized that Edmund had been taking away the last one.

She watched as Simon, Tormand, and the other men began to inch closer to Donnell and Egan. Her cousin was so busy showing James how thoroughly he had fooled him that he did not notice six of his men had been killed and a group of armed men was slowly advancing on him. Yet again she had to wonder how Donnell had accomplished all he had thus far. She then heard an odd note in James' voice and eased herself around the corner to get a better look at him.

It was difficult to bite back a cry of outrage. James was chained to the wall and almost naked. His fine, strong body was covered in welts from Donnell's whip. From what she could see, James was not yet seriously injured. The pain of those whip slashes was undoubtedly great and hard to bear, but he would heal quickly if he was freed before Donnell could inflict any real harm.

Then suddenly Egan looked her way. Annora was certain she could not be seen, but some of the men creeping toward Donnell were no longer hidden in the shadows. Egan abruptly drew his sword and Tormand's men rose up with a battle cry. The noise filled the passageway she was in and she lightly placed her hands over her ears in an attempt to dim it. As the yelling and the running continued, she kept her gaze fixed upon James, praying that nothing happened to him when his rescue was so close at hand.

James watched the shock on Donnell's face as Tormand, Simon, and half a dozen armed men ran into the dungeon a heartbeat after Egan's warning cry. The man was no doubt thinking of all he had confessed in his orgy of gloating. James tensed, wondering how he could defend himself, when Donnell drew his sword and glared at him. But then he simply shoved Egan toward the men and raced up the steps into the keep. A cursing Egan did not wait to see if he could defend himself or surrender; he chased his cowardly laird up the stairs.

"God's tears, get me out of these chains," James bellowed when it looked as if everyone was about to race up the stairs after Donnell and Egan and just leave him hanging there.

"Aye, aye," said Tormand. "I am just trying to find the key to those chains."

"Here," said Edmund as he came out of the shadows of the passageway and handed the keys to Tormand. "That last guard had them on him. Are ye going to tend to him, then?"

"Aye, the rest of ye get up there and see if any of the others need help. We need those gates opened." As the men ran off, Tormand hurried to James' side and began to unlock his chains.

"Do ye have an army with ye?" James asked and then cursed when he was finally set firmly on his feet and found that hours of hanging in chains had left him a little unsteady.

"A small one," replied Tormand as he supported James

while his brother tried to regain his ability to move with some semblance of grace.

"Where did ye get one?"

"A few villagers who had some skill with a sword. About a half dozen of your old guard who ne'er lost their loyalty to ye. Oh, and a few MacLarens."

"MacLarens? We are feuding with them. Donnell's last raid cost that laird his son."

"Simon convinced them that ye and most of the people of Dunncraig werenae responsible for that and if they truly wanted the one who was they had best become your closest, most loyal allies. To swear a form of fealty to ye in front of Simon is much akin to swearing it to the king himself. They want Donnell."

"So do I. Did ye hear all he said?" Feeling steady on his feet, James searched for his clothes and then began to dress, eager to join in whatever battle was going on upstairs.

"Och, aye, and Simon was listening verra carefully. I think he would like Donnell to be captured and nay killed, for he wants the names of those in power who helped him condemn an innocent mon."

As he buckled on his sword, James said, "I want him alive so that others can hear his confessions. Now, how did ye find the way in here? I hadn't yet given ye the directions or a map when I had to flee Dunncraig, and no one else here kens where they are."

"That is nay exactly true," said Tormand. "Your lass does."

"Annora? But she only came through the passage the one time."

"It seems it is all it takes for her to recall every step."

"Astonishing. So, where is she now? I think Egan beat her and I would like to be sure she is all right."

"Weel, she is here." Tormand shrugged when James glared at him. "She couldnae tell us how to get here or draw a map, for she recalls only how to get where she is going when she can see it."

"That makes no sense."

Hearing those words, Annora sighed and, putting her hand on the wall, attempted to stand up. "I have heard that said quite a bit tonight," she said.

"Annora?"

James hurried over to her and then hesitated. Even in the shadowed corner she stood in she did not look well. Gently taking her by the arm, he led her into the brighter light of a torch-lit dungeon. He gaped when he finally got a good look at her and then a hard, cold rage began to fill him.

"Your poor wee face," he said softly as he lightly touched one of her more livid bruises on her high cheeks. "Egan did this to ye, didnae he?"

"Aye. I wasnae giving him or Donnell the answers they wanted," She touched his equally bruised cheek. "Ye arenae looking so verra much better yourself."

"T'will heal."

"As will mine."

"Are ye sure ye are all right?"

She smiled and nodded. Annora could feel his eagerness to go and join in the battle to regain his home and she was not going to hold him back. She did her best to hide the fact that she could barely stand up, locking her knees in place when her legs wobbled from the pain and weakness she no longer had the strength to fight. She had to get James to go and fight before she fell down and he felt compelled to help her instead.

"Go, James," she said. "Go and save Dunncraig."

"If ye need help—" he began.

"Nay, I got this far without your help." He did not need to know that she had had to get a lot of help to get this far. "I ken ye truly want, e'en need to be a part of this fight, so go and fight. But do try nay to kill Donnell as Simon thinks he will be more use alive, at least for a little while."

"I will try, but can I kill Egan?"

There was such a boyish look on his face despite the grim request he was making that she had to smile. "Aye, I dinnae think anyone wants or needs him alive."

He gave her a brief, gentle kiss on her bruised mouth and then bounded up the stairs. Annora looked at Tormand, who was studying her closely. She tried to stand up a little straighter, but his crooked smile told her she was failing.

"He needs to be in on the battle," she said.

"Aye, he does. And ye need to be in bed," he said.

"I can make my way there. James needs ye to watch his back, doesnae he?"

Tormand took her by the arm and started to help her up the stairs. "Edmund and Simon will see to that duty until I can join them."

Annora needed to go up only one step to know that she badly needed his help. He had to give her more and more of his support and strength as they climbed the stairs. By the time he led them through the doorway at the top of the stairs, she was shaking from pain and weakness so badly he was nearly carrying her.

Once in the great hall they saw that a confrontation had begun among Simon, Donnell, James, and Egan. Tormand set Annora on a bench near the doors that led to the kitchens and moved to stand near James. Annora felt a movement at her side and looked to find Big Marta there, Meggie hiding behind her but peeking out from behind her skirts. Meggie looked horrified by Annora's wounds, so she forced her mouth into a smile to reassure the child. A soft grunt from Big Marta told her that that woman did not believe her act in the slightest.

"Shall I help ye to your bed, lass?" asked Big Marta.

"In a wee bit," Annora replied, knowing she was going to have to be carried but not wanting to admit to that much in front of Meggie. "I think I need to see this."

Big Marta stared at her bruised face for a moment and then nodded. "Aye, I think ye do."

"Ye brought MacLarens into Dunncraig!" yelled Donnell as if James was the one who was in the wrong.

They arenae my enemies," said James. "'Tis ye they want to fight and I think they deserved the opportunity to avenge the death of their laird's eldest son." James looked at Egan and saw Annora's battered face. "As for ye, I mean to cut off a piece of ye for every bruise ye inflicted upon Annora."

"So I was right," said Egan, facing James squarely as Donnell stepped back. "Ye have made her your whore."

He knew it was wrong to allow his anger to interfere in a battle, but James heard himself growl in fury and he attacked Egan. It took him just a few swings of his sword to regain the calm that was needed to fight a mon with a sword. Once he did gain control of his emotions he began to coldly and precisely back Egan into a corner.

Egan's style of fighting was rash and consisted mostly of trying to cut a man's head off. James knew he had the skill to beat this man and he began to use it. Within minutes Egan was sweating and bleeding from a dozen small wounds, but he had managed to keep James from striking a death blow.

"Are ye going to surrender?" James asked the man, feeling honor-bound to offer the man that choice.

"For what? To hang beside the fool that confessed all in front of a king's man?"

"Ye might be able to buy yourself some leniency by offering to tell of all the crimes your laird is guilty of."

"I think not."

Egan's sudden attack caught James by surprise and he paid for that with a large gash in his side and a smaller one in his leg. However, Egan did not have the skill to take advantage of that. The moment he regained his balance, James attacked Egan. The resulting battle was quick. Within minutes Egan was faltering so badly that James barely had to think about the swing of his sword that finally cut the man down. As soon as Egan fell to the floor, his life's blood rushing out of a clean cut to his throat, James turned his attention back to Donnell.

"Do ye surrender?" he asked.

To his surprise, Donnell did, throwing his sword at Simon's feet and allowing that man to bind his hands. James staggered, a weakness from a loss of blood and the time he had spent hanging in chains briefly overwhelming him a little, and Tormand was immediately at his side to help him stand and face Donnell one last time. Before he had his wounds tended to, he needed to be certain that this was the end, that he would soon be a free man and have his lands returned to him.

"Did ye hear all ye needed to, Simon?" he asked the man.

"Oh, aye, more than enough. That and the journal and the witnesses we have will be enough to clear your name," Simon replied.

"What journal?" demanded Donnell.

"Mary wrote a journal in which she said a lot about all of your crimes," replied James.

The look on Donnell's face told James that he was rethinking his surrender. It was clear that the man had thought to use his friends or blackmail of important men to get himself out of the dangerous tangle he found himself in. It was not going to work this time. In fact, James would not be surprised if some of the ones Donnell had blackmailed into helping him last time would be eager to see the man hanged for his crimes.

As Simon and Edmund dragged Donnell away, James went over to the bench Annora sat on and waited as Big Marta fetched her simples bag so that she could tend to his wound. When Meggie cautiously approached him James mustered up a smile but it did little to lessen the concern in her brown eyes. There was curiosity there and James had the feeling he was about to be pressed with a lot of hard questions.

"Who are ye?" asked Meggie. "Ye arenae the wood-carver, are ye?"

"Nay, lass, I am Sir James Drummond, the former laird of Dunncraig."

"That was my father's name, ye ken. He was the mon who was married to my mother when she had me and that makes him my father. Doesnae it?"

"Aye, that makes him your father." James saw no sense in trying to avoid this conversation or turn the child's thoughts elsewhere. He suspected Meggie was not a child who would be put off a subject she was interested in or deterred from getting answers to her questions.

Annora watched the different expressions on Meggie's face and felt a little uneasy when she saw a flash of anger in her brown eyes. Ever since Meggie had confessed that she did not believe Donnell was her real father she had sometimes mentioned the previous laird. Since he had been married to her mother, Meggie had already begun to suspect that he had been her father. Annora had offered no opinions, for she knew James had wanted to tell the little girl the truth himself. What James did not know was that Meggie had sometimes thought that her real father had left because of her. Annora regretted not telling him about that, for she feared he was about to be confronted with the fury of a child who thought she had been tossed aside, deserted and unloved.

"So if ye are Sir James Drummond, then ye are my father."

"Aye, I am."

"Why did ye go away?" Meggie demanded.

"Because MacKay had everyone believing I killed your mother and I was declared an outlaw. Have ye not heard that tale?"

"Aye, some of it. Ye didnae kill my mother, did ye?"

"Nay, MacKay did."

"Weel, that doesnae surprise me. He was always killing people."

"And so what do ye think, Meggie-mine?" asked James. "Are ye ready to accept me as your father or are we going to have to discuss it a wee bit more?"

Meggie chewed her lip as she studied the man seated before her. "Ye didnae leave because I was a bad girl?"

"Nay! I left because it was the only way I could stay alive to try and clear my name and regain my child and my land," he said. "I would ne'er have left ye just because ye did something naughty."

She looked at his wounds and then smiled. "Weel then, we had best let Big Marta fix those wounds as I cannae have my da bleeding all o'er the place."

James took her into his arms and held her tightly for a moment, kissing the top of her head. He felt tears sting his eyes but blinked them away, knowing that Meggie could easily misinterpret them. When she started to wriggle in his hold he let her go, knowing it would take time for acceptance to become the love of a child for her father.

"I think Annora needs tending to, Big Marta." Meggie sat down by Annora and very gently began to stroke her hair. "Dinnae ye worry, Annora. We will see that ye are made all better."

"That would be nice," said Annora and then slowly began to slide off the bench, unable to hold back the blackness that had been nudging at her for so long.

James cried out and reached for her, but to his surprise Tormand caught her up in his arms. Before he could say anything he and Annora were hurried up to their bedchambers so that their injuries could be attended to. It was several hours before his wounds were cleaned and stitched and the business of what to do with some of the more immediate problems of Dunncraig were tended to and James was able to turn his full attention on how Annora was faring.

"Did ye see her?" he asked Tormand as his brother strolled into the room.

"Aye, she is sleeping. None of her injuries are serious, just painful."

"I dinnae ken how ye could let her come into Dunncraig with ye when she was so badly beaten."

Tormand sat down on the side of the bed and began to tell James all that had happened since he had been taken captive by Donnell. "So, Brother, ye can see that when the lass decides she has to do something, there is nay stopping her."

Moved by all Annora had done to help him, James was speechless for a moment. To put herself at such risk and push on despite all the pain she had to have been in had to mean that she cared for him. That lightened James' heart in a way he found a little embarrassing if pleasurable. He wanted to see her right away, but knew he had to take care with his own wounds. Lying back in his bed, he came to a decision about Annora. He was never going to let her leave him. He just hoped he could make her agree with that plan.

It took only two days for James to realize that he was going to have to fight hard to get what he wanted. Annora had only come to see him a few times while he had suffered through a short but fierce bout of fever, and he had sensed a difference in her. He had told himself not to read too much into her formal manner as she was still stiff from the results of her beating and she might need some time to accept the change in his circumstances. That lie did not work to calm his growing fear anymore. Annora was slowly but surely pulling away from him.

Chapter Twenty-One

"She is thinking of running away, isnae she?"

When Tormand just shrugged, James scowled at him. There was an all too familiar glint in Tormand's mismatched eyes. His brother was anticipating some entertainment in watching James fumble about trying to hold fast to the woman he wanted. There was nothing the Murray men liked more than watching one of their brethren struggle in the pursuit of his woman. Once James felt confident that he was back to his full strength he was going to pound Tormand into the ground. His younger brother was in sore need of being taught some respect for his elders.

"Where is she?" he demanded, fighting to use the sort of commanding voice even Tormand might feel inclined to obey.

"With Meggie in the gardens," Tormand replied, grinning when James cautiously stood up and had to grab hold of the bedpost to keep from falling. "Need some help?" he asked, knowing the offer would be refused.

"Nay, I am fine," snapped James as he fought against the urge to fall to his knees.

"Of course ye are," he drawled. "I dinnae think ye are in any condition to hunt her down. Ye would just fall on your face in the dirt by the time ye reached her, and that isnae an image a mon wishes to present to his lover."

"Weel, I cannae just lie here and let her run off."

"She willnae run away whilst ye are still weak and healing from your wounds."

"I am nay weak," James grumbled even though he knew full well that he was. "I have but been abed for too long. Makes a mon unsteady."

"Of course it does."

"T'will pass in but a few moments."

"Of course it will."

"Shut your mouth. Wait, hesitate to obey that order until ye tell me why ye think she willnae run until I appear strong and hale again."

"As I said, 'tis because ye are still recovering from a wound."

James found a seed of hope in those words, but it was a very small one. Annora could be lingering at Dunncraig because she needed to see that he was fully recovered before she went away, might even think to care for his poor, battered hide now and again, although he had seen very little of her since everyone had decided he would live. She could also feel that it was her responsibility to continue to care for Meggie until he was able to find his daughter a new nursemaid, aside from Annie. Since MacKay had often used Annora as his lady of the keep, ordering her to see to the care of his guests, Annora could simply be continuing that chore now. He had to find a way to hold her firmly at Dunncraig until he was healed enough to catch her if she ran.

Feeling a little steadier, James took a few cautious steps, wincing a bit at the pull on the still raw wound at his side caused by each step. The stitches had been removed but the wound still ached when he moved too quickly. Considering all he intended to do the moment he got his hands on Annora, James knew he needed a few more days to mend. A man needed to be at his full strength and able to move with some grace when he loved his woman into a stupor. He looked at a grinning Tormand as he sat back down on his bed and struggled not to give away how weak he felt and could tell by the glint of concern and sympathy in his brother's eyes that he was not hiding it well at all.

"Keep her at Dunncraig, Tormand," James told his brother.

"E'en if she wishes to leave?" asked Tormand, moving to pour James a tankard of strong, dark ale.

"Aye, e'en then. Lock her in the cursed dungeon if ye have to." James took a deep drink, welcoming the way the strong ale quickly began to ease his pain and the tension that concern about Annora had roused in him.

Tormand laughed softly. "I dinnae think your wooing will go verra weel if ye imprison her."

"It willnae go weel if I have to hunt her down, either. I dinnae ken why I think so, but I truly believe that Annora can be verra good at hiding."

"'Tis possible. I suspicion the poor lass has had far too many moments in her life that taught her the trick of it. Aye, especially the one where she can seem to just fade into her surroundings."

James nodded slowly. "I fear so. She worries too cursed much about being bastard born and lets the attitudes of self-righteous, or just cruel, people hurt her and make her think less of herself. Aye, and far too many of her cursed kin have done more than speak to her unkindly. MacKay beat her from time to time, at least once so severely that that bastard Egan actually stepped in and stopped him. One kinswoman locked her in small dark places for hours as a punishment when she was a child." He suddenly recalled Annora's very strong fear of the dark. "If ye have to put her in the dungeons to hold her here, keep the torches lit and let Meggie visit with her whene'er she wishes to. And put her cat Mungo in with her."

Crossing his arms over his chest, Tormand said, "I would rather lie to a priest than lock her up in the dungeons."

"Ye *have* lied to a priest," James said absently as he tried to think of some other way to hold Annora at Dunncraig if she tried to leave before he was able to convince her to stay. "Cousin Matthew, I believe."

"He isnae a priest; he is a monk. And I lied to him ere he joined the order. And it was a lie meant to spare his feelings. He didnae ken that the lass he had such strong feelings for was trying to bed down with every Murray within a day's walk of her cottage."

"Just keep Annora here. Watch her closely. Ye will be able to tell when she is thinking of running. The lass has little skill at hiding her feelings when she is around people she feels are no danger to her, people she can trust. She must ken that she can trust ye now."

"Such as people who think to lock her in the dungeons?"

Tormand ignored James' glare. "Why dinnae ye just call the lass in here and talk to her right now?"

"The fool lass thinks she isnae good enough for me, so she may need some persuading to believe that I dinnae care about her being bastard born or her lack of a dowry."

"Ah, I understand now. Weel, dinnae do too much and push yourself so hard that ye end up tied to that bed again. I dinnae want to be following Annora about too much. People may begin to think I am poaching."

James was still shaking his head over that remark after Tormand left. He eased himself back down onto the bed, wincing over the ache that lingered at the site of his wound. Although he was weary of being so weak he had to lie abed for days, he also knew that rest was what he needed. Just as he closed his eyes, the door opened. He felt a brief, sharp stab of disappointment when he saw Meggie in the doorway rather than Annora, but quickly smiled a warm welcome at the child. His smile widened when she skipped up to the side of the bed and grinned at him.

"How do ye feel today, Papa?" she asked.

Hearing Meggie call him father had to be one of the sweetest sounds he had ever heard, James decided. At times he was still stunned at how easily she had accepted him as her father, even though she had made it clear that she did not believe MacKay was. It was as if a small part of her remembered James for all those years they were apart even though he found that hard to believe.

"I am getting better," he replied. "The wound is closed tightly now and I but need to regain the strength I lost whilst lying in this bed."

"So that ye can chase Annora down?"

He laughed. "Aye, exactly. We cannae let her leave Dunncraig, can we?"

"Nay, we cannae and she is thinking about it, ye ken. She keeps giving me that fare-thee-weel look."

"Fare-thee-weel look? What sort of look is that?"

"The one where she looks at ye and smiles but there isnae a smile in her eyes. She looks at ye as if she is making ye a memory."

He had seen the look Meggie described and it had pained him. At first he had not been able to speak of any future because he had not been sure he had one. Then he had had to keep quiet because they had not had any privacy, something he suspected Annora had planned very carefully. Now he was denied the chance to speak to her because she simply avoided him.

"I have seen that look," he said quietly.

Meggie nodded. "So ye must get better and stronger verra soon and then ye can chase her down and tell her she has to stay with us because we need her."

"I intend to do just that, lass."

"I can help ye. I am verra good at tying knots."

James had to bite back a laugh. "I will keep that in mind but I am hoping I can convince Annora to stay here without having to tie her down to do so. Annora MacKay is ours, Meggie-mine, and I mean to make her understand that. This is her home and we are her family and she will stay put."

"Are ye ready to hunt down your woman yet?" demanded Tormand as he entered James' bedchamber three days after James had promised Meggie that he would make Annora stay with them.

James took a final look at himself in the fancy, very expensive looking-glass MacKay had bought to put in the laird's bedchamber. The man had spent far too much of Dunncraig's coin on such needless luxury, but for this precise moment, James was rather glad to have the looking-glass. He was pleased to see his red hair again as well. Putting the coloring in to make it brown and keep it brown had been an unending chore. Except for the scar on his cheek and a few more lines on his face, he looked very much as he had before all of his troubles began. Even naked he would not look much changed despite the ugly red scar marring his side. James just hoped that he looked like a man Annora wanted to love and marry. He knew she wanted him in her bed, but he was after far more than passion now.

"I am as ready as I will e'er be," James replied. "Once the wound closed, my recovery was mercifully quick. Giving ye a wee bit of trouble, is she?"

"At times I think she kens that I am watching if nay the why of it. I swear that once she catches sight of me she begins to do the most boring thing she can think of just to see how long I can stand to watch it. I hadnae quite realized just how many boring things a lass has to do during her day."

"I think she used to do the same when MacKay had guards watching her. They would wander off they got so bored and that got them into trouble with Egan."

"Weel, tedious as that can be at times, today Big Marta set after me. She grabbed me by the ear and told me to stay away from your woman. My back still aches from having her force me to bend down for so long. It took a lot of vowing to behave and sweet words to get the woman to believe that I was just making sure Annora didnae slip away before ye got a chance to corner her and talk some sense into her."

Laughing softly, James shook his head. "I suspicion Big Marta believed ye far more quickly than ye think. She just didnae let ye ken it for a while. That woman takes every chance she gets to put we poor muddled men in our place."

"Then she must have heartily enjoyed herself today," Tormand muttered, rubbing the ear Big Marta had so thoroughly abused. "I came to tell ye that your wee lass just returned to her bedchamber to prepare for the evening meal."

"How wondrously convenient. 'Tis the perfect place to corner her."

"So I thought. Want me to make sure that Meggie doesnae try to come round to see if ye have convinced Annora to stay yet? She has also been keeping a close eye on the woman. And the child has an uncanny skill at spying. Best ye be aware of that."

James grimaced and nodded. "Aye, it might be best to keep Meggie watched now. I certainly dinnae want to try to explain my methods of persuasion to a girl of but five years of age."

Tormand laughed but suddenly grew serious again as he paused in the doorway of the room before leaving. "I ken that ye must have suffered a doubt or two about whether or not Meggie is really yours..." he began. "With Mary having been MacKay's lover for so long, e'en after ye were married—"

"Meggie is mine. By law, by name, and by the fact that I was there to hold her in the first minutes of her life. I dinnae care whose seed bred her."

"That is good because it seems it was yours."

Despite his words of denial and the certainty that he would have loved Meggie no matter what, James felt his heart leap with a joyous hope. "Ye say that with some certainty."

"Weel, I was verra sure before as, despite that verra fair hair—which has some strong hints of red when the sun shines on it by the way—and those big brown eyes, she has a lot of the look of ye in the way she smiles and the shape of her chin. But the real proof is that it seems MacKay was unable to sire a child."

"How can ye be sure of that?"

"I suspicion no one can be completely sure unless the mon has lost his manhood completely, say by the swing of an angry husband's sword, but he ne'er bred a child."

James frowned. "I thought I heard rumors to the contrary."

"Most likely rumors started by him or Egan. Nay, MacKay has been bedding women since he was but a boy of twelve and has ne'er bred a child. A verra high fever and spots when he was just turning from child to mon seems to have killed his seed. Those few bairns he tried to claim as proof of his manliness were bred by Egan."

"That certainly explained his determination to claim Meggie as his own. Do ye ken, I think it explains why he was going to make Annora marry Egan as weel."

Tormand nodded. The need for an heir to the keep he had stolen. Aye, and an heir might weel give the king and his advisers some way to make sure all of the people involved in this mess gain something in the end and allow them to think that they havenae wronged or angered anyone."

"'Tis probably that knowledge that kept Egan safe from MacKay's rages, e'en gave the mon a wee bit of power o'er MacKay although I cannae understand why MacKay didnae just kill the mon as he had so many others who discovered some secret of his. A mon like MacKay would have found his inability to sire a child verra humiliating. How did ye find this out?"

"A woman in the town who many saw as his mistress told me ere she was driven away by the people's anger and scorn of her.

She said that MacKay suddenly told her one night that he had bedded her for so long people were wondering why there was no child. He couldnae have anyone asking that So he made her bed down with Egan secretly for o'er a month until she got with child and then made everyone think it was his. He also made it verra clear that she would also claim the child as his and ne'er mention Egan or she would die a verra painful death."

"Did she take the child with her?"

"Nay, the wee lass is in the village living with a fine family who lost what few children they had and wanted her. It was best for all concerned as this woman would ne'er stop being a whore, although she bluntly says she prefers to be a rich mon's mistress and intends to find herself such a mon ere she loses her good looks."

James shook his head. "The mon had a lot of secrets."

"Aye, and he made sure that nearly every one of them went to the grave with the people who kenned about them. There must have been some bond between him and Egan or that mon would probably have been dead ere he reached full manhood."

"I suspicion we will hear more of those as the years pass. He is dead now and tongues will loosen. All of it can only help me. I may now be widely declared as innocent and the sentence of outlaw lifted, but the blacker MacKay appears the more clear my innocence is." He nudged Tormand the rest of the way out of the door and then started walking toward Annora's bedchamber. "Now 'tis time to have a word with my lady."

"I expect to be able to toast your coming marriage at the meal this evening."

James hoped Tormand would be doing just that but he admitted to himself that he was feeling unsure and nervous. He knew Annora would not share the bed of just any man who could kiss her and touch her in a way she liked. He knew she shared the fierce passion and need he had for her. What he was not sure of was how deep all of that went into her heart and if those urges were born of the sort of feelings one could build a marriage on. What he wanted was for Annora to love him. The next time he took a wife to his bed he wanted to know that she was his in body, in heart, in mind, and in soul.

Annora sighed and sat down on her bed. She knew she ought to be leaving Dunncraig, but she kept finding little reasons to stay just a little longer. There really were none left. James was healed, Dunncraig was running smoothly, the shadows Donnell had filled Dunncraig Keep with were nearly all dispersed, and Meggie was happy beyond words that James was her father. There really was no need for her to linger except to prolong the pain of leaving James and little Meggie.

She would probably even have to leave Mungo behind, she thought and felt tears sting her eyes as she patted her cat's head, for her kinsmen would think it foolish for her to have a pet. "I am such a foolish, foolish woman," she murmured.

Mungo meowed softly and butted at her hand.

Realizing she had stopped petting him, she began to scratch lightly behind his ears. "I love James, Mungo. I love him with my whole heart. The mon is as necessary to me as the air I breathe. But I have to leave him. He is a laird of a fine family and a host of allies gained through the family who took him into their home and their hearts. Many of those allies have power and influence at court, too. A poor, landless bastard is nay the sort of wife a laird like Sir James Drummond takes to wife."

The cat rolled over onto his back in a silent plea to have his belly scratched.

"I ken that ye are little interested in the trials and tribulations of mere people, Mungo, but ye could at least feign a little sympathy." She scratched the cat's belly. "I just need to decide where to go and what kinsmon to inflict myself upon next. I would like it to be one who isnae so verra far away from Dunncraig as I want to be able to see how Meggie fares."

Thinking of Meggie, Annora found she could smile. The child had accepted James as her father with no question at all, her delight in him plain for all to see. There was a rapport between James and Meggie that had been visible from the very beginning when they had all thought he was a wood-carver named Rolf Larousse Lavengeance.

Annora grimaced as she thought of that name. The words of his name meant wolf, red, and vengeance. She should have taken the time to think on that James had not been so very subtle in his choice of that name. If Donnell had taken some time from spending money and bedding women to learn a few things, he would have seen it, too.

"He took a great risk using that foolish name," she muttered. "There could easily have been someone at Dunncraig who knew French and was a close ally of Donnell's or my Cousin could actually have taken some time to learn more than he kenned, small as that was. 'Tis also odd that I have dreamt of a ruddy wolf with green eyes since James was sent running for his life.

"'Tis fate dial I am here and I met him, I suppose. That is what my dream was trying to say, what it was leading me toward. I just wish it had shown me how to help him and Meggie and yet nay lose my heart to either of them." She wiped a stray tear from her cheek and forced the rest back down. "I ken that good has been done and all that, but I wish fate could have chosen someone else to have a hand in it all. Fate is a cruel mistress to send me somewhere to help in my small way and then make me love the ones I have helped only to rip me away from them again."

Mungo suddenly sat up, then leapt off the bed and padded to the door. He sat there and stared at the door but did not yowl as he always did to let her know that he wanted out of the room. She was going to miss her cat, she thought as she stood up and walked to the door. He had been her close companion at Dunncraig since Donnell had allowed her to make no friends.

"And now that I have the chance to make a true place for myself here, to make some friends, I have to leave," she muttered as she opened the door.

"And why do ye think ye have to leave?"

Chapter Twenty-Two

For the space of one heartbeat Annora considered slamming the door in James' face and barring it. He must have seen that thought in her expression, for he gently but firmly pushed her back and after letting Mungo leave, shut the door and barred it himself. Leaving him inside her bedchamber, just where she did not want him. It was dangerous to her heart and her peace of mind to be alone with the man, especially in a bedchamber.

And especially since he was looking so very handsome, she thought, unable to resist the temptation to look him over very thoroughly. She told herself that she was just making sure that he was healthy enough to be standing there frowning at her and herself laughed heartily at that big lie. With his golden red hair and his fine clothes he looked like the laird he truly was, a man ready to take over the rule of his lands and mayhap build a power of his own through allies and friends.

And a good marriage, she thought and hastily turned away from him. Annora suddenly found the sight of him painful, for it only made her all too aware of how far apart they were. She had begun to try and put some distance between them in the hope that it would ease her heartbreak when she left, but seeing him now let her know that that was a very stupid plan. He was a part of her and simply not looking at him did nothing to cure her of that.

When she felt his hands on her shoulders, she tensed. Annora prayed he was not going to try to make love to her. To have a taste of all she craved while knowing she could not really claim it as her own would be more painful than she cared to even think about.

"Annora, what is wrong?"

James turned her stiff body around and pulled her into his arms. She stayed tense as he held her and rubbed her slim back with his hands. He began to feel afraid that she had already cut him out of her heart even though he was not sure why she would do so.

"I am pleased to see that ye are fully healed," Annora said, fighting the urge to cuddle up against him and breathe deeply of his clean, crisp scent.

"I cannae tell that by the way ye stand like an iron poker in my arms," he drawled, "but if ye say 'tis so, I must believe it, aye?"

She tried desperately to shield herself, but she found herself open to his feelings despite all her efforts. He was confused, uneasy, and nervous. Annora's eyes widened slightly as she sensed something else. He was afraid and there was the beginning stir of a pain he fought against feeling. A tiny spark of hope came to life in her heart and she tried not to be seduced by it. Yet, the feelings she could sense in him hinted at more than just desire and respect.

"Aye," she whispered, relaxing a little in his hold. "Believe it."

He leaned back a little and cupped her face in his hands, turning it up until he could look in her eyes. The fact that she had slipped her arms around his waist and had not moved away made him feel a little less uneasy, but there was such sadness and confusion in her eyes, he knew he had a battle ahead of him. Since he did not know what was causing her to feel that way, he was not sure he was going to do or say the right things, the things that might change that sad, confused look in her beautiful eyes to one of love and happiness.

"Ye are planning to leave us, arenae ye, Annora?"

She blushed, feeling strangely guilty. "Aye. Ye are healed now and have all ye lost returned to ye. 'Tis time ye began to live your life as a laird again."

"And ye want no part of that?"

"I cannae stay here as Meggie's nurse anymore. Things will be changing now. Ye will have to work hard to remake treaties with your neighbors and I ken that ye need to establish yourself a little at the court so that ye are kenned weel and trusted by the men with the power. And—"

He kissed her, putting all his need for her into the kiss. For a brief moment she resisted, but the passion he so loved in her rose up and she softened in his arms, returning his kiss. Although he did not have her gift for sensing what others felt, he could almost taste the desperation and the sadness in her kiss. James began to have the feeling that Annora was doing what she thought was best for everyone, not what she truly wanted to do.

"Nay!" she cried suddenly and wrenched out of his hold. "We cannae do that anymore. Ye are the laird again. Did ye nay tell me that the Murrays taught ye nay to make lemans of the servant girls?"

"Annora, ye are nay my leman!" he said, torn between shock and anger. "When did I e'er give ye the idea that ye were just my leman?"

"Weel, what else would I be? Am I nay your lover?"

"My lover and my love."

"Nay, James, I cannae be your love," she whispered, desperately wanting to believe him and yet knowing even if he told the truth that there could be no future for them.

"Why?" James feared that he had been wrong, that her passion for him was simply that, passion, and it did not reach into her heart. "Are ye telling me that ye dinnae want any more from me than a few turns atween the sheets?"

Annora blushed, as much from anger as from embarrassment over his crude words. She was about to respond in anger but then hesitated. The feelings coming from him were strong and they made her wonder if she had been wrong. There was hurt and fear inside James and she had no doubt that she was the cause of both of those emotions. There was also something else, something strong and warm that she dared not put a name to.

For just a minute she considered doing or saying something that would make him leave and then she would flee Dunncraig. The cowardice prompting that thought was enough to appall her and she stiffened her backbone. She was done with being a coward. There might be a lot of pain ahead for her if she forced this conversation to continue, but she would do it. When and if she did leave Dunncraig she did not want to do so with a lot of unanswered questions.

"If I was that sort of woman I wouldnae have been a virgin, would I?" she said calmly.

"Annora," he said in a softer voice, fighting to calm the fear growing inside him, a fear that caused him to lash out with angry words, "I have ne'er thought of ye as my leman." He cautiously put his hands on her shoulders again. "If I was all that sort, would I have kept pushing Mab away? So much easier for me to have just let her have her way if all I sought was a good sweaty rutting."

That was true, she thought, and then grimaced. "I wasnae so verra hard to seduce, James, though it shames me to say so."

"Considering how quickly and fiercely I wanted ye, it seemed like a verra long time to me." His fear eased just a little when she smiled fleetingly. "It was just ye that I wanted e'en though I kenned it was nay a good time to go a-wooing."

"A-wooing?" she whispered, her heart pounding with a renewed hope.

"Aye, lass. I ken the circumstances didnae make it seem as though that was what I was doing, but it was. Annora"—he pulled her into his arms and breathed a sigh of relief when there was no tension in her body this time—"I need ye. I need ye to stay here with me. I need ye to keep the darkness from my soul."

He kissed her and she melted in his arms. He had not spoken of marriage or a future, but at that moment, she did not care. The words he had said had banished all of her resistance. Annora knew he had not said he loved her exactly, but she could not understand what else all his sweet words could mean.

"Annora-mine," he said in a thick, hoarse voice as he kissed her throat.

"Aye, I feel die same. Tis like a fever."

He said nothing else as he rapidly rid them of their clothes. Annora was amazed that she could laugh as he nearly threw her down on the bed and then fell on top of her. The need possessing her was so great and so fierce, laughter seemed to have no part in what was about to happen between them. Yet, she also felt such joy to be back in his arms that she supposed laughter was a fitting response. And then he began to make fierce love to her and without another thought she gave herself over to the passion they shared.

When James finally thrust inside her he groaned with the force of the pleasure he felt. "This is where I belong," he said as he leaned down to kiss her while he moved in and out of her body. "This is what I need."

"I need it, too, James. I fear I always will."

"Ne'er fear that, my love."

She clung to him as he rode her with a ferocity that they both seemed to need. Annora wrapped her arms and legs around him and held on tight as he drove them to passion's summit with a speed that was exhilarating. The release that tore through her was so fierce and beautiful she nearly screamed out his name. She also screamed out how much she loved him. The flare of concern over that confession did not last long as she was overcome by the joy only James could bring her.

James washed them both clean of the remnants of their passion and then cautiously slipped into bed beside an ominously silent Annora. The only thing that kept his fears from returning in full force was the memory of the words she had yelled when her release had held her in its grip. She had said she loved him. Whatever else troubled her and had her thinking to leave Dunncraig, he felt sure he could overcome.

"What troubles ye, love?" he asked as he tugged her into his arms.

"Ah, James, ye are a laird again."

"And that is what troubles ye? Ye dinnae like the fact that I can provide for ye?"

"Nay, that isnae it. I am bastard born—" she began but he ended her speech with a hard kiss.

"I dinnae care about your birth. I dinnae care if ye have lands or coin or an old auntie who talks to the birds." He smiled faintly when she laughed. "Ye are mine, Annora."

"Donnell bled Dunncraig nearly dry, James. There is so much

that needs to be fixed and replaced. Ye need a fine rich wife with lands and powerful relations."

He pushed until she was lying sprawled beneath him and then he placed his hands on either side of her face. "I need ye, Annora. And ye need me. Are ye going to deny that ye said ye loved me?"

"Nay, I cannae, can I? I screamed it like a banshee. But I am sure ye can find other women who would love ye as I do." Annora did not think she had ever said anything as difficult as that, for the very last thing she wanted to think of during her lonely future was James being loved and loving another woman.

"I am glad to hear that ye nearly choked on those words. Are ye nay heeding what I am saying, woman? I need ye. Ye are the other half of me." He almost smiled when her eyes began to widen and he realized he needed to be more exact in what he said about how he felt. "I love ye, Annora. I love ye as I have ne'er loved anyone else and will ne'er love again as I love ye. Now do ye understand? Ye are my mate, my perfect match."

Afraid she was going to burst into tears before she could make everything perfectly clear, she asked in a voice that was so soft and unsteady it was nearly a whisper, "Are ye saying ye wish to marry me?" She blushed, a little afraid that she had mistaken his words and just thoroughly humiliated herself.

"Aye, lass, I am, in my crude way. I will admit that the moment I kenned ye were my mate, I just assumed we would be marrying once all the trouble with MacKay was settled. I apologize for that arrogance. So, Annora MacKay, will ye marry me?"

"Oh, James, are ye verra sure? Ye could do so much better than me for a wife."

"Nay, I couldnae. I already tried marrying the sort of woman everyone felt was perfect for a laird, havenae I? And we see how weel that worked."

"Did ye think Mary was your mate?"

"Never. I was but weary of looking for my mate and I wanted the family, the bairns, and all of that. I also have ne'er liked, weel, the sort of things a mon does to sate his manly hungers. I wanted a loving woman in my bed, one I didnae have to worry about getting with child or paying in the morning. I wanted one who could give me that something special that changes rutting into making love."

"And ye got Mary," she said, feeling sorry for him for just a moment.

"Aye, and a great deal of trouble, but I cannae regret all of that. In the end it brought ye into my arms. Now, tell me, lass. Are ye meaning to stay here? Will ye marry me and have my bairns?"

"Oh, aye. I cannae do aught else as I love ye and it was killing me slowly to think of leaving ye. I just hope your family doesnae think too poorly of your choice."

"They will love ye because ye love me."

"I hope it is just that simple."

It was just that simple, Annora thought a few hours later as she was enthusiastically welcomed to the family by a grinning Tormand and a few of James' cousins. All they seemed to care about was that James was openly happy, grinning much like a fool in fact, and she would shyly confess to loving him whenever anyone asked. There was only one small impediment, she mused as she looked around for Meggie.

"She is o'er by the window looking a wee bit cross," said James.

"Did ye tell her that ye had asked Annora to marry ye and nay just stay here?" asked Tormand as he waved to his niece, who gave him a rather wan wave back.

"Nay, I suppose that was a mistake," said James.

"I think ye best speak to her now and make your most sincere apologies ere the official announcement is made. She has probably heard something already and that is why she is looking so cross."

Annora nodded and took James by the hand. "I think Tormand may be right. We didnae tell her our plans to be married or e'en let her ken that ye had asked me ere ye announced it to everyone else. She could be feeling a wee bit hurt by that."

The sulky greeting they got as they reached Meggie told Annora that the child was indeed hurt by not being told of Annora's plan to marry James, at least before everyone was in the great hall celebrating the news. "I am sorry I didnae come and tell ye, Meggie. I fear I was just so excited and, weel, stunned a wee bit that I didnae think of anything except James and getting married."

Meggie stared at her and then at James for a minute and then she rolled her eyes. "Ye mean ye just got all silly because of a handsome mon."

"That says it quite nicely. Aye, I got silly o'er your verra handsome da."

"Aye, I suspicion he is handsome," Meggie said cautiously, her gaze fixed upon James, "but were ye nay married to my mother?"

"I was," James said as he crouched down so that he could look her in the eye. "As I think ye already ken, I was falsely accused of her death and then branded an outlaw. I had to flee for my life. For three years I have been trying to find a way to clean the stain from my good name, find the real murderer, and regain all that was once mine."

"Dunncraig?"

"Aye, Margaret Anne. Dunncraig and ye. Ne'er think elsewise. I ne'er forgot my wee lass and always intended to come back for ye. That is why I first came to Dunncraig. It was but my good fortune that I met Annora here. Will ye allow me to marry her?"

Annora was moved by the understanding James showed for a little girl's fears. Meggie had to be uncertain of what her place would be now. By asking her permission for her newfound father to marry the nursemaid she had depended on for three years, he was making her a full part of that decision. Annora prayed the child did not balk and said she approved. Any other answer could cause them a lot of trouble with the child, for Annora felt certain James would not change his mind; he would just become determined to change Meggie's. What he did not know was that little Meggie could match him in stubbornness.

"And we will be a family?" Meggie asked.

"Aye, lass, we will be a family," said James and he briefly glanced toward Tormand. "A verra large family."

"I would like to be a family again."

"So ye approve of my plan to marry Annora?"

Meggie grinned and hugged him. "That will certainly make sure she stays at Dunncraig, aye?"

"Aye, it certainly will." James stood up and began to say, "And once Annora and I are married she must be called—"

Annora clapped her hand over his mouth and smiled at Meggie. "Whate'er Meggie wishes to call me. I leave that decision up to ye, Meggie-love."

"Thank ye. I will give it a lot of thought." Meggie did not wait to speak to James again but skipped away toward her uncle.

"Why did ye stop me from saying that she must call ye her mother when we marry?" James asked. "Ye will be her mother and so she ought to call ye such."

"Only in the eyes of the law. Meggie kens that her mother was Mary and, aye, she was a verra poor mother, but that doesnae matter. I dinnae want Meggie ordered to call me her mother. I want her to choose to call me that."

James sighed and wrapped his arm around her shoulders. "As ye wish. Shall we make this announcement? Everyone already kens that we are to be married as soon as possible, but this is something they expect a proper announcement for."

"A proper announcement and then a lot of ale," murmured Annora as they walked to the head table.

"'Tis tradition."

The hall went silent when James rapped his goblet down on the table several times. Annora stood by his side holding his hand as he told all the people gathered there that he had asked Annora MacKay to be his wife and she had said yes. As soon as the cheering for that had eased, he also told them that the marriage would happen as soon as possible and there would be a very grand wedding feast.

"My, I hadnae expected the news to be greeted with quite that much enthusiasm," Annora said as she sat down next to James.

"They love ye, lass, as I do." James gave her a quick kiss. "They ken that ye belong here and are pleased that their laird had the good sense to see that, too."

Annora blushed and looked around at the people gathered in the great hall. She had thought that because of the way Donnell had kept her so apart from everyone, the people of Dunncraig did not know or care for her. Most of this cheer was probably for the fact that James was hale and hearty and Dunncraig was back under his care, but she knew that many of the people were honestly happy for her as well. With tears in her eyes, she looked at James when he brushed a kiss over her cheek.

"Ye are home now, lass," he said softly. "Ne'er forget that."

And that, she realized, was the source of the joy she felt. At long last she had found a home.

Epilogue

One year later

"Isnae she done yet?"

James looked down at his daughter and, despite his growing fear for Annora and the child she was struggling to bring into the world, he almost smiled. Meggie had her hands on her hips and was scowling up at him through a tangle of golden curls. She seemed to think Annora would just retreat to her bedchamber with a few women and shortly thereafter call them in to see Meggie's new brother or sister. His daughter did not understand the many dangers of childbirth and he had no intention of enlightening her just yet. He prayed that Annora would not be doing so, either, that she would emerge from this trial hale and holding a fine, healthy child.

He thought back to the day Meggie was born and did not recall feeling so afraid for Mary or the child she carried. Mary had carried on loudly and continuously, repeatedly declaring for all to hear that he was a cruel man for making her suffer so much pain and torment. James supposed that the noise and complaints ringing through the halls of Dunncraig had sounded so strong and healthy it had been difficult to become concerned for Mary's health. What fears he had begun the day with had been quickly stomped down by all of Mary's bellowing.

Annora had remained unsettlingly quiet and James did find that frightening. He had started to move toward the door of the great hall so that he could rush up the stairs and demand to see Annora when someone grabbed him by the arm and held him back. He looked at his brother Tormand only to catch the man grinning at him, an expression of amusement in his mismatched eyes. It was an expression that James thought needed to be pounded right into the mud.

"What do ye want?" he demanded of his brother. "And cease that cursed grinning."

"I just wanted to stop ye before ye charged up those stairs, burst into your bedchamber, and scared poor Annora half to death," Tormand said. "Ye had that look."

"What look are ye talking about?"

"The look of a crazed mon who thinks his wife is being tortured and he must get to her to make sure that all the dangers of childbed stay far, far away. Doesnae work, brother. Ne'er has. Ne'er will. Only adds to the fears the poor lass already has."

Tormand's voice had grown very soft and James took a quick glance toward Meggie only to find her watching him very closely. "Aye, ye are right," he said and strode over to one of the big windows that lined one wall of the great hall and looked out toward the gates. "We have heard our kinswomen say the same thing often enough that I should have recalled the advice ere now."

"Is it true that MacKay wanted to make these windows of stained glass like they have in the kirk?" asked Tormand. "Who did the fool think he was?"

"A laird who could become a king if he was clever enough." James thought of the large stained glass panels that had arrived at Dunncraig a few months after MacKay had died. The idiot had spent too many years in France seeing all the excesses of the nobility o'er there and he wanted to recreate something similar here. A verra vain mon."

Looking at Tormand's far too innocent expression, James inwardly cursed. It was easy to guess the game his brother played, the one where someone distracts the poor fretting husband from where his wife is and what is happening to her. What really annoyed James was that it had worked for a little while. Even worse, he suspected Tormand could play the game again and it would work again. James reluctantly admitted to himself that he was eager to be distracted, but that did not mean he had to like being manipulated.

"I think the moment MacKay set his arse in the laird's chair his mind began to rot," James said. "Aye, he wanted stained glass windows. I got some huge panes of it delivered here nay so long ago. All paid for so there is nay sending them back to their maker. I cannae put the cursed things up in my windows, for they would block all view of the bailey from here. They would also cut out what little sunlight we get into this room. But the biggest reason I willnae be using them is because of what is depicted in the panels of the windows."

"Ah, 'tis all naked women frolicking, is it? Scenes of rampant debauchery."

"Weel, aye, but what makes them so appalling is that the mon in the center of all the lewdness shown in the picture is MacKay, Eagan seated at his right. Both naked. Both being weel attended by buxom women. And, if I may say so, both with endowments worthy of some mythic bull."

Tormand laughed so hard he slumped against the wall to keep from falling down. "Ye jest."

"Sad to say, nay, I dinnae."

"If this is what they have in France, mayhap I have been remiss in nay visiting our kinsmen o'er there."

"I doubt they have such nonsense in France."

"Ye must tell me where ye have put them. I need to look at such wonders."

"Annora saw them and laughed so hard I feared she would drop the bairn right there and then."

"They are that amusing?"

"'Tis all good work, beautiful colors and all, but 'tis the way MacKay arid Egan are drawn that makes what might have been a beautifully arousing painting into little more than some grand, expensive jest. I have a few men coming in later in the summer to look at them and see if there is any way to, weel, fix them, clean them up a wee bit, shall we say? Several pieces are verra good despite the lechery depicted, and because they were to be but one part of a large scene, the king and his jester with their endowments arenae there."

"I shall have to take a look at them, I think. I may e'en buy one from ye if 'tis as good as ye say it is."

"Ye want to put windows in your home that depict rampant debauchery?"

There is naught that says the piece must be part of a window. It just needs light shining through it to see the best of the colors, aye? So that might be arranged in some other way and thus the panels nay blessed with MacKay's and Egan's godlike personages could be treated as, weel, just a picture done in glass."

James thought about that for a moment and slowly nodded. He could think of one or two of the pieces that were beautiful, the lechery that was depicted only a small part of what intrigued one about them. He was certainly not going to tell Tormand that, once the laughter had passed, he and Annora had studied some of the panels and become very aroused. They had shut and barred the storeroom door and made love right there on the floor.

There was even one panel in particular he would not mind keeping just as it was, for the woman featured the most clearly looked very much like Annora, much to her horrified surprise. James suspected that, despite his cruelty to his cousin, MacKay had recognized her beauty. He just thanked God that MacKay had never let that beauty stir his lust to the height where he had tried to take her. The man had obviously had a few lustful thoughts about her, however, as that sultry woman depicted in the stained glass panel revealed. The fact that a man who looked a lot like him in his Rolf guise was in another one of the pictures was something he did not really care to think about, although Annora had found it intriguing once she had gotten past the jealousy stirred by seeing him shown with other women. And James had no intention of sharing some of the exquisitely drawn books showing various ways to make love or the tapestry hanging in the laird's chamber that also showed scenes of debauchery.

"MacKay didnae like the usual religious scenes or moral allegories or e'en hunting scenes depicted in most art," he said, smiling faintly. "S'truth, I hadnae realized more, shall we say, earthy matters were e'en shown in stained glass or stitchery."

"If the one doing the work is skilled enough, he or e'en she can make a picture of whate'er is wanted," Tormand said. "'Tis just that MacKay seemed to want what would make everyone else turn their gazes away. I have seen things that show the more earthy things as weel, although it appears MacKay was planning on making Dunncraig Keep some bastion of lewd works." Tormand suddenly grabbed hold of James' arm again. "Big Marta has arrived."

Since Big Marta was one of the women tending the birth of his child, James tensed and realized Tormand had grabbed his arm to steady him. Mayhap even to keep him from doing something foolish. James stood with his hands clasped tightly behind his back in an effort to look calm. He glanced down when a weight suddenly settled against his leg and he found Meg leaning against him. His daughter was obviously not completely ignorant of the fact that there was an ever-present danger hanging over the birthing bed. He unclasped his hands and wrapped his arm around her short, thin body as best he could.

"Weel, laddie," said Big Marta as she stopped right in front of him obviously savoring the fact that everyone gathered in the great hall had gone silent upon her entrance and waited for her to speak, "ye got yourself a good little breeder there. E'en her pains werenae all that bad, the worst coming in only the last hour or so."

Although he felt almost weak-kneed his relief was so great, James managed to sound calm as he asked, "Annora and the child are weel, then?"

"Aye, that they are. Ye have a fine, big son," Big Marta announced and grinned around at everyone when they cheered. "And, aye, your lady is fine, naught but tired from a hard day of work."

Big Marta had barely finished speaking when James began to run for the stairs leading up to the bedchambers. It took him a moment to realize that there was a weight on his left leg making his movements awkward and the laughter echoing in the great hall was far too boisterous to be no more than a reaction to an anxious new father racing to see his wife and new son. James stopped and looked down into Meggie's laughing brown eyes. She was clinging to his leg with her arms and legs, hanging on tightly as he ran. Laughing, he picked her up and tossed her over his shoulder, then began running again. Tormand was right at his heels, for he had been the one chosen to look at the new heir to Dunncraig and then take word back down to the great hall and the various cousins waiting there.

Annora's eyed widened with surprise as James burst into the bedchamber, a grinning Tormand right behind him, and a giggling Meggie draped over his broad shoulder. Once her surprise eased, however, she grinned back at them as they all gathered around the bed where she lay with her new son in her arms. She had been terrified of giving birth, recalling far too many bad ones and ones ending in the woman's death, but it had all been rather easy.

Although she knew she was very fortunate, she also knew that she had James' foster family to thank for some of that ease. Knowing they might not be able to be at Dunncraig for the birth, James' tiny, sweet mother, Bethia, and several of his cousins had all come to visit several months ago. The instructions they had given Big Marta, Annora, and several other women had proven their worth. Annora knew in her heart that many babies and mothers at Dunncraig would be saved in the future because of the knowledge those women had shared.

"Why isnae he all red and wrinkly like Morag's wee sister, Mama?"

Hearing the word *mama* on Meggie's lips nearly caused Annora to burst into tears. She had been waiting almost a year to hear it, waiting to know for certain that Meggie had accepted her as her mother. Glancing at James, she saw the faint sheen in his eyes, knew he had heard that final, full acceptance of her as well, and was feeling nearly as emotional as she was. There was a glint of uncertainty in Meggie's big eyes and Annora knew she had to hide her tears and save them for later.

She smiled at Meggie. "He is a big lad, Meggie-love. I think that makes a difference. Morag's sister was a verra wee lass." One who would have certainly died if the Murray women had not arrived at that precise time and quickly offered their skills to help Morag's mother keep her child alive.

"What is my brother's name? Mungo?" asked Meggie as she peeked under and around the baby's swaddling.

"Nay, we arenae naming our son after a cat," said James, lightly swatting Tormand when the younger man laughed.

"It isnae a cat's name," protested Annora. "It was the name of my childhood friend."

Then ye shouldnae have given it to a cat. I offer ye the choice of Niocal and Quinton."

He was being a little arrogant about the naming of their child, but Annora had already decided not to argue with him over the name. "Quinton, then. Quinton Murray Drummond."

"Ah, now, that is a fine name and shall please the elders," said Tormand as he grasped Meggie by the hand. "Come, my wee beauty, and help me tell the cousins the news."

Meggie tugged free of his hold and dashed over to Annora's side of the bed to give her a quick hug and a kiss. Annora lovingly returned it. A moment later she was alone with James. She watched as he sat on the bed beside her. He kissed her in a way that made her toes curl with pleasure despite the fact that her body still ached from giving birth. Then he held out his hands for Quinton and she did not hesitate to put their child in his arms.

She waited patiently as he unwrapped the baby, for she had done the same right after Big Marta had put the baby in her arms. Right along with James, she silently counted each little finger and toe all over again. By the time he reswaddled their child and looked at her, she knew her eyes were as wet with tears as his were. He blinked his away as he settled himself on the bed beside her, wrapping his arm around her, and holding her close by his side, little Quinton still snuggled safely in the crook of his other arm.

"Ye have done me proud, Annora-mine," he said quietly and pressed a kiss to her forehead.

Annora rested her head against his shoulder, her gaze fixed upon their sleeping child. "Quinton is a miracle we had an equal part in making."

"But ye did most of the work."

"Weel, I willnae argue that."

"And ye arenae in too much pain?"

"Nay. I but ache and am verra tired."

"I began to fear that something was wrong, for I didnae hear ye make any sound."

"Oh, I made plenty of noise, but nay the screaming that can carry to where the father waits." She reached across James' broad chest to stroke her child's soft cheek. "He was worth every pain, every grunt and groan, and all the offenses to my modesty."

"Och, aye, and he was worth every white hair I grew in the last far too many hours of feeling utterly helpless." James grinned when she laughed and then ever so lightly touched Quinton's hair. "He has your thick black hair. Blue eyes?"

"For now, but I am hoping they will be green. Meggie called me Mama," she whispered, feeling choked with tears for a moment.

"Finally, but ye were right. It was best to allow her to decide and choose her time. I but felt that ye had always been more of a mother to her than Mary e'er was or e'er would have been and wanted ye to have the honor of that name immediately."

"It means more when it comes from her heart, and nay just because her beloved da told her to do it."

"Aye, I felt that, too, when I heard her say it. I just always want what I want immediately and then I have to talk some sense into myself. I have ye to do that for me now."

"Aye, ye do, but I understand wanting something immediately. I wanted ye immediately. The moment I kenned I was carrying your child I wanted him in my arms immediately. 'Tis a strong temptation to want what ye want right away."

"Weel, I shallnae be tempted again. I have all I want now."

She looked up at him and murmured her pleasure when he kissed her. "As do I. I have my big ruddy, green-eyed wolf." He blushed a little just as he had the first time she had told him about her dream.

"I love ye, Annora-mine."

"And I love ye. I loved ye when I first saw ye. I loved ye when ye saved me from Egan, especially when ye were ready to give all this up and take me to France just to keep me from the mon. And each day I love ye more. Ye have given me all I have e'er wanted."

"I have?"

"Aye. Ye have given me a family. A big, loud, loving, laughing, arguing, tramp-mud-into-the-great-hall family. Ye, me, Meggie, and now Quinton and whate'er other children we are blessed with are the heart of that family, but the rest of them, blood kin or nay, are a pure joy. Thank ye, husband."

"Ah. Lass, I am the one who should be the most grateful. Ye gave me back my heart and took the darkness from my soul."

She cuddled up against his side again, deeply moved by his words and the deep, unwavering love she could feel inside him, one that perfectly matched what rested in her heart "We are a perfect match, my wolf."

That we are, lass. That we most certainly are."

ABOUT THE AUTHOR

Hannah Howell is an award-winning author who lives with her family in Massachusetts. Since *Amber Flame*, her first historical romance, was released in February 1988, she has published over 25 novels and short stories, with more on the way. Her writing has been repeatedly recognized for its excellence and has "made Waldenbooks Romance Bestseller list a time or two" as well as was nominated twice by Romantic Times for Best Medieval Romance (*Promised Passion* and *Elfking's Lady*). She has also won Romantic Times' Best British Isles Historical Romance for *Beauty and the Beast*; and, in 1991-92 she received Romantic Times' Career Achievement Award for Historical Storyteller of the Year. Hannah loves hearing from readers and you may write to her through her website (www.hannahhowell.com).